RULES OF COMBAT

PRIMARY RULES

1. The objective of Arena 13 combat is to cut flesh and spill blood. Human combatants are the targets.
2. No human combatant may wear armour or protective clothing of any kind. Leather jerkins and shorts are mandatory; flesh must be open to a blade.
3. An Arena 13 contest is won and concluded when a cut is made to one's opponent and blood is spilled. This can occur during combat or may be a ritual cut made after a fight is concluded. If it occurs during combat, hostilities must cease immediately to prevent death or serious maiming.
4. If death should occur, no guilt or blame may be attached to the victor. There shall be no redress in law. Any attempt to punish or hurt the victorious combatant outside the arena is punishable by death.
5. The right to make a ritual cut is earned by disabling one's opponent's *lac* or *lacs*.
6. The defeated combatant must accept this ritual cut to the upper arm. The substance *kransin* is used to intensify the pain of that cut.

7. An unseemly cowardly reaction to the ritual cut after combat is punishable by a three-month ban from the arena. Bravery is mandatory.

8. Simulacra, commonly known as lacs, are used in both attack and defence of the human combatants.

9. The min combatant fights behind one lac; the mag combatant fights behind three lacs.

10. For the first five minutes combatants must fight behind their lacs. Then the warning gong sounds and they must change position and fight in front of them, where they are more vulnerable to the blades of their opponent.

11. A lac is disabled when a blade is inserted in its throat-socket. This calls the wurde *endoff*; the lac collapses and becomes inert.

12. Arena 13 combatants may also fight under **Special Rules**.

SPECIAL RULES

1. **Grudge match rules**

   The objective of a grudge match is to kill one's opponent. All **Primary Rules** apply, but for the following changes:
   - If blood is spilled during combat, hostilities need not cease; the fight continues.
   - After an opponent's lac or lacs have been disabled, the opponent is slain. The throat may be slit, or the head severed from the neck – the decision belongs to the victor. The death blow is carried out by either the victorious human combatant or his lac.
   - Alternatively the victor may grant clemency in return for an apology or an agreed financial penalty.

2. **Trainee Tournament rules**

    The objective of this tournament is to advance the training of first-year trainees by pitting them against their peers in Arena 13. For the protection of the trainees and to mitigate the full rigour of Arena 13 contests, there are two changes to the **Primary Rules**:
    - The whole contest must be fought behind the lacs.
    - Kransin is not used on blades for the ritual cut.

3. **A challenge from Hob**
    - When Hob visits Arena 13 to make a challenge, a min combatant must fight him on behalf of the Wheel.
    - All min combatants must assemble in the green room, where that combatant will be chosen by lottery.
    - Grudge match rules apply, but for one: there is no clemency.
    - The fight is to the death. If the human combatant is beaten then, alive or dead, he may be taken away by Hob. Combatants, spectators and officials must not interfere.

SECONDARY RULES

1. Blades must not be carried into the green room or the changing room.
2. No Arena 13 combatant may fight with blades outside the arena. An oath must be taken at registration to abide by that rule. Any infringement shall result in a lifetime ban from Arena 13 combat.
3. Spitting in the arena is forbidden.
4. Cursing and swearing in the arena is forbidden.
5. Abuse of one's opponent during combat is forbidden.
6. In the case of any dispute, the Chief Marshal's decision is absolute. There can be no appeal.

Also available by Joseph Delaney

THE
SERIES

THE WARDSTONE CHRONICLES

THE STARBLADE CHRONICLES

JOSEPH DELANEY

RED FOX

ARENA 13
A RED FOX BOOK 978 1 782 95405 7

First published in Great Britain by The Bodley Head,
an imprint of Random House Children's Publishers UK
A Penguin Random House Company

Penguin
Random House
UK

The Bodley Head edition published 2015
Red Fox edition published 2016

1 3 5 7 9 10 8 6 4 2

Penguin Random House is committed to a sustainable future for
our business, our readers and our planet. This book is made from
Forest Stewardship Council® certified paper.

MIX
Paper from
responsible sources
FSC
www.fsc.org   FSC® C018179

Set in 13/17pt Bell MT by Falcon Oast Graphic Art Ltd.

RANDOM HOUSE CHILDREN'S PUBLISHERS UK
61–63 Uxbridge Road, London W5 5SA

www.**randomhousechildrens**.co.uk
www.**totallyrandombooks**.co.uk
www.**randomhouse**.co.uk

Addresses for companies within The Random House Group Limited
can be found at: www.**randomhouse**.co.uk/offices.htm

THE RANDOM HOUSE GROUP Limited Reg. No. 954009

A CIP catalogue record for this book is available from the British Library.

Printed and bound in Great Britain by CPI Group (UK) Ltd, Croydon, CR0 4YY

For Marie

The dead do dream.

They dream of the world of Nym and twist hopelessly

within its dark labyrinths,

seeking that which they can never reach.

But for a few, a very few, a wurde is called.

It is a wurde that summons them again to life.

Cursed are the twice-born.

PROLOGUE

Within that thirteen-spired citadel dwells Hob. He is
    thirsty for blood.
We will give him blood until he drowns.

Amabramdata: the Genthai Book of Prophecy

Hob is waiting for the woman in the darkness; waiting just
beyond the river, under the trees where the pale light of the
moon cannot reach him. He sniffs the air twice, exploring
it tentatively until the sharp scent of her blood is carried
towards him on the breeze. Now he can taste her on the back
of his tongue.

Shola is alone. Her husband and child are left behind in
the farmhouse at the top of the hill. Her son is sleeping; the
husband, Lasar, can do nothing to help her now.

The summons is strong; more powerful than ever. Shola
must answer Hob's call. Her will deserts her, and she runs
down the slope until she reaches the river. She knows
exactly where to go. She kicks off her shoes, lifts her dress
to her knees and begins to wade through the shallow water
towards the waiting darkness of the trees. At one point she
almost loses her balance on the slippery stones. The water

is cool and caresses her feet like the touch of a silk scarf, but her brow is hot and fevered and her mouth is dry.

The woman is at war with herself. One part of her wishes she could remain behind with her family, but she quickly dismisses the thought. If she does not go when summoned, then Hob will climb the slope to the farmhouse and kill her son.

Hob has threatened this.

Her husband would be unable to defend their son.

Better to suffer the will of Hob.

Tonight, as the sun went down, Lasar carried the battered leather case down from the attic, limped across the flags and placed it on the kitchen table. He drew from it two blades with ornate handles, each crafted in the shape of a wolf's head.

These were the Trigladius blades; the blades he'd once wielded in Arena 13 in the city of Gindeen, a lifetime ago.

'Don't go to him!' His voice was filled with anger. 'I will go in your place. Tonight I will cut the creature into pieces!'

'No!' Shola protested. 'Think of our son. If I don't go, Hob will kill him. He's warned me of that many times. You know that even if you were able to kill him this night, another would replace him tomorrow. You can't fight them all. You above all must know this! Please! Please! Let *me* go to him.'

At last, to Shola's relief, Lasar relented and replaced the blades in the leather case. He wept as he did so.

Now, as she steps out of the moonlight, she sees the outline of Hob's body against the sky. His eyes glitter in the darkness, brighter than the stars. He is huge; larger than she has ever seen him before.

She stands before him, trembling; her heart is pounding and the breath flutters in her throat like a soul ready for flight. She sways but does not fall. Hob has moved closer now and has gripped her hard by the shoulders.

He will just take a little of her blood, she tells herself; her heart will labour for a while and her legs will tremble. There will be some pain, but she will be able to endure it. It will be just like the other times, soon over, and then she will be free to return to her family.

But this is different. This is the time she has always feared – the last time he will ever summon her. She has heard the tales; she knew that it would come to an end eventually . . . One night Hob would not allow her to return.

His teeth pierce her throat very deeply – too deeply. The pain is worse than ever before. He is drinking her blood in great greedy gulps.

This is the beginning of her death.

As her vision darkens, memories of her husband and child flicker into her mind and she is submerged by a wave of sadness and longing. She struggles to block them out. Memories bring only pain.

And as she falls into darkness, she experiences something even more terrible. It is as if a hand is reaching deep within her to snatch and twist and loosen; reaching beyond her heart, beyond her flesh, to draw her essence forth like a tooth.

It is as if something is sucking forth her very soul.

Some call him Old Hob. Others whisper Pouke to frighten children. Some name him Gob or Gobble. Women call him Fang.

By any name he is an abomination.

A creature such as this deserves to be cut into pieces and scattered to the winds.

But men are weak and afraid, and here Hob rules.

For this is Midgard, the land of a defeated and fallen people.

This is the Place Where Men Dwell.

Stick-Fighting

Sticks and stones may break my bones,
But wurdes are far more deadly.

The Compendium of Ancient Tales and Ballads

I watched the two stick-fighters circling each other warily. The boy with the blond hair was tall and fast, a local champion who was taking on all comers. I'd already watched him beat four opponents with ease, but this fifth one was giving him a harder time. He was squat and muscular but had surprisingly rapid reactions.

These fighters were a couple of years older – maybe seventeen or eighteen – and much bigger than me. Could I beat the champion? Was I good enough? I wondered.

Blows had already been exchanged, but none had struck home where it counted; a blow to the face or head would result in immediate victory.

They were fighting on waste ground at the outskirts of the city, within an excited circle of spectators who were punching the air and shouting, clutching betting tickets they'd bought from the tout who was watching the contest from a distance. Mostly the crowd was young – teenagers like myself – but there were middle-aged people there too; they displayed the same degree of enthusiasm, waving and shouting encouragement to the fighter they supported.

Betting against the champion was risky: you were likely to lose your money. Though if by chance you won, you received four times your stake. I wouldn't have risked a bet against this champion. Despite the skill of his adversary, he looked certain to triumph.

Even if I'd wanted to, I couldn't bet because I had no money. I'd been walking for almost two weeks and had only just arrived in the city of Gindeen. I'd eaten nothing for over a day and desperately needed food. That's why I'd come to watch the stick-fighting. I hoped to take part. The tout arranged the bouts so that he could make money from the betting, but only paid the winning fighter.

Suddenly the short, muscular boy threw caution to the wind and attacked wildly, driving his opponent backwards. For a few seconds it looked as if his aggression and speed would prevail. But the tall blond boy stepped forward and smashed his stick hard into his opponent's mouth.

As the polished wood made contact with flesh and teeth, there was a hard *thwack* followed by a soft squelching sound.

The loser staggered backward, spitting out fragments of tooth as blood poured from his mouth to drench the front of his shirt.

That was it: over. Now it was my time – or at least, I hoped it was.

I joined the back of the small queue of spectators who were waiting to collect their winnings. At last I reached the front and stared up at the tout. He was wearing a blue sash diagonally across his body; the mark of his trade – a gambling agent. His strong jaw and close-set eyes made him look tough; moreover, his nose had been badly broken and squashed back against his face.

'Where's your betting ticket?' he demanded. 'Hurry up. I haven't got all day!'

As he spoke, I saw the missing and broken teeth. I guessed that he'd once been a stick-fighter himself.

'I'm not here to bet,' I told him. 'I want to fight.'

'From down south, are you?' he sneered.

I nodded.

'New to Gindeen?'

I nodded again.

'Done much stick-fighting before?'

'A lot.' I stared up into his eyes, trying not to blink. 'I usually win.'

'Do you now?' He laughed. 'What do they call you, lad?'

'My name's Leif.'

'Well, you've got spirit, Leif, I'll give you that. So I'll let you have a chance. You can fight next. The crowd like to see a bit of new blood!'

I'd got my opportunity more easily than I'd anticipated.

He led me to the centre of the patch of muddy grass and put his big beefy left hand on the top of my head. Then he pointed to the tall blond boy, whose previous opponent was no longer to be seen, and beckoned him forward to stand on his right-hand side.

'Rob won again!' he cried. 'Will this lad ever be beaten? Well, maybe his time has finally come . . . This is Leif, who's new to the city. He's fought before, down south. He's fought and he's won. Perhaps a provincial boy can show you city lads a thing or two. So come and place your bets!'

A moment or two passed before anybody reacted. Over two hundred pairs of eyes were judging me. Some of the spectators were grinning; others were staring at me with open contempt.

Meanwhile I sized up my opponent. His white shirt gleamed in the late-afternoon sunlight and his dark trousers and leather boots were of good quality. In contrast my green checked shirt was smeared with dirt from the journey and my left trouser knee had a hole in it. People were now staring down at my shoes, the soles flapping free of the toes. My skin was also darker than that of anyone else present. Some spectators simply shook their heads and walked away.

If nobody wanted to bet, I wouldn't get to fight. I needed to fight and I needed to win.

However, to my relief, a small queue soon formed in front of us and bets were placed.

Once that was over I faced my next problem.

'I haven't got a stick to fight with. I don't suppose some-body would lend me one . . .' I asked the tout, pitching my voice so that the crowd could hear as well.

I'd left my fighting sticks back home with my friend Peter. I hadn't travelled to Gindeen to become a stick-fighter. I'd thought those days were behind me.

The tout rolled his eyes and cursed under his breath, and some of the queue fell away, suddenly uninterested. But then someone placed a stick in my right hand, and moments later I faced the champion while the crowd formed a circle around us. Immediately I saw that I faced yet another dilemma. It was late afternoon and the sun was quite low in the sky. I was looking directly into it.

My opponent moved towards me in a crouch, a dark silhouette against the sun. I squinted at him, waiting for his attack, and he lunged forward. He was fast and I barely avoided the blow. I twisted left and began to circle while he tracked me with his eyes.

The crowd began to chant his name: 'Rob! Rob! Rob!'

They wanted him to win. I was an outsider.

I continued to circle until I was no longer blinded by the sun and stared back into the blue of his eyes. He wasn't crouching any more, and I noted again just how tall he was. His reach would be far greater than mine. I needed to make him over-commit and then get in close.

He attacked again, and I ducked away as his stick flashed over my right shoulder. He'd almost caught me that time. My shoes weren't helping. With each step I took, the loose soles slapped down on the damp, slippery grass.

Concentrate, Leif, concentrate, I told myself.

The next time he attacked I wasn't quick enough. He dealt me a painful blow on my right arm and I dropped the stick.

Immediately the crowd gave a great cheer of glee.

One rule of stick-fighting is that, whatever happens, you must not drop your weapon. Do that and it's as good as over – your opponent can move in close and strike you without fear of counterattack. The blow had struck a nerve and numbed my right arm, which now hung uselessly at my side.

I'd begun with a degree of confidence – I remembered all my victories back home – but maybe I'd misjudged the situation. After all, the city was far more populous than the rural area I came from. It stood to reason that, with more stick-fighters, the standards would be higher.

Rob was smiling, his stick raised as he approached. I wondered if he would go for my mouth – if so, I'd probably lose my teeth.

The crowd began to chant again, louder and louder: 'Run, rabbit, run! Run, rabbit, run! Run! Run! Run!'

They were laughing as they chanted. They wanted me to give up and run away.

Running would have been the sensible thing to do. Why wait here to have my teeth smashed in?

I never found out whether Rob was aiming for my fore-head or my mouth. I dived in under the blow and rolled close to his boots, snatching up my stick with my left hand. I was already on my feet before he'd turned to face me.

Then I kicked off my useless shoes – first the right one and then the left. Time seemed to slow, and I heard each one slap down onto the grass. I spread my toes and gripped the grassy surface. That felt better. Next I took a firm grip on the stick. My right arm was still numb, but that didn't matter. I favour my right hand but I'm almost as good with my left. I can fight with either.

I attacked.

Rob was fast, but I am fast too – very fast. Maybe I wasn't as quick in my bare feet as I'd have been wearing a good pair of boots, but I was quick enough. I caught him on the right wrist, then high on his left shoulder – not hard enough to numb his arm and make him drop his stick, but I succeeded in enraging him, and that was exactly what I'd wanted.

I had good reason to be angry myself. I'd been hurt, and there were very few people watching who wanted me to win. Only about four people had bet on me. But a stick-fighter whose vision clouds with anger has taken a big step towards defeat. When I fought, I always tried to keep calm, but I could see that my opponent was furious. No doubt he was rarely hit. Maybe he felt shamed in front of his supporters and wanted revenge. Whatever the reason, now I'd got under his skin and he became reckless. He came at me, swinging his stick as if he wanted to strike my head from my shoulders.

He missed three times because I was dancing away, retreating across the grass. But after his third attempt I suddenly stepped inside his guard.

For a second he was wide open – so I took my chance.

I could have struck him in the mouth – repeating what he'd done to the previous combatant. Some fighters were brutal and liked to inflict the maximum damage on their opponent. But I really liked stick-fighting, preferring to exercise the skill and speed that led to victory rather than deal the blow that ended the bout.

So I hit Rob with minimum force; just a quick strike to the forehead which didn't even draw blood.

It was enough.

Rob looked stunned. The crowd fell silent.

I'd won. That was all that mattered.

The tout was smiling when he paid me out. 'You are good. Very fast!' he said. 'Come back tomorrow at the same time and I'll find you someone even better to fight.'

'Maybe,' I said with a smile, just to be polite. I'd no intention of doing so. Stick-fighting didn't figure in my plans.

I was now able to buy food and had a little money left over – enough to get my shoes stitched back together.

That night I slept in a barn on the edge of the city. I was up at dawn and washed at a street pump, trying to make myself as presentable as possible for the meeting I had in mind – with Tyron, one of the most important men in the city of Gindeen.

I had a winning blue ticket. It gave me the right to be trained by the best – and that was Tyron.

I wanted him to train me to fight in Arena 13.

Tyron the Artificer

Whom the gods wish to destroy they curse with madness.
Whom the gods wish to flourish they bless with luck.

Amabramsum: the Genthai Book of Wisdom

'Sit down, sit down!' commanded Tyron, nodding impatiently towards the chair opposite his desk.

No sooner had I done so than he shook his head fiercely and pointed back at the open door behind me. 'We don't want everybody knowing our business, boy.'

He had a point. This was a public building, the Wheel's administration offices, and the corridor outside was busy.

Having closed the door and sat down once more, I waited for Tyron to speak. I was doing my very best to be patient. I'd given him my blue ticket early in the morning, explaining what I wanted. Now it was less than half an hour before sunset; he'd had plenty of time to make up his mind.

What would he decide to do? Why had it taken him so long?

The room had no windows: suspended from the ceiling was a three-branched wooden candelabrum, the stubby yellow candles burning steadily in the still air. There was an odour of tallow and sweat.

Tyron shuffled papers about as he searched his large leather-topped desk. My chair was much lower than his so that, even if I'd been as tall as him, he'd still have been able to look down at me. I felt sure this wasn't an accident.

I could have taken my winning ticket to any of the trainers in Gindeen, but I'd chosen to present it to Tyron. Everybody in the whole country seemed to think he was the best. Even back home people knew his name. He looked different to the man I'd imagined: he was thick-set, with a ruddy complexion, and greying hair cut very short to disguise the fact that it was thinning at the front. Character was etched into his face: here was someone who had lived a lot and knew things.

'Look, you've won the right, boy,' he said now, holding my ticket aloft. 'I can't take that away from you. But how much is it worth?'

I didn't know what he meant. You couldn't sell a winning ticket. It couldn't be exchanged for money. And it was only valid once it had been checked and signed by the overseer of the gambling houses. I'd seen to that, so now it could only be used by me.

'Supposing I find you a trade apprenticeship instead?' he suggested, and my heart sank. 'Something nice and steady. The city's becoming more prosperous. You could be a builder or a joiner. When you come out of your time five years from now, you could earn a good living. Be set up for life. All you have to do is put this ticket back in your pocket and forget all about it. I'll even pay for your apprenticeship, your accommodation and food – and you won't owe me a penny.'

Why would he do that? I wondered. Why did he want to get rid of me so badly that he would pay my keep elsewhere? After all, giving me what I wanted wouldn't cost him anything. The gambling houses supported five trainees each season. This was partly funded by the thousands of tickets sold to young hopefuls. Or, more usually, to fathers who bought them on their behalf. Blue tickets were expensive.

Arena 13 in Gindeen attracted those who sought excitement and a chance of fame; the opportunity to earn real money, rather than being bound to some trade or, even worse, stuck in the drudgery of unskilled labouring. This was why I wanted to fight there too – though I had another, more personal reason that I wasn't prepared to divulge to anyone yet – not even Tyron.

'Well, what do you say?' he asked. 'What trade would you like to follow?'

'I want to work for you, sir,' I repeated. 'I want to learn how to fight in the arena.'

'What's your name again?' Tyron demanded.

I took a deep breath and gave him the information for the third time. 'My name is Leif,' I reminded him.

He got to his feet. 'Look, I don't want you, Leif.' His voice was louder now, and edged with real anger. 'Why should I give you a place when I've dozens with proven ability already clamouring at my door? The system says that your winning ticket gives you the right to be trained, but that doesn't necessarily mean trained by *me*. You're just trying to live out a dream like lots of other young lads from the provinces. The reality of this life is not what you've been led to believe. None of it is. I bet you've never even been inside the Wheel or seen any of the arenas.'

I bowed my head. He was right. This was my first visit to Gindeen.

'I only arrived yesterday. I haven't had a chance to see anything yet.'

'Who brought you here?' Tyron demanded. 'Whose wagon was it?'

'Nobody brought me.'

'Nobody? You'll be telling me next that you walked!'

'Yes, I did. I walked.'

'What! All the way from Mypocine?'

I nodded.

Tyron raised his eyebrows in astonishment. I thought he was going to make some comment, but instead he asked, 'Tell me about that ticket, boy! Who paid for it – your father?'

'My father's dead and so is my mother.'

'Well, I'm sorry to hear that. But I asked you a question. When I ask a question, I expect to be answered.'

'Two weeks ago a merchant came to Mypocine,' I explained. 'He had a big convoy of five wagons, and everyone came for miles around to barter or buy. Late in the afternoon the men started drinking and he joined them. After a while he suggested that the local lads should put on a bit of a show for him and he'd give a prize to the winner. So we started stick-fighting, three against one.

'As usual, I won, but I was really disappointed when my prize was only a blue lottery ticket—'

'Hold it there a minute,' Tyron interrupted. 'What did you say?'

I thought I'd spoken clearly but I repeated, 'I said I was disappointed because I'd only won a blue—'

'No, not that – it was your first two words that caught my attention. You said you'd won *as usual*. Did I hear you right?'

I nodded. I wasn't showing off; just telling the truth. 'I was the best stick-fighter in Mypocine – the champion. Since turning fourteen I've only ever lost once. That was because it was wet and I slipped in the mud – though that's no excuse. If you want to win, you don't slip.'

'And how old are you now?'

'I was fifteen last week.'

'So you usually fought alone against a team of three boys?'

I nodded. 'Yes, mostly it was one against three, just like the lacs in Arena 13. But occasionally it was one against one.'

'Go on with your tale. You said you were disappointed with your prize. Why would that be?'

'Because I'm just not lucky,' I told him. 'I never have been. Only five of all those thousands bought each year are winning tickets. But the Chief Marshal pulled mine from a lottery orb. I'd won! So I set off for the city straight away. As I told you, I walked all the way and it's taken me since then to get here.'

'This merchant – describe him!' commanded Tyron.

'He was a big man, probably about your age. He had red hair and a red beard.'

Tyron sighed long and deeply, and the expression on his face made me think that he knew the man I'd described.

There was an uncomfortable silence and I ended it, talking fast.

'I've walked all the way from Mypocine. Doesn't that show how much I want to be here and fight in the arena? I want to be trained by the best – that's why I chose you!

I want to be one of the greatest and most successful combatants ever. That's been my dream since I was a child. Please give me a chance. I'll work as your servant without pay until you see what I can do.'

'What do you mean by that?'

'Until you see me fight.'

'You can't fight until you've been trained, and I've already told you that I'm not prepared to train you. So I'm not going to waste any more of my breath. Now, off you go, boy! Go and bother somebody else!' Tyron snapped, pointing at the door.

I got to my feet and pushed back my chair to leave, filled with a mixture of emotions. I stared at him for a moment before turning and heading for the door.

'Here!' Tyron shouted. 'Catch!'

As I turned back towards him, he snatched something from his leather belt and hurled it at me.

It was a dagger.

It spun towards me, its blade gleaming in the candlelight. End over end it came. Concentrating, I noted that it was aimed a full hand-span to the right of my head. Tyron didn't want to hurt me; just to shock me. This was a test.

I reached up and plucked the dagger out of the air, walked back to the desk and set it down on the black leather, the hilt towards him. Then, slowly and quite deliberately, I bowed.

When I lifted my head again, Tyron was staring straight into my eyes; it was a long time before he spoke.

'Well, Leif, that earns you a visit to the Wheel,' he said at last. 'But that's all. I've a two-year-old grandson who can catch as well as that!'

The Stench of Blood

Victory is marked by a ritual cut to the arm of the
    defeated combatant.
Although, in combat, the intention is not to kill,
    accidents do happen.

The Manual of Trigladius Combat

As I followed Tyron through Gindeen's deserted narrow streets, it was getting dark, though the rain that had been pouring down when I arrived in the city had finally stopped. My heart felt as heavy as lead. Yes, it would be good to visit the Wheel. But I wanted more; much more . . .

It was still early in the spring, and all day long, hauled by teams of heavy dray-horses, wagons had been churning fresh furrows into the city. Running along outside the houses were wooden walkways, but many were in a bad state of repair, with missing planks and rotten boards; piles of rubbish obstructed some of the alleys between them. What I could see was a far cry from the big city of my imagination. I'd expected impressive buildings, order and tidiness.

While waiting for Tyron to make his decision, I'd spent part of my day watching the flow of traffic. Some wagons were loaded high with coal or wood, while others were huge canvas caravans, each home to some hopeful combatant from the provinces.

The Trig season started today and would last until early in the autumn. My father, who had fought in Gindeen, had told me that during this time the population almost doubled.

The sun still hadn't gone down, but from our vantage point on the hillside, the streets looked dark, with just the occasional lantern suspended from a hook. I had a feeling that we were being watched from the shadows. Maybe Tyron felt it too, because he was striding at a fast pace across the city.

Suddenly, out of the corner of my eye, I saw something move. To my left a monstrous shadow twitched across the whole width of an alley.

I came to a sudden halt. Could it be Hob? I wondered.

I remained frozen to the spot, and Tyron turned, frowning with annoyance.

'What is it, boy?'

I pointed to the shadow and the frown left his face. He took a cautious step into the alley, paused for a moment, and then beckoned me to his side, indicating a window which I could now see was the source.

It was the only one on the gloomy street that was illuminated, and through a gap in the curtains I saw someone staring out into the alley. The broad face was coarse and brutal, the nose flattened, the mouth open and devoid of teeth. A candle flame projected the man's shadow, distorting him far beyond human into some dark grotesque ogre. He was big and, although toothless, not far past his prime.

The candle stood behind him, and now he turned and reached for it, lifting it out of its holder. He pulled the flame close to his mouth as if he intended to eat it, but then a sudden paroxysm shook his whole body and he pursed his lips, expanded his cheeks and blew out the flame, plunging the room within into utter blackness.

'I saw a big shadow and thought it was Hob,' I said. 'Sorry.'

'There's no need to be sorry. For all we know, that *could* be Hob,' Tyron whispered, picking up his pace again. 'Hob could certainly be abroad on a night like this,' he went on. 'There are lots of tales about him. Mostly it's just superstition, but they're often based on truth.'

Hob was the djinni who terrorized the whole country of Midgard, though this city was the focus of that terror. He lived in a citadel on a hill high above Gindeen. It was fear of Hob that forced people off the streets during the hours of darkness. I didn't comment on what Tyron had said. I knew all about Hob. Who didn't?

We walked on in silence.

The city was built on the slopes of a great hill, the buildings constructed of wood, like almost everything else in Midgard. In fact, Gindeen was the only city in my country; Mypocine, far to the south, where I was born, had the second largest population, but compared to this it was tiny. I'd never seen so many houses, such a maze of streets. Even so, I could have found my own way to the Wheel. Rivalled only by the huge dark block of the slaughterhouse to the east, it was the most impressive structure on view, rising high above the city.

The Wheel was where the thirteen arenas were located. It was also where the gambling houses had their headquarters;

the centre of activity in a city that largely depended on arena combat and gambling for its prosperity. All the other wealth came from the surrounding farms and the cattle that were sold in the markets and driven to the slaughterhouse to feed the city's inhabitants.

The Wheel was a vast circular wooden edifice. The curved walls reared up into the sky like a cliff, topped by a high copper dome which was now bathed in a red glow from the last rays of the setting sun. It was far bigger than I had imagined; it took my breath away. The city had been a disappointment, but this was beyond my wildest dreams.

Above it, at least a score of black vultures circled ominously, soaring in slow widdershins spirals against the sun. It was said that the vultures spent the day haunting the slaughterhouse and the meat-wagons, but as the sun sank into the Western Ocean, they descended like harpies to the dome, flocking there when someone was about to die in Arena 13.

As I approached the entrance to the Wheel, I noticed a couple of large men in blue uniforms standing on either side of it. They glanced at me with a scowl, although Tyron just went in confidently as if they weren't there.

It was a shock to leave the cool, quiet, deserted streets and find myself in the hot, noisy, packed interior of the Wheel. I could almost taste the sweat. It was full of specta-tors jostling and pushing each other, with the loud buzz of conversation echoing back from the high ceiling above us. My head whirled with the excitement. Never had I seen so many people crammed together in one space, all struggling desperately to worm their way through the queues, but continually held back by the throng. The only time anyone halted was to exchange coins for tickets – which I knew meant that they were placing bets on likely victors in the various arenas.

I halted for a moment and stared up at the inside of the massive dome.

It was a big mistake.

When I looked down again, Tyron was almost out of sight, leaving me behind. A large, grim-faced man wearing a red diagonal sash was making straight for me. He carried a club at his belt and I was fairly sure he wasn't planning on giving me a friendly welcome.

Was it the way I was dressed? I wondered. The man scowled at me as the guards outside had done. I'd noticed a queue to enter the Wheel. Maybe, unlike Tyron, ordinary people had to pay an entrance fee.

Just in time, Tyron stepped back and grabbed hold of me.

The man bowed to him. 'Sorry, sir. I didn't realize he was with you.'

Tyron gave him a curt nod and the man moved away, satisfied.

'The red sashes tell you that he's a marshal representing the Wheel Directorate,' Tyron explained. 'Inside the Wheel, they're the law. Outside, as you just saw, it's the Protector's Guard, the big men in the blue uniforms, that you need to be wary of.'

The Protector ruled our country. He was rarely seen outside his palace. Those who had glimpsed him said that he looked like a middle-aged man, but there was speculation about his origins; some believed that he was a djinni. He had surely lived too long to be human.

'I haven't seen many guards before today,' I told him.

'You wouldn't, I suppose, out in the provinces. It's different here, very different. There are several thousand in barracks just north of the city. Keep a low profile and never look them in the eye, that's the key. They're bored, and sometimes that's all the excuse they need to find a problem with you.'

Tyron led me through a narrow door to a flight of steep stone steps. 'Follow me, boy,' he said as he began to descend. 'Before we visit any of the arenas I want you to see something else.'

At the foot of the staircase we entered a large cellar, a great gloomy vault lit only by a single flickering candle near the door.

Snatching it up, Tyron headed towards a long bench that stood against the far wall. My mouth went dry with fear, for upon it lay what looked like several dead bodies.

Was this a morgue? Why had Tyron brought me here? I wondered. I'd thought I was here to see the fighting.

'These are some of the lacs that I own,' Tyron said, gesturing towards the bench. 'They're used by Arena 13 combatants who work for me.'

I felt foolish. Of course they were lacs. Even so, a strong sense of unease took hold of me. I saw that some were covered with sheets, but Tyron led me towards one that was dressed in full armour. It lay on its back, the chain mail, helmet, mask and armoured plates on shoulders, arms, chest and knees in place.

I'd met people back in Mypocine who, like my father, had worked in Gindeen and encountered lacs. However, their descriptions hadn't prepared me for the thing that disturbed me most: the stink of the creatures.

There was a repulsive mixture of different odours: an animal smell that reminded me of a wet dog, along with rotting vegetation and foul straw. There was also a faint stench of excrement. I wondered what the lacs ate and if they were ever washed. There was so much that I didn't know.

'This is a simulacrum, but everybody uses the abbreviation "lac". It's a creature fashioned in the image of a man. Its flesh is similar to ours: it will bleed if cut and bruise if struck, but its mind is very different. It is not aware as we are aware. Its behaviour and actions are informed and executed by the patterning language called Nym – a language controlled by humans.'

Most of what Tyron was telling me was stuff I already knew, but I listened attentively, eager for even the smallest piece of new knowledge.

'A human combatant isn't permitted to wear armour in the arena,' Tyron continued, 'but lacs are different. Here one important piece of armour is still missing. Look . . .'

The lac had a thick muscular neck, and where Tyron now pointed I saw a vertical slit in the bare throat, the wound a dark purple that showed up against the white skin.

'That's the throat-slit – and this contains the socket that fits inside it . . .' Tyron bent down and picked up a large collar. He spat onto the narrow metal socket and eased it gently into the creature's throat-slit. As he did so, the lac groaned deep down in its belly.

Once that was done, he snapped the collar into place about the broad neck. There was still a slit to receive a blade, but now it was protected by a metal sheath.

'Now the slit is held slightly open to receive a blade,' explained Tyron. 'Because of that metal sheath the flesh cannot be cut. Usually there is only minimal bruising.

'The metal protects the soft flesh and makes it easier to effect a clean insertion. Of course, the socket displaces and constricts the gullet somewhat, causing the lac discomfort. Most believe that this makes it more eager to seek an early victory. It's always the last piece of armour to be fitted – and the first to be removed.

'When a blade is inserted in the throat-socket, it brings about a complete shut-down of the defeated creature's nervous system. We call this "endoff" – but it isn't death for a lac as it would be for a human. Take out the blade and, with a wurde, a lac can be returned to consciousness, ready to fight again.'

Despite my unease, I reflected that I would have to get used to working with beings such as this if I wanted to fight.

Tyron now placed his open palm on the metal armour that covered the forehead of the lac. 'Awake!' he commanded softly.

The lac sat up very suddenly, stretching its long arms like a man awaking from sleep. It drew in a deep breath, and behind the narrow horizontal slit of the face armour, the eyes flickered rapidly. The creature looked menacing and my heart gave a lurch – I found myself taking a step backward. Luckily, I don't think Tyron noticed because he was still concentrating on the lac.

'Selfcheck!' he snapped. 'Now I've instructed the lac to get busy checking its own mind and body; it's going over the complex patterns that give it the skills to fight in the arena.'

I nodded – though I didn't really understand all of what Tyron was saying. For the first time since I'd left home, I felt overwhelmed by the challenge I had set myself. The expression on my face obviously gave me away because Tyron smiled. 'In time trainees learn to pattern, but to begin with, they work with lacs that have already been patterned and trained.'

'Can it see us?' I asked nervously, studying the lac's flickering eyes.

'Oh, it can see us all right. And it can think. But it's the patterns that do the thinking. It's not conscious as we are. Some people think they're called "lacs" because they lack sentience and aren't aware, but that's a load of nonsense. Five hundred years ago, master artificers patterned lacs that were sentient – just as alive and aware as you and me. We can't do that any more. That knowledge has been lost over time, unfortunately. A lac is faster and stronger than a man, but always remember that it's not sentient, so don't go worrying about that. Anyway, boy, let's go up and look at a couple of the arenas now.'

We left the cellar and went back up the steps. When we emerged, we had to push our way through the crowd and I felt the buzz of excitement. Tyron gestured upwards. 'Above that ceiling there's a large circular hall. That's where the Lists naming the combatants who are to fight are posted. On this level, the floor is divided like the spokes of a wheel into thirteen combat zones,' he explained. 'You access each from the corridor set within the outer walls.'

It was difficult to hear what Tyron was saying. Not only were people jostling us and shouting to be heard as they passed, there was now also a distant roar of chants and cheers, and what sounded like the steady rhythmical beating of a drum.

Tyron led me into the first zone, and I saw that each of these spokes was on two levels. Below us was a windowless wooden box, open at the top. The spectators stood above, looking down on the action.

We joined the rabble jostling for position on the sloping viewing balcony. The ones right at the front were squashed hard against the metal safety rails; it seemed to me that they were at very real risk of broken ribs or worse. I was glad that Tyron seemed content to stay to the rear.

Almost all the spectators were male. They were coarse and loud, shouting obscenities and spitting down into the arena below. Surges of anger or excitement rippled across the crowd as if it was one great beast with myriad backs but a minuscule mind.

Tyron forced me to look down, beyond the spectators. 'That's where the action is, boy.'

The small square arena below couldn't have been much more than ten paces by ten paces. Within it I saw two huge lumbering figures clad in crude bronze armour. They clashed together with a wild locking and swinging of arms, butting heads and roaring loudly.

'You can make a good living here in Arena 1,' said Tyron, shouting into my ear. 'Some of my trainees concentrate just on patterning creatures such as these. So if you've the brains for it, there's no need to set foot in Arena 13. Why not let the lacs do it for you? In all the other arenas the lacs fight each other. Men aren't involved at all. It's only in Arena 13 that you risk your life.'

The two battling figures below were creatures like the one we'd just examined in the cellar. With a hand on my arm, Tyron steered me away from the viewing balcony and back into the long curved corridor. We walked clockwise, passing the open doors that led to other arenas.

'Move with the clock,' Tyron told me. 'As you go round, each arena represents a higher level of skill. People new to this game begin by entering lacs at the lowest level. Then they gradually work their way up. Some never make it – or want to make it – but the very best reach Arena 13, where the Trigladius method of combat takes place.' His voice was now almost a whisper.

'Trigladius is an ancient word meaning "three swords". Except on formal occasions, everyone simply calls it the Trig.'

My father had explained what fighting in Arena 13 involved. In fact, it had seemed to me that he barely stopped talking about it until the difficult, terrifying months before his death, more than three years ago.

One human combatant stood behind three lacs – known as a tri-glad – in what was called the mag position, while his adversary was defended by a lone lac in what was called the min position. It didn't seem fair, but that was the way it was done. It was obviously much harder for the one to defeat the three, and therefore the odds were always against the former.

That was where the gambling came in. If you bet on the min combatant and he won, you won too – a lot of money.

I knew that my father had been a min combatant. You needed great skill and speed to win from the min position, so that's what I wanted to do too. I wanted to be the best.

Finally Tyron opened a door and I took a deep breath as we stepped inside. 'Here we are.'

Arena 13 was far larger than I'd expected after seeing the first arena – fifty paces long by twenty-five wide – and the steep rake of the gallery seats made it easy to look down into it. Here there was no standing room, but it still held at least two thousand spectators.

The tiers of seats were richly upholstered in red leather, and the outer pillars were adorned with intricate carvings; torches were embellished with gold and silver and the wood of the curved walls was a dark, rich mahogany. The smell of wood and leather was everywhere; it suggested tradition, polish and manners.

The Arena 13 gallery already looked full, but Tyron led the way confidently down to the front. He was well-known, and people waved or nodded to him as we passed. When we reached the front and pushed our way along to our seats, people leaned across and patted Tyron on the back with evident warmth and enthusiasm, though they eyed me with interest.

The nearer to the rail we got, the greater the finery worn by the spectators: I could not take my eyes off the women. They were dressed in rich silks unlike any I'd seen before, either inside or outside the city. They wore elaborate ribbons in their hair, rouge upon their cheeks, and in every case their

lips were painted black. Their escorts wore diagonal sashes
of different colours.

'What are the sashes for?' I asked Tyron as we took our
seats.

'A few indicate ranks, but most are just the formal sashes
of the various trade guilds – armourers are green, butchers
are brown, and so on,' he explained.

'Why don't you wear a sash?' I asked him.

He pointed to his broad leather belt and to the clasp
which bore a number fashioned out of bronze:

13

'That tells everybody exactly what I am, boy. This is my
territory. This is where my stable of combatants fight. I'm
the best there is in this city. I'm no braggart. That's the plain
truth.'

The sweet scent of women's perfume floated upon the still
air, mixing with the smell of ancient wood and leather. And
there was something else now. An underlying smell of sweat,
yes, but something metallic and sour too.

With a start, I realized that it was the stench of blood.

The Grudge Match

Grudge matches usually end in the decapitation of
  the loser.
Sometimes the throat is only cut.
These are the preferred methods.
An untidy death results from multiple cuts to the body.

The Manual of Trigladius Combat

Everywhere there was excitement. It tingled in the air,
fluttering on the lips of the women and trembling on the
restless hands of the men. But nobody could have been more
excited than I was. At last I was looking down on Arena 13!
My whole body quivered with anticipation. There were so
many questions I wanted to ask, but I couldn't trust myself
to speak. I knew I would stammer or sound foolish; Tyron
was testing me: I needed to look, and sound, confident.

Money was changing hands; a lot of money. Wagers
were being taken by the gambling agents who were
busily working the aisles, accepting last frantic bets and
issuing red tickets.

Our seats were in the first row. Below, in the arena, a
huge candelabrum that held thirteen torches was being
slowly lowered from the high ceiling so that it cast

flickering yellow light upon the combatants, who had already emerged from the two doors – the min and the mag doors – and were taking their positions. The first contest was about to begin.

Somewhere out of sight a bass drum sounded; a slow, steady rhythm like the beating of a monstrous heart.

A tall figure dressed in black and wearing a red sash moved amongst the combatants. The drum halted very suddenly and a hush fell over the gallery.

'That's Pyncheon, the Chief Marshal,' Tyron whispered to me. 'He has full control within the Wheel, but in Arena 13 his function is mainly ceremonial. He'll get out of there before the action starts. If there's a problem during the bout, he will make any necessary ruling.'

The Chief Marshal moved between the two opposing groups. The lacs were dressed in metallic armour from head to toe, the horizontal slits in their helmets enabling them to see. They were identical to the armoured one Tyron had shown me below.

The two humans, who were standing behind their lacs, wore no protective armour. They were dressed in leather shorts and jerkins, the former cut high above the knee, the latter close to the armpits.

This was something else that my father had described to me. Their unprotected flesh was the target of the lacs' blades.

His hands held theatrically aloft, Pyncheon looked up towards us. Then, in a loud voice, he addressed the gallery: 'This is Arena 13,' he boomed. 'This is a fight to the death. Let those who die die with honour. Let those who live remember them. Let it begin!'

Had I heard correctly? What was happening? I couldn't believe it. Why were they fighting to the death?

I saw that the two combatants were just boys, barely older than me. I looked at Tyron, trying to catch his eye, but he was staring down into the arena.

The Chief Marshal turned and headed for the mag door. Here he paused and lifted a long silver trumpet to his lips: a high shrill note emerged. Immediately the two doors rumbled shut.

The crowd was utterly silent. Not one of the figures in the arena below had even moved.

'What colour are the tickets being sold by the touts, boy?' Tyron asked.

I didn't need to check; I'd noticed them as we came in.

'They're red,' I answered.

'Yes, they're red, boy, and that's because this is a grudge match. You heard what the Chief Marshal said. It's one in which someone usually dies. That's why I brought you here. I wanted you to see just how bad things can get.'

'But why are they fighting to the death?' I asked. 'What possible reason could there be for it?'

'Sometimes it's a dispute over a woman. Here it's plain stupidity. They got drunk one night and traded insults. It got out of hand, and too many bitter words were exchanged. So they've chosen to settle it here. Now blood will be spilled!'

The combatants came together hard, with a deafening clash of metal upon metal; immediately the min combatant seemed to be in trouble. His feet began to thump desperately on the boards, signalling new movements to his lone lac, which was hard pressed to defend him from the blades trying to cut his flesh.

My father had actually fought in this arena. He had told me that a combatant told his lac what to do by beating on the floor with his boots. It was a sound-code, a system called *Ulum*.

'The human fighter in trouble is Kanus,' Tyron said, shaking his head, 'and he won't last much longer, the way he's shaping up. Sandor's too good for him.'

It was obvious that his opponent, fighting behind three lacs, was far better prepared. At first the bout was very one-sided, with Kanus steadily pushed back. Then, at last, things changed: Kanus seemed to regain a measure of control and the struggle became more even.

A rapid, intricate dance began. Patterns began to form. I was almost hypnotized by the rhythmical surge and ebb. Sharp blades gleamed in the torchlight. Sweat glistened on the brows of the two human combatants, each dancing warily behind the armoured lacs that protected them.

'This is worth watching.' Tyron interrupted my thoughts, his voice animated. Things on the fighting floor had changed again. 'Watch Sandor's three lacs. They're taking up a position known as the stack.'

Sandor was now sandwiched between two defensive lacs, one before him and one behind. They became the diameter of a wheel that began to rotate, first widdershins and then clockwise. While it was spinning, Sandor's third lac launched a ferocious attack so that Kanus was driven back against the far wall.

And then a gong sounded, stunning me as the noise

reverberated through the floor. In response, the combatants disengaged and changed position.

Now the two combatants were standing *in front* of their lacs rather than behind them.

What was happening? I was sure that my father had never told me about this!

'Now it gets even more dangerous, boy,' Tyron explained. 'After five minutes of fighting behind the lacs, the combatants must face each other directly, making themselves vulnerable to the blades of their opponent and his lac or lacs!'

As the fight began again, it seemed impossible to me that the two human combatants could survive more than a few seconds. After all, the lacs were armoured but the men only wore shorts and jerkins. Surely their flesh would be cut to ribbons . . .

But it seemed that although the two men were desperately trying to cut each other, they could never get quite close enough.

The arms of the lacs were far longer than human ones. The two men danced with their backs almost touching the chests of their lacs, which used their long arms to reach forward and fend off any attack.

It continued like this for several minutes. How much longer could it be before one of them was badly cut? I wondered.

No sooner had the thought entered my head than a blade came in hard, forcing Kanus backward into his lac; they were now pushed right back to the arena wall.

Kanus was cut again, and he gave a scream even shriller than the trumpet blown by the Chief Marshal. It seemed too high to have come from a human throat. The knives were flashing, and I saw a blade sink into the throat-socket of Kanus's lac. Then they were slicing into the man's body again, and blood was spraying everywhere.

The spectators were roaring and cheering in excitement. Most had leaped to their feet. Meanwhile Tyron and I remained seated. I was struck dumb with horror, while he was shaking his head at the spectacle below us.

Together the armoured lac and the man slid down the wall. But long before they crumpled into a heap at its foot, blades were arcing downwards, cutting into the flesh of the screaming Kanus.

Blood began to pool under his body, spreading outwards across the boards, and his screams gradually became fainter.

At last the crowd fell silent. All I could hear were faint whimpers from the dying combatant, and after a few seconds they ceased altogether.

I couldn't help noting the reactions of the spectators around us. Some stared with open mouths and wide excited eyes, almost drooling at the spectacle of the man's death. Others, like the old man on my left, simply shook their heads sadly. I heard him mutter the word 'untidy' to himself.

Below us, the victor raised his hands to receive the applause, while the dead man was dragged away without ceremony. A trail of blood marked his exit from the arena.

'The night's fighting is far from over,' said Tyron, 'but I think you've seen enough for now.' He got to his feet, beckoned me to follow and led the way out of the arena, climbing the rows of tiered seats until we reached the exit.

'Men die in Arena 13 . . .' He spoke slowly and deliberately.

'That's not the main intention, but it happens. You saw those stains on the floor. That's blood. Some of it's very old. Some of it's just from last season. And there'll be more added soon.'

He halted and turned to face me, staring into my eyes. 'Have you seen sense and changed your mind, boy?' he asked.

I opened my mouth to reply, but before I could speak he let out a long sigh. 'I can see it in your face! Your eyes are shining with excitement. Even after what I've said, the things you've seen, you still haven't changed your mind, have you?'

I shook my head. 'I want to fight in Arena 13.'

'You're stubborn, I'll give you that, boy. And despite my efforts, nothing I've said has deterred you. It's something I do with all my potential trainees – I have to be sure that they are fully committed.'

I felt a surge of hope. Did he intend to take me on? I wondered optimistically.

He pointed downwards. 'Right, boy, let's get ourselves back to my house. Are you hungry?'

I nodded.

'Well, you'll eat a good supper tonight. All my trainees eat well.'

Two Important Rules

The gods reward ambition,
For without it we are but dust.

Amabramsum: the Genthai Book of Wisdom

As we approached Tyron's house, I realized that the streets had changed. We were climbing, and I had already noticed that the wooden walkways were in a far better state of repair here. After a while they were replaced by stone flags, as the muddy roads gave way to wider cinder streets. Soon we entered an avenue of trees with fresh green leaves. This was where the prosperous city-dwellers lived.

Few of the wooden houses in this area were higher than one storey, but Tyron's house proved to be different.

It had four storeys and was the tallest house I'd seen in Gindeen. He took a key from his pocket and opened the door, stepping inside, then turning and facing me as if to bar my way.

'I'm going to give you a month's trial,' he said. 'The days will be long and will include both practical fighting skills and Nym theory, followed at the end of the day by basic maths. There'll also be a smattering of other subjects, including history.'

Now he'd confirmed it beyond all doubt. I was to be given the opportunity I'd dreamed of.

'There are three important rules to remember: firstly, I don't allow my trainees to drink alcohol. It slows the mind and the body – which is the last thing an Arena 13 combatant needs. I catch you drinking and you'll be out on your ear. Secondly, you have to take an oath before entering the arena for the first time. It's the law. You'll have to swear before the Chief Marshal never to use a steel blade as a weapon outside the arena. However, I take it a stage further and ban stick-fighting as well. That's my own rule for those who work for me. Understand? Or will that be too much for the best stick-fighter in Mypocine to stomach?' he asked drily.

'Can I ask why you ban stick-fighting?' I asked.

Tyron raised his eyebrows, and for a moment I thought he was going to tell me off. But then his face relaxed.

'To be successful at stick-fighting, you need speed and skill. But much of that type of combat is spontaneous. You can't afford to fight like that in Arena 13. You need discipline to work in partnership with lacs. Stick-fighting creates bad habits that may cost a combatant dearly in Arena 13. Not everybody thinks the same way as me, but I enforce the rule in my stable. So I'll ask you again, Leif. Will you abide by it?'

I nodded. 'I'll keep to your rules,' I told him, my heart thudding with excitement. 'I gave away my sticks before I set off for the city. Thanks for giving me a chance to prove myself. I promise not to let you down.'

'Well, boy,' Tyron said, 'your training begins tomorrow, but now it's time for supper. Your own clothes will have to do for now, but I'll sort out something better in the morning.'

We entered what was obviously the dining room, and I saw that supper was already being served. Tyron was clearly a wealthy man and could afford servants, who now bustled about the long table placing hot, steaming dishes of meat and vegetables at its centre. The food smelled delicious. My mouth began to water.

'This is Leif.' As Tyron addressed those seated at the long table, he pointed at me. 'He's my new novice. Sadly his father and mother are dead so he's travelled here alone. I'm sure he's going to do well. Let's make him feel welcome!'

The announcement was greeted with smiles, but nobody spoke. Tyron sat at the head of the table and directed me to its foot. As we waited for the servants to finish serving, he introduced me.

'This is my daughter, Teena,' he said, nodding towards the young woman seated on his right. 'She's been married four years and has already provided me with my first grandchild. But you won't meet him until tomorrow as he's been packed off to bed.'

'It's nice to meet you, Leif,' Teena said, giving me a friendly smile. 'I hope you'll be happy here. We'll be your family now.'

She was a very attractive woman, with blonde hair and blue eyes. I could tell at a glance that she was warm and generous and very genuine. I liked her immediately.

'And this is her husband, Kern,' Tyron continued, placing his hand on the shoulder of the man seated opposite Teena. 'Kern is about to begin his fifth season fighting in Arena 13.

This year he should build on his previous successes and rise very high in the rankings. You'll get to know him well as he'll be carrying out part of your training.'

Kern was a tall man with very dark hair; he seemed as open and friendly as his wife.

'I'm looking forward to working with you, Leif,' he said. He looked like he really meant it.

I started to relax, but when Tyron turned his attention to the other diners, the atmosphere wasn't quite as warm. There were two lads about the same age or slightly older than me; they stared at me, eyebrows raised.

'All my new trainees spend their first season under my roof. After that they have quarters in the Wheel. This is Palm,' Tyron said, pointing to the fairer boy. His hair was cut very short and his back was stiff. Had we both been standing I'm sure he'd have looked down his nose at me, for he had an air of superiority. 'Palm is the elder and more experienced, and already has several months of training behind him. He wants to fight behind three lacs. Luckily his father can afford it − it's very expensive to buy and maintain them.'

Palm nodded in my direction. He forced a smile, but only with his mouth, not his eyes. I could sense that he didn't welcome my presence.

The other, smaller, boy was introduced as Deinon. He had darker, mousier hair and was very slim. He seemed nervous and unsure of himself. Even though he seemed more friendly in his greeting than Palm, his eyes were wary.

'Right, let's begin. Help yourselves!' invited Tyron, looking directly at me. 'It's bad practice to train on a full stomach, so we have a light breakfast and just a snack at noon. So eat well because this is the main meal of the day.'

I didn't need a second invitation, so I filled my plate with slices of beef and a mound of potatoes and vegetables, and was generous with the gravy too. There was water to drink, but I noticed that, despite his rule for the trainees, Tyron drank red wine.

There was laughter and conversation at the far end of the table; I'd have been far happier chatting to Tyron, Kern and Teena. The two boys next to me were too busy eating to talk; I feared that it would prove difficult to get to know them.

A clatter at the door grabbed my attention, and I looked up from my plate for a moment to see someone else enter the room and take a seat next to Teena. It was a dark-haired girl of about my own age; she wore loose trousers tied with black ribbon at the ankles, above what looked like the same type of boots worn by the combatants in Arena 13. Her hair was pulled back into a bun, making her face look hard and angular.

'This is my younger daughter, Kwin, who makes a habit of being late for meals.' Tyron gave his daughter a long searching look. 'Kwin, this is my new trainee, Leif.'

Kwin didn't even fake a smile. She stared at me with hard, hostile brown eyes. To my surprise, I saw a scar on her left cheek, running from just below the eye almost to the corner of her mouth. Although the scar hadn't distorted her face, her otherwise attractive features were twisted; twisted with anger at my presence.

But at least, unlike the two trainees, she was honest.

There were three people in the room who clearly didn't want me here.

After supper, at Tyron's bidding, I followed Palm and Deinon upstairs to our sleeping quarters.

The three beds stood in a row down the long narrow room. Next to each bed was a small chest of drawers with a single flickering candle. On the left was the only window; the long green curtains were already closed.

'This is my bed, that's Deinon's – and that's yours,' said Palm, pointing towards the bed furthest from the window. There was another closed door next to it, and I noticed that it had a keyhole but no handle.

Something else caught my eye – a framed painting that hung over Palm's bed. It was a scene from Arena 13. In the foreground a combatant was facing forward; at his back stood a lac. The man held his arms out wide, blades gleaming in his hands. Behind him, the lac's blades were held at an angle of forty-five degrees, so that together they looked like one creature with four arms – a powerful, dangerous entity that hurled a challenge right at me.

'Do you like it?' Palm asked. 'It cost a lot of money to have that painted. Do you know who that is . . . ?' He pointed to the combatant.

I shook my head.

'It's Math, the great hero of Arena 13. He defeated Hob fifteen times!'

I stared at the picture and swallowed. My mouth was very dry. Suddenly I felt like I was about to fall, so I went and sat down on the edge of my bed.

No sooner was I seated than I was overcome by a wave of exhaustion – the journey here and the adrenalin of the day finally taking over. But my two roommates obviously weren't ready to let me sleep; they stared me, as if waiting for me to speak. I couldn't think of anything to say and the silence seemed to go on for a long time.

'Where are you from?' Palm asked at last.

'I lived just south of Mypocine,' I replied.

'You certainly look and sound like you come from down south.'

He spoke with the clear, clipped accent of the north. My first impression had been right: there was superiority in his every syllable. He was referring to my accent, with its broader vowels, and my darker skin colour. The expression on Palm's face said that I was to be pitied.

'What did your father do?' he asked.

'He was a farmer.'

'My father owns one of the largest farms north of Gindeen,' Palm said, as if he hadn't taken in what I had just said. 'I'm going to fight behind a tri-glad, and Tyron has promised to pattern it for me himself. He's already begun the work. The three lacs should be ready in a few weeks – I'll have time to get plenty of practice in before the TT. You do know about the TT?'

The boy was obviously demonstrating how much more experienced than me he was. I didn't need him to tell me, but I shook my head – it was best to be honest.

'It's what we call the Trainee Tournament. Later in the season there's a tournament for all the trainees and I'm going to win it. Even though you're the novice here, you'll have to enter as well. It's compulsory. Are you going to fight from the min?'

I nodded, noticing as he spoke a faint click at the end of some words. I wondered if he had something wrong with his jaw.

Palm gave me that pitying look again. 'So is Deinon,' he said, grinning at the other boy. 'But it's hard to beat a good tri-glad, so you'd better get used to being defeated – Deinon can tell you all about it.'

He suddenly got to his feet and went over to the wall, placing the palm of his right hand flat against it, just above my headboard.

'This wall is hot!' he declared loudly, grinning again. 'Come here, Leif! Feel it and tell me what you think!'

I could tell that this was some kind of trick, but I had to play along. I knew I'd be spending a lot of time with Palm and Deinon so I didn't want to appear hostile at our first meeting. I'd have to make an effort to be friendly and get on with them. I walked across and placed my hand flat against the wall as Palm had just done.

'What do you think?' he asked. 'Am I right or not?'

The wooden wall did feel mildly warm, but that was all.

Before I was forced to give my opinion, Palm asked me another question. 'Why do you think it's so hot?'

I shrugged.

'It's because a girl sleeps in the next room,' he added, his grin wider than ever. 'That's why. She makes the walls burn!'

'Who is she?' I asked. 'What girl?'

'Why, Kwin, of course, Tyron's younger daughter. What do you think of her scar?'

'How did she get it?'

'Kwin's crazy about the Trig. She never stops practising the steps. It's a waste of time, of course, because women aren't allowed to take part – they can't even set foot on the arena floor. But she won't be told – she practises like she really believes that she'll be allowed to fight there. It's just nonsense. Anyway, one day she went down to the cellar and activated a lac. Not just a practice one either. It was a lac that had been readied for Arena 13. She fought it blade against blade and almost lost an eye. Lucky for her, Tyron came down just in time to save her life. She could have been killed.'

Palm was still grinning and I started to go red. What was so funny about almost being killed? I felt embarrassed and angry. Everything he'd said so far seemed to be a long joke at my expense. And why was Deinon so silent? Had he nothing to say for himself? His silence began to annoy me.

Suddenly there was a loud knock on the wall above my bed. It was followed by two more.

'I'm number one, Deinon's number two and you're number three. Three knocks! That means you!' Palm shouted with glee. 'Kwin's knocking for you. Better not keep her waiting!'

I stared at him in astonishment.

'Don't look so miserable,' he jibed. 'Kwin can be fun. And if you want to stay on the right side of Tyron, you need to keep her sweet. She argues with her father a lot in public because she likes to be seen as a rebel. But, believe me, they're pretty close. Cross her, and you'll be out of here!'

I got to my feet.

Kwin

Her feet practise a tinker shuffle picked up on the
    street.
Like a long-legged fly upon the stream,
Her mind moves upon silence.

The Compendium of Ancient Tales and Ballads

A key turned in the lock and I watched the door next to my
bed open slowly, allowing a shaft of yellow candlelight into
the room.

I felt the eyes of Palm and Deinon watching me.

'Go on! Don't keep her waiting. Kwin gets annoyed very
easily!' said Palm.

For a moment I hesitated. Was Kwin in on the joke too?
Would all three of them soon be laughing at me?

I decided to go along with it. Did it matter? It was surely
just a bit of fun; probably some kind of initiation rite that all
new trainees went through. So, still feeling foolish, I walked
towards the door, opened it wider and entered the next room.

'You took your time!' Kwin snapped, an annoyed expression on her face. She strode past me to close the door and
turn the key in the lock once more.

I glanced at her angry face, then quickly scanned the

room. It didn't look like a girl's room at all. A pair of crossed blades was fastened to the wall directly over her bed, and the far wall was covered with sketches – clearly scenes from Arena 13. They immediately drew my attention and I walked over to examine them.

'They're great!' I said. 'Did you draw them yourself?'

Kwin nodded. A smile lit up her face and she suddenly seemed quite different to the girl who'd scowled at me during supper. For one thing, she was wearing a dress – a purple sheath that fitted her like a second skin. It was short, with small black leather buttons down the front, and only just covered her knees; the long sleeves came down almost to the end of her thumbs. Her hair was loose, softening her face. On the right side it was very long, but on the left it had been cut far shorter, almost as if to draw attention to her scar.

But the most striking thing about Kwin was her lips.

I had seen the women in Arena 13 earlier – they had all painted their lips black; that seemed to be the fashion. But only Kwin's upper lip was black. Her lower lip was painted the vivid red of arterial blood.

She came very close and took hold of my shirt collar, rubbing it between her thumb and forefinger, as if feeling its texture.

She was so close that I could feel the heat from her body and almost taste the scent of her skin on the back of my tongue. I caught my breath and my heart began to beat faster. I was strongly attracted to her, but I felt embarrassed by my clothes. I knew I smelled of stale sweat.

'You're dirty,' she said. 'I like that. It's authentic. Some of the kids tear their clothes and don't wash, but it's all an act.'

'I've been travelling for more than two weeks,' I explained. 'I walked here from Mypocine. Your father said he'd find me some clean clothes tomorrow.'

'Shame,' she said. 'Try not to make too much noise. My father's a light sleeper, but this staircase doesn't pass his room.'

Without further explanation she led the way out of her bedroom, and soon I was tiptoeing downstairs after her. Moments later, we'd left the house and were walking through the streets at a brisk pace.

'Where are we going?' I asked.

'The Wheel, of course,' Kwin replied. 'Where else is there to go at this time of night?'

I wondered why she was taking me there. 'I've just been to the Wheel,' I told her. 'Your father showed me round.'

'I'll show you what he hasn't,' she said. 'There are places there he'd never go.'

I decided to let her lead for the moment. She knew this city well; there was lots that she could teach me about it. After all, I needed to learn all I could.

Now that the sun had gone down, the Wheel's dome was invisible; without Kwin ahead of me I would have struggled to find my way there. We took a winding route that led us through the very darkest and narrowest of streets. We seemed to be the only people out and about. I thought of the danger from Hob and started to feel nervous.

Where the narrow streets intersected, lanterns hung from cowled wooden posts, but to my surprise they'd already been extinguished. Anything could have been watching us out of the darkness. At one point I thought I heard footsteps following us.

This was the only city in the country of Midgard, and the streets were unlit; even back home in Mypocine the torches had burned until long after midnight.

'Keep up!' Kwin called, and I realized I could only just make out her figure ahead of me. I ran, managing to catch up with her before she turned the next corner.

'Aren't you scared of Hob?' I asked. He could be anywhere, lurking in the shadows.

'Maybe it's you who should be scared.' Kwin sniggered. 'Hob's a shape-shifter djinni. He could be living amongst us unnoticed. Watch yourself: *I* could be Hob!'

Her flippant response irritated me and I wished I'd stood my ground and refused to come with her. 'Do you think Hob's a joke?' I asked angrily.

Kwin rolled her eyes at me and didn't answer; she simply hurried on.

Rather than making for the front entrance of the Wheel, as I had with Tyron, Kwin led me round to the back. People were gathered outside and I saw that she had been right: this was somewhere the residents of Gindeen came to socialize at night. From the midst of the largest group, a deep male voice called her name.

He was a tall, well-muscled young man, maybe a couple of years older than me, and Kwin determinedly ignored him. I glanced at him as I followed her through a narrow door and saw that he looked hurt and disappointed. I wondered about the history between the two of them.

Once inside, she turned and addressed me. 'This is the level directly below the arenas,' she said. 'We could go lower – into the Commonality – but it's dangerous at this time of night.'

'What's the Commonality?' I asked.

'It's where most of the lacs are stored. There's stick-fighting down there almost every night. Serious bets and everything. It's very big – easy to get lost. You need to go in a big gang to be really safe there. Maybe you could get Palm and Deinon to take you with some of the other trainees.'

I couldn't imagine Palm making me his friend and I wasn't sure I wanted to be his. As for Deinon, he had nothing to say for himself and wouldn't be good company. I said nothing, and continued to follow Kwin down a long broad corridor, with doors every twenty paces. Most of these were closed, but at last she halted outside an open one.

I made to step through, but Kwin grabbed me and pulled me back.

'What?'

She just stared at me as if there was something obvious I was missing.

I looked about the large, dimly lit room. It seemed to be some kind of bar, and was furnished with huge chairs and couches upholstered in brown leather. Servants in purple jackets hovered, carrying trays of food and drink to the customers.

'It looks expensive,' I said.

'Of course it's expensive, but those who enter can afford it. That's not the reason we can't go in there.' There was anger in Kwin's voice.

Suddenly I realized why that was.

'There are no women here,' I said. Females weren't allowed to practise professionally, either as artificers or as combatants. 'Can't you even enter as a guest?' I asked.

'No, I can't! So tell me what you think, Leif,' Kwin challenged. 'Why shouldn't women fight in Arena 13?'

I couldn't think of a reply; we stared awkwardly at each other for a moment before Kwin shook her head, obviously as disgusted with me as she was with the rest of the world. I was struggling to find the right words around her – even more so after her next demand:

'What do you think of my body?'

I opened my mouth but no words came out.

'I'm working hard to perfect it. Look!'

To my surprise, Kwin began to unbutton the front of her dress, moving upwards from below her waist. I glanced left and right; to my relief nobody was approaching. By now she had undone three of the buttons and pulled her dress wide open to reveal her stomach.

I managed to nod. The muscles were visible, there beyond all doubt.

'I'm fast too,' she said. 'Very fast. If you train all year, it won't do you any good. I'll still be faster than you.'

Her eyes were full of fire. I couldn't resist responding.

'Maybe we should put that to the test.'

She raised her eyebrows. 'Me against you, then!' she challenged. 'Shall we see who's the better stick-fighter?'

'If that's what you want,' I said, relishing the idea of something that was familiar. But no sooner had I spoken than I remembered Tyron's ban. I wasn't allowed to fight with sticks now that I was being trained by him. However, I didn't want Kwin to think I was pathetic; I'd spoken hastily and now it was too late to take my words back.

She held out her hand to me, and there was just a moment

of hesitation before I shook it. 'That's settled then,' she said. 'But not now.'

I felt a strange mix of relief and disappointment.

'We can't fight tonight. Come on – I'll show you the other lounge.' And she led me on down a flight of stairs.

This turned out to be more like a cellar; it was certainly less smart than the lounge I'd seen upstairs. There were at least two or three hundred people there; in the background drums could be heard, an insistent rhythm that rose and fell in volume. The kind of drums that forced you to change the pattern of your steps, making walking difficult.

Everyone seemed to be drinking, dancing or both. A girl gyrated wildly on a table, her legs a blur, to the distant drum-beat and to the claps of the spectators. With a shriek, she launched herself out over the hard wooden floor as if executing a dive into water. She was neatly caught, and another eager woman was lifted up to take her place.

'Buy me a drink,' Kwin shouted in my ear. Having her so close made me forget how to talk again. 'A glass of red wine.'

'I haven't any money,' I managed, turning red with embarrassment.

This reminder of another of Tyron's rules told me that I shouldn't have come here. It was exciting and interesting to be in such a place – I'd never seen its like before. But I also felt uneasy. I was sure that Tyron would be angry with me if he knew.

Kwin pushed me towards an empty table in the corner as if I were a child, and then made her way through to the bar. I sat down, and a few moments later she came back carrying two small glasses of red wine.

She placed one in front of me and sat down facing me, raising her own glass to her lips. After her third sip she leaned forward. I had to lip-read: 'What's wrong? Why aren't you drinking?'

'Your father doesn't allow it!' I shouted back.

'One glass'll do you no harm.' Her mouth twisted up at the corner in amusement.

I shrugged, and when I made no move to pick up the wine, she reached across and placed it next to her own. Ten minutes later both glasses were empty and she rose to her feet. She walked away abruptly without so much as a glance at me. For a moment I wondered if she was going back for more wine, but when I saw her heading for the door, I quickly followed her.

Hearing me behind her in the corridor, she halted and turned to face me, speaking as if I had done exactly what she had always known I would. I wondered if this was all part of the same initiation rites that Palm and Deinon had gone through with her when they were new to Tyron's house. I didn't know what the point was, but there was something about Kwin that drew me to her. I wanted her to think well of me.

'Have you got a good head for heights?' she asked me now.

'Well, I've climbed a lot of trees back at home,' I said, attempting to make a joke of it.

'This is much higher than trees, Leif. I'm going to show you the view from the top of the dome. Follow me – unless you're scared . . .'

Obviously I went after her. I couldn't let her think that.

She led me along corridors and through doors, using an ornate key to open any that were locked. Finally we began a long hot climb up a staircase that took us through a narrow opening in the ceiling to emerge in the gloom of the high dome of the Wheel. I found it almost impossible to keep up with Kwin on the steep spiral, and the atmosphere was thick with the oppressive odour of dust and ancient wood.

After about five minutes she halted and looked back at me impatiently, and then I saw beads of sweat on her brow too. I took advantage of the pause to look down into the circular hall that sat on top of the arenas far beneath us, where people scurried about like ants.

'We've further to go yet, but at least it'll be cooler outside.' Kwin hurried us on, continuing her ascent.

I was relieved when we emerged at last into the chill, late-evening air of early spring. I looked up and saw that a full moon illuminated the city. On the outside of the dome, with only a slender hand-rail for reassurance, we continued our climb until we came to the apex, where a broken flagpole jutted towards the heavens like a spear-tip.

I gazed out over the city, marvelling at the fact that I was here on top of the Wheel's dome; that I'd been taken on by Tyron. So much had already gone according to plan – though I quickly reminded myself that I'd only taken a few short steps along a very long road.

Far above, the vultures still circled, but my eyes were drawn to the west.

Here I could see the dark shimmer of the sea and, beyond it, a segment of the Great Barrier that encircled Midgard and sealed it off from the outer world. It looked like a wall of mist or cloud, but it wasn't a natural phenomenon. It had been placed there long ago by the enemies of mankind; placed after the last battle by the djinn who'd destroyed the Human Empire.

Kwin gestured at the city. 'This is a view that few get to see.'

It was breathtaking. Despite the late hour and the empty streets we'd followed on our way here, I could see narrow plumes of smoke rising from the smithies and, beyond the huddle of wooden roofs, the crisscross patterns of cattle pens. Far above the slaughterhouse, a lone sea-bird was soaring. Judging by its enormous wingspan, it was an aulburte. They could fly for weeks without landing; some people even believed they could soar over the Barrier itself.

All my life I'd wondered what lay beyond it. Was the landscape changed beyond all recognition? What were the djinn like, and how had they shaped their own world? What did they do? How did they live? Surely they weren't all like Hob, who so cruelly preyed upon the land of Midgard from his citadel on the hill above Gindeen?

'That's the Protector's palace,' Kwin told me, pointing north towards a tall building with pillars at its entrance. 'It's the only building in the city not made of wood. That porch with marble pillars is called a portico. There's no marble anywhere in Midgard, so the stone must have come from the other side of the Barrier. The barracks is somewhere beyond it.'

Out of the corner of my eye I saw her staring at me, but when I turned towards her, she looked away. I felt a strong attraction to her. Maybe she felt the same. I wondered why she'd brought me up here.

We looked out over the city for some time without speaking again, drinking in the magnificent view. After a time Kwin drew my attention westwards, where the stone and bronze citadel rose on the summit of the hill. Its thirteen bronze spires of varying heights gleamed in the moonlight, some twisted strangely. She jabbed her forefinger towards them. 'Know what that is?' she asked.

I knew what it was – everybody did – but I didn't answer. I wanted to hear it from the lips of a city-dweller.

'Hob's citadel,' Kwin hissed. 'It's the lair of the djinni that terrorizes this city.'

Yes, I knew all about Hob. I had made it my business to learn all I could.

'In answer to your earlier question,' Kwin said angrily, 'no, I don't think Hob is a joke. But you have to laugh and joke, or the fear would drive you mad. Don't you see that? In winter, during the hours of darkness, people stay in, their doors barred. Well, not me. I do the opposite. I go out! There is real danger, Leif. There are frequent murders. Hob kills people. He drains their blood. Girls disappear, sometimes for weeks. They return whole in flesh but with their minds completely blank, just like a lac fresh from the Trader. All their memory is gone; some return unable to speak.'

The horror of what she was saying filled me with anger. My hands started to tremble.

'Hob has stolen their souls. And people are right to be scared – but they resort to superstitious rituals that don't work. Farmers sprinkle pig blood along their perimeter fences to keep Hob at bay. Some city-dwellers believe that he's afraid of brambles and nail thorns to their doorways.'

I said nothing, simply waiting for Kwin to continue. My hands were still trembling and I felt incapable of speech.

'Well? Cat got your tongue? Haven't you anything to say?'

'I may be new to the city but I do know about Hob . . .' I took a deep breath to keep my voice measured. 'He's terrorized people as far south as Mypocine. He's killed there too.'

'Can I ask you something?' Kwin asked.

I nodded.

'Why have you come here? Looking forward to fighting in Arena 13, are you?'

'Of course I am. That's what I want more than anything else. That's why I left Mypocine.'

'You should know that there's a special danger from Hob in Arena 13. My father doesn't always tell his novices, but I think you should be warned. Every so often, Hob visits and challenges a min combatant there. He places an enormous wager and the gambling houses are forced to accept it. These days, Hob always wins . . . Dead or alive, the loser is taken up to Hob's lair and is never seen again. One day that could be your fate . . . Still want to fight there?'

If anything, what Kwin had just told me made me even more determined. 'Yes, I still want to fight in Arena 13. The danger from Hob doesn't put me off.'

'I feel exactly the same way,' said Kwin. 'I wish I could fight there.'

A Bit of a Disappointment

The stack is the term for a sequence of Nym code.
A patterner might add to or subtract from it.
New code is always placed at the summit of a stack.

The Manual of Nym

We left the heights of the Wheel but didn't descend as far as the steps. Kwin led me out through a different door.

'We're now on the roof of the thirteen arenas,' she said, pointing across the great circular hall: I saw a huge wooden post that rose vertically from the centre, to be lost in the dark shadowy vastness of the dome somewhere far above our heads.

'That is called the Omphalos,' Kwin said, indicating the great post. 'It's the centre of the Wheel – some say that it's the very centre of Midgard.'

Fastened to the great post were a series of notices covered in names and numbers.

'Are they the Lists?' I asked as we walked towards it. I remembered Tyron telling me that they were on this floor.

'Yes,' answered Kwin. 'New ones go up every week. Up there now is the order of combat for this week – the first week of this year's Arena 13 season. Some are challenges made publicly; others have been placed there by those in authority who decide who should fight who according to their rankings. Look at that one . . .' She pointed to one which bore just two names on paper that had a thick black border. 'That signifies a grudge match; one that'll end with someone losing his head or being cut to ribbons!'

'I saw one earlier,' I told her, shaking my head. 'I can't believe they do that. It doesn't make sense!'

'Some people are stupid!' she hissed. 'It happens two or three times a season. Someone who fights in Arena 13 takes a dislike to you and challenges you to a fight to the death. Accept, and your life's at risk. That's another thing my father doesn't allow. None of his combatants are allowed to fight grudge matches. I think that's one of his good rules.'

I smiled and nodded, and we returned to the steps. A few minutes later we were back at ground level, emerging in the shadow of the huge Wheel, its high wooden walls curving away before and behind us. The night air was cool.

'You've been a bit of a disappointment,' Kwin told me as we walked. 'You're not what I expected at all.'

'What *did* you expect?' I asked angrily, taken by surprise. I thought we'd been getting on well: Kwin had seemed to open up to me at the top of the dome, but she was totally unpredictable.

'I expected someone fun who'd take risks and make life in this godforsaken place more interesting,' she said. 'But you were too scared of my father to take even one sip of wine. Well, boys who keep to the rules are boring!'

I simply shrugged and left it at that.

Why get into a petty argument and say things that I'd regret later? What would it achieve?

Groups of people still loitered here, and I now saw a number of large wagons parked nearby. The mood between us soured now, Kwin hurried across the cinders and I followed in silence, my shoes crunching as I walked.

Suddenly, out of the shadows between the wagons, a figure stepped into our path, heading for Kwin. I wondered if she knew him, but the tense set of her shoulders made me doubt this. Though the man's face was in darkness I could see that he was large. He began to sway a little as he moved closer until he was standing right in front of Kwin. Even from behind I could smell the sour ale on his breath. This did not seem like a friendly approach.

I began to move forward, intending to put myself between him and Kwin. But I didn't get the chance.

As the man lurched towards her, I saw something glitter in the moonlight. Kwin was holding a knife in her right hand.

There was a quick flurry, and then it was over. Kwin lunged towards him and the man fell sprawling back on the cinders. He groaned and clumsily got to his feet, and I saw the dark blood running down his forehead into his eyes. Kwin took another step towards him, threatening him with the blade.

'You've made a big mistake,' she hissed. 'Either make things worse or back off! It's your choice!'

He held up both hands and backed away, quickly fading into the shadows.

'You cut him!' I blurted out in astonishment.

Kwin shook her head, smiling grimly. 'No, I just hit him on the forehead with the hilt. Head wounds bleed a lot. They look far worse than they are – as a stick-fighter, you should know that.'

'Do you always carry a knife?' I asked.

'Always! This is a Trig blade. I'd feel naked without one.'

I watched as she slipped the knife back up inside the long sleeve of her dress.

'Carry one yourself,' she advised. 'One day you'll need it.'

'I have to take an oath,' I told her, 'never to use a blade outside the arena.'

'Well, I don't need to worry as they won't allow *me* to take that oath,' Kwin said bitterly.

We walked back to Tyron's house in silence. I followed Kwin up to her room, then used the connecting door into my own. As she locked it behind me, I heard laughter from the darkness to my right.

'Well, you're back soon,' Palm jibed. 'I wouldn't hope for a second invitation!'

I ignored him and climbed into bed. It was a long time before I managed to get to sleep.

'This room smells of sweaty socks. It's time to get up!'

I opened my eyes to see the curtains being pulled back, flooding the room with daylight. Then the window was opened with a bang, and I felt cold air on my face.

Teena's face smiled down at me. 'Good morning, Leif,' she said. 'I've put a change of clothes at the foot of your bed.'

Before I could wish her a good morning in return she had swept out of the room, closing the door behind her.

'She never knocks,' Palm grumbled, crawling out of bed. 'There's no privacy at all in this place.'

I didn't know why he was grumbling. Teena was really nice – it was good to have a woman like that being pleasant and taking care of you. I felt a sudden pang as I remembered my mother and how she had loved and cared for me. Sometimes I thought I'd come to terms with her death, but then the grief came from nowhere with an intensity that was almost unbearable.

'Where did Kwin take you last night?' Palm demanded.

'To the Wheel,' I answered.

'What did she show you?'

'We went to a bar where people were dancing. Then, after we'd been right to the top of the dome, she showed me the Omphalos.'

Palm made no comment, simply stared at me, a look of astonishment on his face. Maybe he hadn't had the same initiation as me.

I dressed in the clothes Teena had left me. They were on the large side, but at least they were clean and fresh. My own dirty threadbare clothes had vanished. They probably weren't worth washing.

Before I could fasten my shoes Palm had left. I'd never seen anyone dress so quickly.

'What's the rush?' I asked Deinon.

There was a long silence. I thought he wasn't going to answer, but then he spoke.

'You don't get long for breakfast. And if you're late down, you don't eat . . .' Suddenly he gave a little smile. 'You've just upset Palm,' he said. 'Kwin takes every new trainee out to show them the Wheel, but neither Palm nor I got to go to the top of the dome. She must have used one of her father's keys.'

Tyron was standing by the door as I followed Deinon into the dining room. If the food was as delicious as dinner last night, then I wanted to make sure I had my fill.

'I'll see you all on the training floor in ten minutes,' Tyron announced. 'Don't be late! You'll need to take your shoes and socks off before you enter, Leif. Bare feet will give a better grip. I'll get you Trig boots at the end of the month – if you're still with us.'

With that he was gone.

Palm, already seated at the table, didn't bother to disguise his delight at Tyron's parting shot to me, and a wave of anger flooded through me. I'd been reminded that I was only here on trial – that was fair enough. But I suddenly realized that Palm *wanted* me to fail.

Breakfast was merely toast and a couple of boiled eggs, but I was hungry and every mouthful tasted good.

Palm wolfed his down and rushed out without a word. 'He likes to be down first to keep in with Tyron,' Deinon said. 'But it makes no difference – Tyron is fair. As long as you don't dawdle over breakfast I don't think he cares who's first down.'

I smiled at Deinon and nodded. He'd spoken without being prompted. Perhaps he was shy; it would just take time to get to know him.

The training floor had no windows and was lit by torches high on the walls rather than a candelabrum. Nor was there a gallery – or the two huge doors through which combatants entered. Apart from that it was an exact replica of Arena 13: fifty paces long by twenty-five wide, taking up the whole first storey of Tyron's house. It was seriously impressive and I was filled with excitement about what awaited me.

Tyron and Kern were standing side by side. Palm was facing them with his hands clasped behind his back. In one corner I saw a lac standing perfectly still with its head bowed. Its armour was scratched and dented as if it had seen a lot of fighting, possibly from the losing side. There was a particularly deep gash in the helmet just above the eyes, as if somebody had used an axe to try and cleave its head in two.

I followed Deinon across the floor to stand beside Palm.

'This is the best training floor in the city,' Tyron told me proudly. 'You'll put in a lot of hard work here; work that'll pay off later. My days are very busy and I spend a lot of time at the Wheel training my adult combatants and patterners, and at my office in the administration building. So Kern will be your primary trainer here. You'll have the pleasure of my company on Thursdays. Now, Leif,' he went on, 'I have a question for you. What are the rules when fighting in Arena 13? You saw the Trig in action. Now tell me succinctly what it's about.'

'Three lacs fight together against a single lac . . .' I chose my words with care, replaying in my mind the fight I'd seen last night. 'A human combatant stands behind the three lacs in the "mag" position, and his opponent is defended by the lone lac in the "min" position. After five minutes, signalled by the gong, the combatants must move in front of their lacs and fight from there instead. To draw human blood means victory. Usually this is achieved at the end of the contest, a safe ritual cut to the defeated combatant. But in a grudge match the aim is to kill.'

'That's a good explanation, Leif,' Tyron said. 'Now, have you any questions for me?'

'Why do we need the lacs at all?' I asked. 'Why don't the human combatants just fight each other face to face, as in stick-fighting?'

There was a long silence, and out of the corner of my eye I could see Palm smirking. I felt the heat rise to my face. My question suddenly seemed foolish. It was just the way things had always been done. Maybe Tyron would think me an idiot.

But his reply was unexpected. 'Why don't you give some careful thought to it, Leif, and arrive at your own answer. At the end of your month's trial, before I decide whether or not to keep you on, you can tell me your conclusions and I will share mine with you. Now, your training will begin!'

He walked towards the door in the corner of the room, but instead of leaving, he leaned back against the wall, watching us. He obviously wanted to see how my first training session went, I thought with a stab of anxiety.

What happened in the next few minutes would play a big part in deciding the outcome of my month's trial.

The Bow

The wurde is the basic unit of the ancient patterning
    language called Nym.
Wurdes contain other wurdes.
To call one wurde is to call all that is embedded within
    it, both manifest and hidden.

The Manual of Nym

Kern smiled at each of us in turn. Finally his eyes settled
upon me. 'Welcome, Leif. Most of what takes place in this
first session will obviously be new to you, but for Palm and
Deinon it will be revision. I'm sure they won't mind.'

He went over to face the armoured lac.

'Awake!' commanded Kern, and the lac raised its head,
eyes flickering behind the horizontal slit in the face armour.

I felt a slight stirring of unease, but less than when I'd
first encountered one. That was good. I needed to feel
comfortable around these creatures. I'd be working with
them a lot.

Kern turned back to face me. 'That command – *Awake* –
was just one wurde of Nym,' he explained. 'Nym is the name
of the language we use to pattern the lacs. Note the spelling,
w-u-r-d-e, not to be confused with *w-o-r-d*, which refers to

units of ordinary human speech. Now that the lac is awake and responsive, I'll command it to check its own readiness for combat and then report back on its condition.

'Selfcheck,' Kern ordered; and a few moments later, 'Report!'

'*Ready*,' said the lac.

I'd never heard a lac speak before – I didn't even know they could – and the voice that came from behind the metal mask was harsh and guttural.

'Combat Stance!' Kern said.

The lac obeyed, and Kern turned his back and went over to the assortment of weapons and pieces of armour that hung on the wall. He reached up and drew two short-bladed Trig knives from their leather scabbards.

He strode past the lac, holding the blades with their points down towards the floor. With an almost careless gesture he dropped the blade in his left hand. The point buried itself in the wooden floor and vibrated in the flickering torchlight. The lac didn't move.

'Get Weapon!' Kern commanded softly – but as the lac bent to obey, with his foot he slyly pushed the handle of the blade down until it was bent over, almost touching the floor. He suddenly withdrew his foot, causing the knife to spring back up and oscillate wildly. Three times the creature's fingers fumbled for the blade. It had almost come to a stop when, at last, the lac was successful.

Kern turned towards us. 'As you can see, its reactions have been deliberately slowed. This is for training purposes – to make it easier for you. But not *that* easy,' he added, smiling grimly.

I saw that Palm was smirking again. Deinon was grinning too. They knew what was going to happen in this training session and were no doubt waiting to see how I coped. Tyron was still standing there watching. He would be judging me as well.

Kern turned back to face the lac, raising the blade in his right hand towards it. With the bunched fist of his left hand, he struck himself hard on the chest.

'Seek Target!' he commanded. 'Cut Flesh!'

As the lac lifted the blade and advanced menacingly, Kern shuffled two steps left and then two steps right. It was like the steps of a dance.

Now he began to retreat, moving diagonally right, his boots drumming rhythmically on the floor. The creature attacked suddenly, lunging with its blade towards Kern's chest. But even as it moved for him, Kern had already reversed direction. There was a sudden flash as his own blade reflected the torchlight.

He thrust upwards and buried his blade in the lac's throat-socket. It immediately collapsed in a cacophony of clattering metal, its heavy fall reverberating across the wooden floor.

'Endoff,' said Kern, turning back to face us. 'Endoff is a wurde that renders a lac unconscious. It is called automatically once a blade is inserted into the throat-socket. As I said, boys, this is a lac patterned for practice. Anyway, watch again what I did . . .'

Alongside Palm and Deinon, I copied Kern as he took two steps to the left and two to the right, executing them slowly, aware of Tyron's eyes on me.

'This sequence allows you to keep your options open. The reverse diagonal can be made to the left or the right, but I'll do it to the right again, the same as before . . .'

Once again, Kern's boots thundered on the boards, we three trainees copying. Then he reversed, brought himself back almost to the same point and stabbed upwards with his blade.

'In Arena 13 combat, your opponent and the lac or lacs who defend him know these patterns; they will attempt to predict which ones you will use next and precisely where that will position you on the combat floor. Dancing with your own lac, you will attempt to deceive and out-think them. Your aim is to be elsewhere when they attack. Then you counter, positioning your own lac where it can do most harm. The steps are very old, Leif . . .' He looked directly at me. 'They are the basic building blocks of much more complex patterns. You'll practise these until they're perfect, even if that perfection takes a long time coming. Your fellow trainees know this to their cost.'

I saw from the looks on the faces of Palm and Deinon that Kern had made them go over and over this until they were sick of it.

'Now,' Kern continued, 'we'll play a little game. There's no chance of getting seriously hurt. View it as a bit of a challenge.'

He bent down and withdrew the blade from the throat-socket of the lac. It still didn't move. 'Awake! Stand!' he commanded, and as the creature lumbered to its feet, he replaced the dagger in its scabbard on the wall. He returned carrying a leather ball about the size of a human head.

He threw it towards me without warning. Snapping into action, I caught it, my hands sinking into the leather. It was soft but heavy, and I noticed that it had a strip of leather sewn to it, designed for a hand to slip inside.

'For now, the lac will use this instead of a blade. Even so, perform badly and you'll end up with a headache. You first, Palm.' Kern handed him the blade and gave the leather orb to the lac.

Palm executed the steps flawlessly, as light on his feet as Kern had been. At the end of the reverse right diagonal, he struck upwards with the blade. He was good; very good. My heart sank. His superiority was based on skill. Sparks flew as the blade's point jarred against the edge of the metal throat-socket – but it didn't go in.

Palm tried to duck, and almost succeeded, but the lac swung the leather ball, caught him a glancing blow on the side of the head, and it was over.

'Good. Well done! You're getting closer,' said Kern, generous with his praise. 'It won't be long now before you succeed.'

Palm grinned, showing his teeth. He was obviously pleased to hear that.

Deinon showed just how good Palm had been. He was relatively clumsy in his movements, and the heavy leather ball smacked into his face with such force that he was lifted clean off his feet. He sat down hard, dazed, and Kern had to help him back up while Palm smirked in the background. Good-naturedly, Deinon shook his head to try and clear it as he got to his feet, throwing a wry smile at me.

'Well then, Leif,' Kern said, handing me the blade. 'Let's see what you can do . . .'

I accepted the blade and took up my position facing the lac, my heart thumping hard. I felt self-conscious, aware that the eyes of everybody in the room were watching me intently to see what I could do. The presence of Tyron bothered me the most.

None, however, scrutinized me as closely as the scary eyes of the lac, which flickered behind the horizontal black slit in the face armour.

I stared back into those alien eyes, took a deep breath, then moved into the pattern of the dance, bringing all my concentration to bear upon it. Two steps to the left. Two steps to the right.

The lac was already moving towards me, but instead of retreating, I took another two steps to the left. I was doing it, not thinking it. My feet were leading my mind. I began to retreat diagonally, but to the left rather than the right.

The lac came after me fast, already starting to swing the leather ball. I reversed suddenly, my bare feet slapping hard against the boards. I ducked and the ball passed very close to the top of my head; the draught from its passing felt like fingers smoothing back my hair, but it didn't strike me.

I moved in close to the lac and lunged towards its throat-socket. The blade went home hard, jarring my hand, the shock travelling all the way up to my shoulder. And that was that.

As the lac fell, the blade was torn out of my grasp, the creature collapsing with a crash as the wurde *endoff* was called, the patterning within the mind of the lac bringing about that automatic response.

Elated, I bowed low towards the lac; it was something that

my father had done when we fought with sticks, and which I had adopted and did automatically after each stick-fight. After a while it had caught on, and all the lads back home had done it as well.

I heard the door closing, leaving a silence in the training area. As I straightened up, I saw that Tyron had gone. Kern was gazing at me in astonishment, Deinon too. But in Palm's eyes there was only envy and hatred.

I'd just made an enemy.

For Absolute Beginners

Artificers are adepts skilled in patterning the wurdes
of Nym.
The first artificers were ur-human.
They developed their power to its height in the
Secondary Epoch of Empire.

The Manual of Nym

The morning had gone well. I had a real sense of triumph at having brought the lac to its knees. It was something that Palm had failed to do, despite having been trained for months while I was a complete novice.

The afternoon was devoted to the skill of patterning; it was something I was certainly not looking forward to. I fully expected to find it difficult.

We each had a small study in which to work. Kern gave me a slim textbook: it was an introduction to patterning in the language of Nym for absolute beginners.

He patted me on the shoulder and smiled. 'Just read through the first couple of pages and absorb as much as you can, Leif. Even in this simple form it's not easy. So don't worry. Just do your best. Anything you don't understand we can discuss later.'

He left me alone, so I opened the book and began to read.

THE DICTIONARY OF NYM

The TOTAL DICTIONARY of Nym (informally termed 'Fat Nym') is continually growing, exists in no single location and is potentially infinite. It is also widely distributed. Here are a few locations where segments of it are to be found:

1. Wurdes are embedded within each simulacrum bought from the Trader.
2. New wurdes are created by combining existing wurdes.
3. New wurdes can be created from primitives by a skilled patterner.
4. Some wurdes are created by a patterner and, until embedded within a simulacrum, exist only within his brain.

The CORE DICTIONARY of Nym (informally known as 'Slim Nym') exists within the mind of each simulacrum bought from the Trader.

I read that first page about three times, trying to understand it. Then I turned to the second page, dreading what I would find.

It was even worse.

CREATING A NEW WURDE

This is how to mark the beginning of a new wurde definition.

Begin with **:** which is voiced as **Colon**

End the new wurde definition with **;** which is voiced as **Semi**

Here is a list of some existing wurdes which can inform and direct the movement of a simulacrum:

StepF1 {this means take one step forward}

StepR3 {this means take three steps to the right}

StepL2 {this means take two steps to the left}

Seektarget {this means decide which is the best available target (opposing lac or human combatant) and attack}

Cutflesh {this modifies the former command and directs the lac to attack the human combatant}

Now we see below the creation of a new wurde, 'Reckless', which combines a selection of the above pre-existing wurdes. Note the use of * to link the wurdes within the definition.

: Reckless – StepL2 * StepR3 * StepF1 * Seektarget * Cutflesh ;

The above names the new wurde as 'Reckless'. It commands your lac to take two steps to the left, three steps to the right and then one step forward followed by a direct attack on your human opponent.

The new wurde needs to be **COMPILED:**

Utter the wurde **COMPILE** {this places the new wurde within the brain of the lac in a form that can be **Called.** To call a word is to command your lac to implement it}.

Now **CALL** the wurde. The wurde is called by simply uttering its name (**Reckless**). Of course, this is not spoken aloud in combat. It is signalled to your lac by using **ULUM**, a code drummed by your boots onto the floor of the arena.

I sighed . . .

Deinon was starting to become a little more talkative, and during lunch, while Palm had sulked at the far end of the table, he had explained 'Ulum' to me.

You didn't speak to your lac during combat as Kern had done during our training session. Instead of shouting out a wurde to control its movement, you beat on the floor of the arena with your boots. The drumming was a code that you had to develop yourself and memorize; something that your opponent and his lacs would not understand. So I got the general idea. But as for the rest, I was totally demoralized. It was just too difficult – I knew that I could never become a patterner. Yet even if you were a combatant, you still needed a basic level of competence in patterning. You had to understand how it worked.

Would I ever manage that? It seemed a big obstacle to successfully completing my training.

One after the other we went down for our private lesson with Kern. Deinon returned from his session and rapped on the door to tell me that it was my turn. I thanked him and went downstairs.

Kern had a study twice the size of mine. On the wall hung a painting of Teena holding their son. She was smiling out of the photo and looked very happy. It was extremely life-like.

I faced him across the wooden desk. He smiled at me warmly. 'How did you find the textbook?' he asked.

There was no point in pretending otherwise so I told him the truth.

'I found it really difficult. I couldn't understand some of it at all. That wurde it showed – why is it called "Reckless"?' I asked.

Kern smiled. 'The textbook is being slightly humorous. If you commanded your lac to "Cutflesh", as it was defined there, from the min position, it would almost certainly be defeated in seconds. There would be three lacs defending your opponent and it would ignore all defensive measures and go straight for him. It would be a stupid thing to do, but it was just demonstrating how a new wurde is put together.

'Look, don't let it worry you, Leif. You may never become a patterner. Very few of us have the ability to develop that skill to the highest level. I certainly don't. But you don't necessarily need to pattern wurdes – you just have to be able to use those which have been created for you. I know enough to teach you the rudiments, but if you had enough talent, then Tyron would have to take over at a later stage. He is easily the best patterner in the city.'

This wasn't the way I wanted to go at all. I wanted to fight, and my face must have given me away, for Kern continued, 'From what I saw earlier, judging by your speed and agility, I suspect that you're more likely to end up fighting in the arena. But you can never take it for granted – only time will tell. In the meantime, you still need some basic skills and knowledge of what Nym is all about. So I'll begin with a little history today.'

'Do I need to take notes?' As instructed, I had brought writing materials with me.

'You'll be given assignments and essays to write on the things we discuss, but I would advise against taking notes now,' said Kern. 'It's best to concentrate and commit what you learn to memory. Practise using your brain in that way. The best patterners and artificers hold whole sequences of wurdes inside their heads. That way you own them and never have to look things up. They are immediately accessible. And ask as many questions as you like as we go through; you need to get this straight in your mind.'

I got straight in. 'I'm not quite clear about artificers. How are they different from patterners?' I asked. I felt more comfortable asking questions of Kern. He had none of the stern gruffness of Tyron.

'Artificers are master patterners, highly skilled in the language of Nym. Often, like Tyron, they employ many others and have a whole stable of combatants, some of whom are skilled in patterning and some in fighting. Let's begin now by considering Nym and how it developed. The ancients had a different name for patterners – they called them "programmers" or "coders". We believe that they used their fingers in some way to pattern moving combat machines that were made out of metal. We don't know how it worked but suspect it was something like this. They did this on something called a "keyboard".'

Kern demonstrated by placing his hands next to each other on the desk and drumming rhythmically with his fingers on the wood.

'Of course, now we use an AUI, which means Audio User Interface. We use our voices and speak words directly to lacs which they can hear and absorb, then fitting them into the basic patterns they already have within them.'

'How were the first lacs created?' I asked. I wished I had spent more time asking my father about these things so that I would be more prepared. There were so many things I wanted to ask him, but now it was too late.

'That's a good question, Leif. As far as we know, the military were responsible. They started by programming metal war machines called "ibots", but then replaced them with lacs, which are really prototype djinn but inferior to even the lowest of those creatures. Eventually djinn were developed. We think it likely that the flesh of both lacs and djinn was grown in big vats. It's sometimes called "false flesh". About that time the patterning language called Nym was developed. It evolved out of several programming languages, but mainly out of "FORTH", which was created long ago by a programmer called Charles H. Moore.

'The rest is history – although there are several versions of the actual events, depending on which historian you read. The most commonly held belief is that after the wars between nations of humans, they used djinn to fight for them. The djinn rebelled and then fought against humans until we were defeated. Then they built the Barrier and imprisoned the few human survivors within it. They appointed a protector to rule Midgard on their behalf. A lot of knowledge was lost. We could no longer grow our own lacs, but were allowed to buy lacs from the Trader. Only he can pass back and forth across the Barrier. However, we no longer have the skill to make the lacs we buy sentient.'

The session ended with Kern attempting to teach me a few of the Nym primitives – the building blocks of the language. He was a good teacher with a lot of patience, but I was a poor pupil. I had never been good with language and reading, and this was the most complex thing I'd ever tried to learn. Some of the wurdes were difficult to pronounce and were uttered in the clipped, clear accent of the north. My southern accent was going to make that difficult. If I couldn't say them correctly, how could I hope to speak to a lac and pattern it?

Perhaps I would never gain the skills necessary to complete my training . . .

That night, when I was just about to get undressed, I heard three knocks from Kwin's bedroom.

Deinon gave a little smile and raised his eyebrows at me, but Palm's jaw dropped almost to his boots. He hadn't expected Kwin to summon me again. He hadn't spoken to me at all since our morning in the training room, and now his eyes almost turned from blue to green with the intensity of the anger in them.

I wondered what the problem was. It made sense for him to feel annoyed that I'd successfully floored the lac in the training room when he hadn't managed it yet, but what about now? Did he like Kwin? Maybe he'd hoped for just one knock, meaning that she was summoning *him*?

I simply shrugged as if I didn't care one way or the other. I was still annoyed with Kwin for the way she'd turned on me after our night out, but I couldn't suppress a quiver of excitement.

I was standing by the door even before the key turned in the lock. Kwin was unpredictable and aggressive, but I couldn't ignore the fact that I wanted to see her again.

Once more I entered her room – only this time she wasn't wearing her dress. Her trousers were secured at the ankles with black ribbon, above what were definitely Trig boots, and her hair was pulled back tightly. Once more her lips were painted black and red. Even her scowl was identical to the one she'd given me the first time I saw her.

'Me against you, then, Leif – a stick-fight to see who's the best. Still want to do it?' she demanded. 'I heard you put on quite a show in the training room this morning. Come on, I want to see you in action!'

My heart sank. 'Your father said he doesn't allow it,' I told her, regretting the deal I'd made with her the night before. 'I could get kicked out.'

'He's all talk. He wouldn't dare. Don't worry – if he ever finds out, I can bend him round my little finger.'

'Are you sure?' I asked. I *was* worried, and with good reason. My dream of fighting in Arena 13 felt a lot nearer after my first day of training – even though the theory had been hard. I didn't want to jeopardize it all.

'Just as sure as I am that I'll beat you . . .'

I took a deep breath. There was no reason for Tyron to

find out. Kwin knew the city well and I could learn from her. Complicated as she was, I liked being around her – and I certainly wasn't making a friend in Palm. Plus, I found it hard to resist a challenge. Part of me wanted to fight and put Kwin in her place. I knew that I could beat her and I was looking forward to seeing the expression on her face as I did so.

I nodded. 'If that's what you want ... I haven't got a stick, though. I gave mine away to a friend. I didn't think I'd be using them again.'

Peter had been a good fighter and a close friend. I missed him and the other lads I'd hung around with. I found it hard to believe that I'd ever find that sort of companionship here.

Kwin's face softened and she almost smiled. She picked up a leather package. 'You can take your pick from what I've got here,' she said. 'Let's go and fight!'

The Bone Room

A blow to the head means victory; only the malicious
and cruel target the eyes or mouth – such a blow is
without honour.

Amabramsum: the Genthai Book of Wisdom

Soon we were crossing the city again, tonight's waning moon
still almost full, and very large and bright on the horizon.
We took a different route to the previous night, and when I
commented on this, Kwin told me we were heading towards
the slaughterhouse rather than the Wheel. The houses gave
way to a patchwork of cattle pens, most of them empty, while
overhead the dark block of the huge building began to fill
the sky, blocking out the moon and eating the stars. There
was an overpowering smell of animal manure and sweat
that made me breathe through my mouth rather than my
nose.

'Surely there's a better place to fight than this!' I said.

'Inside, it's well-lit and it's quiet at this time of night,'
Kwin said, noticing my revulsion. 'After dark, it's one of
the safest places in Gindeen. Nobody will disturb us. Fight
anywhere else and we'd attract attention.'

As we approached, I saw a few workers dressed in

bloodied aprons, but they took no notice of us, and we weren't challenged.

The stench of blood and excrement was much worse – almost overpowering – as we stepped inside.

'They kill the cattle over there.' Kwin pointed to a huge door which was open to the night sky. There were pools of blood on the floor and two huge hammers propped up against the wall. From overhead hung a long chain with sharp hooks. It went up at an angle of forty-five degrees to disappear through a big hole in the high ceiling. There was an identical chain near the far wall.

'It's all over very quickly,' Kwin explained. 'One blow and they're dead. Two seconds later, the carcasses are hauled up there and they cut their throats. Then the chain begins to move, carrying them up to the butchers on the next floor. But we're going up even higher. Down here, they never clean up properly and it's always slippery with blood.'

Kwin seemed to delight in giving me all the gory details; she could tell from my expression that I didn't like it. Did she intend to make me uncomfortable and put me at a disadvantage?

Bile rose in my throat and I swallowed hard, fighting to control my stomach. Hoping that I wasn't going to embarrass myself by being sick, I followed Kwin to the far corner of the vast room and we began to climb. It wasn't as bad as going up onto the Wheel's dome, but it was a long way to the very top floor.

'This is the bone room,' Kwin told me. 'By the time animals get up here there's not a shred of meat left on them. There are big vats where they boil it off. Some of it gets turned into paste or soup – it's cheap food for lacs.'

In the gloom I saw bones everywhere, heaped so high that they almost touched the ceiling; some were dry and yellow, clearly very old.

The smell of death wasn't so strong here, and my stomach was starting to settle. I followed Kwin between the mountains of bones until we reached the far corner. Here, a broad shaft of moonlight shone through a big high opening, making it bright enough for us to see clearly.

Kwin indicated a wide wooden chute close by. 'The bones go down two floors,' she told me. 'Some are ground up for glue, but most are for fertilizer. Nothing gets wasted here.'

She knelt down and untied the leather parcel she had been carrying before opening it out on the floor. 'Choose a stick,' she offered.

Inside it were four sticks, very similar to the ones we'd used in Mypocine. Slightly longer than a Trig blade, they were thick at the end and rounded to lessen the chance of serious injury. Stick-fighting was still dangerous, though. I knew a lad who'd lost an eye. I knelt, chose a stick, then waited for Kwin to make her own choice.

'So this lac you downed today . . .' she said as she stood up to face me. 'It's pretty good you managed that on day one, but it won't be good enough. I've downed one too, but mine was the real thing, readied for the arena. Yours was just patterned for training. It would have been slow.'

'Was that the one that cut you?' I asked, my eyes lingering on the scar on her face.

Kwin nodded. 'But it was worth it,' she said. 'Men who fight in Arena 13 only have scars on their arms. I've gone

one better. It missed my eye because I was too fast for it . . .'

This was different to the version I'd heard from Palm – that her father had arrived just in time to save her – but she obviously didn't want to say any more about it.

'Let's go over there.' She pointed away from the chute. 'There's more space and it's brighter. Nobody comes up here during the night shift. We won't be disturbed.'

She stared at me for a long time before moving away, and my heart was beating hard.

I followed her into the shaft of moonlight where there was a clear area of floor.

As extraordinary as the circumstances were here, inside me excitement surged, as it did before any fight. It was strange to be fighting a girl, but that didn't change the most important thing – I always fought to win.

'Ready?' asked Kwin. 'Best out of three?'

I nodded, but then, without warning, she attacked.

I'd been wondering about what had really happened when Kwin faced the lac. Who should I believe – Kwin or Palm?

Within seconds I knew the answer.

I was in a real fight, and Kwin was fast. Faster than anyone I'd ever fought before.

She lunged forward, going for my head. When I moved away, she danced after me, whirling and spinning, and jabbed towards my left temple. I ducked to the right.

Too late, I realized my mistake. The stick was now in her left hand and it caught me above my right eye, bringing me to my knees. The blow was hard and made me feel sick to my stomach.

Kwin took two steps backwards. 'First blood to me,' she said.

She was right, I realized. Blood was running down into my eye. I brushed it away with the back of my hand and readied myself for her next attack.

This time I watched her more carefully. Moving the stick from hand to hand was a trick I hadn't seen before, but I wouldn't be caught out by it again.

Kwin smiled and passed the stick quickly from her right hand to her left, then back again. It was slick, really skilful; she must have spent hours and hours practising the move.

I concentrated hard, taking in everything about her: the dancing feet, the posture of her body; then her eyes, especially her eyes.

I was ready for her next attack.

Kwin lunged for my jaw. I stepped back out of reach, then reversed. She was fast, but I was the best stick-fighter in Mypocine.

Kwin didn't retreat fast enough and I struck her on the forehead with a quick back-handed blow, just above her right eye. The wound was almost identical to the one she'd inflicted on me. She staggered but didn't fall. The blood was already trickling down into her eye.

She smiled at me.

She was caught directly in the shaft of moonlight, and as she smiled, her face became transfigured. When I was very young, my mother had once shown me a picture of an angel in a book. The angel had huge, majestic wings, but it was the face that had stayed with me. Kwin's face possessed that same unearthly beauty now, as she rejoiced in the thrill of the fight.

The third bout was the hardest. It went on for a long time . . . Kwin was obviously desperate to win – but then, so was I: I matched her step for step and blow for blow. Twice she got through my guard, only my speed managing to save me.

Sometimes we used steps copied from the Trig, but mostly these were moves from the street.

The end, when it came, was almost a disappointment.

Without realizing it, we'd made our way to the very edge of the clear floor space. I'd been forcing Kwin backwards, further and further, and then I lunged towards her left temple.

Suddenly she found bones under her feet and lost her balance. If she hadn't slipped, she'd probably have avoided my blow completely, but with her body weight off, instead of catching her on the temple, my stick struck her right in the mouth.

She went down into a mound of bones and they cascaded over her head and shoulders. When I pulled her clear, I saw that her mouth was bleeding badly, her lips already beginning to swell.

I cringed at the sight, the elation of victory immediately giving way to regret. I was disgusted with myself; it wasn't just that I hated to see Kwin in pain – I was sure the blow would cause lasting damage. I couldn't believe her mouth would ever look as pretty again. Just as quickly, my thoughts turned more selfish. What of the consequences for me? What would Tyron say and do when he saw his daughter's face? And what would happen when he found out that I was responsible?

However, Kwin's eyes were shining. 'I think one of my teeth is loose,' she said, wiping the back of her hand across her bloody lips.

'I'm so sorry,' I managed. 'That doesn't count. You slipped.'

She shook her head firmly. 'No. Slip in the arena and it's over. You'd be cut in seconds. Same rules apply here. You win.'

As the winner, I bowed, just as they did in Arena 13.

'I've never seen a stick-fighter bow, Leif. Did they do that back where you lived?'

I nodded. 'My father once fought in Arena 13. He taught me stick-fighting and we used to bow when we won. I started doing it when I fought other boys; it caught on, and soon we were all doing the same!'

I'd expected her to be angry at being defeated, but all the bitterness seemed to have left her. She looked almost happy. She even twisted her bloody mouth into another smile.

'Thanks for fighting me, Leif,' she said. 'I enjoyed that.'

The way she spoke my name and the look in her eyes made me feel warm inside. We stared at each other for a moment.

Just one thing spoiled it.

Kwin was Tyron's daughter.

Nobody Fights a Girl

Some believe that Nym itself is sentient; that it is the
*   sum of all the patterns in existence.*
Others believe Nym to be a goddess; one who chooses
*   a mortal to be her champion.*
All are correct.

Amabramsum: the Genthai Book of Wisdom

'What have you been up to? What a mess you are!'

The jeering voice jerked me out of a deep dreamless sleep and I looked up to see Palm grinning down at me. I sat up slowly. My head hurt, and when I touched my forehead it came away sticky with blood. My pillow was soaked in it. The events of the night before came flooding back in a rush.

'How did you get that?' he asked. 'It looks nasty.'

The other two boys had been asleep when I crept back into the room last night.

'A stick-fight,' I told him, trying to clear my mind. It was difficult to think. My head began to throb.

'Looks like you lost,' he said smugly.

'No. It was the best of three,' I answered without thinking, annoyed by his attempt to score points off me.

'Who did you fight against? Did Kwin take you down to the Commonality?'

I shook my head. 'No, we went somewhere else. I fought against Kwin.'

Immediately I realized I had made a mistake in telling him that.

I'll never forget the expression that came over his face. It was a mixture of amazement and what looked like triumph. Then, slowly, it changed to contempt.

'You fought Kwin . . . ? You fought a *girl*?'

I nodded. When I moved my head, it hurt. Everything hurt.

'Nobody fights a girl,' Palm said, shaking his head and looking at Deinon as if he couldn't believe it. Deinon avoided my eyes completely.

I'd assumed that Kwin had fought them both – as well as taking them to see the Wheel. Perhaps I'd been wrong and Kwin hadn't challenged them at all.

'Wait until this gets around!' Palm jeered. 'You'll be the laughing stock of the city. You should be ashamed! You're finished here. You're finished even before you've begun! There's no way you'll be able to hide that from Tyron.'

With that, he left the room, no doubt planning to be first down to breakfast as usual.

I glanced at the painting of the Arena 13 combatant over his bed.

I'd probably thrown away my chance to fight there, I reflected sadly.

Palm's prediction was soon proved correct. I was finished, and the end came even faster than he had anticipated. No sooner had I got dressed than a servant came with a message.

Tyron wanted to see me downstairs. He was waiting in the yard behind the house.

As soon as I saw his face, I knew it was bad news. When I stepped out into the early morning sunshine, he was standing with his back to me. I spotted the bundle of clothes tied with string at his feet and my heart sank. I recognized my shirt, the one I'd worn travelling up from Mypocine.

When he turned to face me, Tyron looked sad rather than angry. 'You've let me down, boy,' he said. 'I don't allow stick-fighting. You knew that. Didn't you listen? I made it plain enough.'

'I'm sorry,' I heard myself say, knowing that it wouldn't make any difference. Why had I let Kwin talk me into fighting her? My dream had been within my grasp and I'd lost it because of a stupid stick-fight.

'Sorry? *You're* sorry? How do you think *I* feel? You have talent, boy, but now it's all gone to waste. Your career in the Trig is over before it properly began. Once you leave me, nobody else will take you on. It's bad enough to betray my trust, but ten times worse to do it with my own daughter. The girl's daft enough without getting encouragement from you.'

He picked up my bundle of clothes and tossed it over. Then, without another word, he went inside, slamming the door behind him.

I stood there in the yard for several minutes, unable to move. I couldn't believe what had happened. I fought hard to stop the tears overflowing down my cheeks.

At last, taking a deep breath, and not knowing what else

to do, I picked up my bundle of clothes and walked out into the street. Without so much as a glance at the Wheel, I headed south. What else could I do?

There were few people about and I felt trapped in my misery. I'd not gone very far when I heard someone running behind me, the steps getting closer and closer. When I turned round, I saw that it was Kwin.

'I'm sorry, Leif, really sorry.' She was fighting for breath.

'Sorry isn't good enough!' I snapped. 'I thought you said it would be all right? That you had him wrapped around your little finger?'

'I've never seen him so angry. He just won't listen. I think it's because of this,' she said, pointing to her swollen mouth. 'I tried to stay out of his way this morning – I didn't go down to breakfast – but Palm had already told him about our fight and he came up to my room ranting and raving.'

Palm . . . of course! I'd been so stupid to tell him the truth about my head wound.

'I denied everything, but he wouldn't believe me. Look, please don't leave. Just give me time to work on him. I'll talk him round, I promise. Trust me. I can do it.'

'What will I do until then?'

'Find work. The slaughterhouse hires people by the day. You're big and strong for your age – they'll take you on. Then, when my father's cooled down, I'll know where to come and find you . . .'

I couldn't give up on my dream if there was still a chance, so within the hour I'd joined a queue of men looking for work outside the slaughterhouse.

I got a job collecting offal in big buckets and emptying it into a vat, and I stuck at it all through that long day. It was dirty, smelly and back-breaking. The stink of blood and excrement was everywhere, and when I finished, long after sunset, I carried that stink away with me.

As the days passed I tried not to even think about the short time I'd spent as one of Tyron's trainees. The contrast between that and my present occupation was too painful. That had been heaven; now I was in hell. I couldn't believe I'd been so foolish as to throw it all away.

Each morning I had to rejoin the queue to be hired again. Some days I didn't get work, and then I had little to eat. Sometimes I was lucky and got a night shift, which paid more, but whether I had money or not, I was forced to sleep amongst the cattle pens. Because of the Trig season there was no accommodation left in the city.

I gradually got used to the stink and began to find the work easier. I could feel myself getting stronger, building muscle, and eased into a routine.

One night the foreman led me into a storage area to show me which buckets of offal needed to be dealt with first. I heard a movement in one of the dark corners and glanced over, assuming it was another rat. There were plenty of them about – big, grey-whiskered and ravenous. They fed well in the slaughterhouse.

But the foreman frowned and suddenly strode towards the noise, plucking a torch from the wall as he passed. Intrigued, I followed him, and I will never forget the sight that greeted us. A girl dressed in rags was kneeling before a bucket of offal. She was eating that raw mess, her cupped hands full of it; thick dark blood trickled down from her mouth. I couldn't believe what I was seeing.

'Be off with you!' cried the foreman, raising his fist.

The girl rose to her feet and opened her mouth as if to speak. But then she let out a shrill cry and a sequence of sounds that might have been words but came out as a mixture of moans and gibberish.

'Get out of here, or you'll feel my fist, you dirty, disgusting thing!' the man cried, stepping towards her.

I was appalled by the girl, but even stronger was my instinct to help her. What had happened to reduce her to this? I stepped closer, but she looked terrified and turned on her heel, running off into the darkness, leaving only bloody footprints behind.

The foreman glared at me angrily. 'She's vermin, and probably riddled with disease. She's been touched by Hob, so keep well clear!'

'Touched?'

'Hob snatches girls off the streets. No doubt she was foolish enough to stay out after dark. And, yes, he touches them – sucks their souls from their bodies. All that's left is an empty husk.'

This was one of the girls Kwin had told me about. 'What about her family?' I asked. 'Shouldn't she be with them?'

'She's no longer their daughter. She's an animal without a mind. But don't you worry, boy – she won't be around for long. The tassels will come to collect her. That's the way of things.'

'Who are the tassels?' I asked. I'd never heard of them.

'The servants of Hob,' answered the foreman. 'Sometimes

they walk the city after dark – another reason to stay indoors once the sun goes down. Some have been changed by Hob and are no longer fully human. They're ugly as sin, and you wouldn't believe how fast and strong they are. When they're around, nobody is safe.'

I found it hard to concentrate on my job the rest of that night.

I never saw the girl again.

Your Sort

True Genthai may be recognized by their facial tattoos.
True Genthai are warriors.

Amabramsum: the Genthai Book of Wisdom

One morning, as the sun was rising, I came out of the slaughterhouse to find someone waiting for me.

For a moment I didn't recognize him. Maybe it was because he usually wore a sad, nervous expression and now he was smiling. I rubbed the sleep from my eyes and looked again. It was Deinon!

I felt a sudden flash of hope. Had he come to take me back to Tyron's house? I wondered. Had Kwin managed to persuade her father to change his mind?

But Deinon quickly dashed my hopes into the dust.

'Kwin's sent me with a message,' he said. Even at the sound of her name, my insides churned. I'd often thought of her, veering between anger and something else I wasn't fully ready to admit. 'She asked me to tell you that her father is slowly coming round to her way of thinking. She said don't give up, she'll get there.'

How long could I carry on doing this job? I sighed. 'Tell her thanks for trying,' I replied.

I was about to brush past Deinon. I didn't like him to see me like this, splattered with muck from head to toe. But he went on, 'I'm sorry this has happened, Leif.'

I paused and looked at him. He seemed sincere.

'You don't deserve this. I told Palm he was wrong to have told on you,' he continued.

I knew it must have taken a lot for Deinon to stand up to the other boy like that and I appreciated it – even if it had done me no good.

'You're not the only one who fought Kwin. Palm and I both fought her, but nothing came of it. Not like this. In my case, Tyron didn't even find out. He did find out about Palm, but *he* got his father to come and see Tyron and make it all right. He's a rich man. No doubt he gave extra money for Palm's tuition.'

I was overcome with rage at the unfairness of this world, and then, suddenly, I felt completely exhausted. I wanted to sleep. 'Thanks for telling me that, Deinon.'

The boy nodded. 'I hope I'll see you again soon.'

And with that he returned to the comfort of Tyron's house while I searched for a quiet corner in which to sleep.

The days became weeks, and despite her message, Kwin still didn't come looking for me; I began to give up hope.

I certainly didn't want to go home. It would be good to see my friends again but I couldn't work on a farm now I'd seen what the rest of my life might be like. One possibility I'd been considering was taking up stick-fighting here in the city. I felt confident that I was good enough, but I wasn't sure how much money I could make. And it was a betrayal of my dream of succeeding in Arena 13. Once I started stick-fighting, I would have burned my bridges. Tyron would never take me on again after that.

One evening I walked right around the Wheel, listening to the shouts and cheers from inside. I felt lower than I ever had before.

I was heading back towards the slaughterhouse, my thoughts dark, when I saw ahead of me three members of the Protector's Guard; they were coming straight towards me. One, on horseback, was clearly an officer; he wore a long sword at his hip. The other two were on foot, daggers at their belts, each carrying a long stick and a flickering torch.

I remembered Tyron's advice – that you should never look them in the eye, never give them an excuse. So I looked down at the muddy street and made to walk by.

'Where do you think you're going?' a voice demanded.

I kept my head lowered but raised my eyes to his face.

The officer sat high on his horse, his blue uniform immaculate, his blue eyes full of disdain. He made no attempt to disguise what he thought of me. I knew I was a mess; despite the apron I wore, every day I ended up streaked with blood and offal. Sleeping outdoors made it hard to wash myself and my clothes, and as time went by I'd been making less and less of an effort.

'I'm going back to work,' I told him, as politely as I could. 'I'm on the night shift.'

'No you're not. There's no work for your sort here. That's where you're going,' he said with a sneer, pointing south. 'Back home where you belong.'

The other two men were on me in a second, striking me with their sticks. I didn't have the energy to even try to fight them off. I ran.

They chased me down the street for a while, the officer laughing somewhere behind them. I soon managed to lose them, but as I slowed down to a walking pace, I kept moving in the same direction. South.

Physically, I wasn't badly hurt. Most of the blows had fallen on my back. But I felt more humiliated and ashamed than I had ever done before.

It was time to give in.

I was going home.

I walked south until I'd left the city behind, and then, at dawn, I rested. I looked back towards Gindeen, watching the sun rise above the city, committing to memory the way the bright rays lit Hob's citadel. They gleamed on the thirteen twisted bronze spires. A new day had begun, but tonight, as the sun set, the rays would throw their deformed, threatening shadows eastwards across the city, shadowing the rooftops and reaching as far as the Wheel.

I had often watched those pointed shadows; they were like dark blades seeking out the lives, the very souls of Gindeen's inhabitants.

Somehow Hob had to be stopped . . .

Somebody had to do it. He *had* to be stopped. After all that had happened, after coming so far, I couldn't give up so easily, I told myself. I just couldn't.

So I turned and retraced my steps to the slaughterhouse.

*

I was too late to get work that day, but the following morning, just after dawn, I was standing in the queue when somebody came up to me.

It was Kwin. And she was grinning.

Was this it? Surely she wouldn't be here for any other reason?

Kwin grabbed my arm. 'Come on,' she said. 'My father's changed his mind. He's going to give you another chance.'

In a daze, I let her drag me away from the slaughter-house. I couldn't believe I was actually going back to Tyron's house. Kwin had done it; she'd actually talked her father round. All the anger and resentment I'd been feeling towards her was gone and we fell into an easy banter.

'You stink,' she said, wrinkling up her nose.

'I thought you liked dirt.' I smiled cheekily. 'It's taken you long enough to persuade your father,' I told her. 'I almost gave up and went home.'

'I did my best, but I've never known him to be so stubborn. When I fought Palm, he didn't make half as much fuss. Then, yesterday, he suddenly changed his mind. I searched everywhere but couldn't find you. I thought I'd give it one more try today. To be honest, I wasn't sure you'd have stuck it out for so long.'

'Did you beat Palm when you fought him?' I asked.

'Of course I did,' Kwin said with a smile. 'Have you noticed that sound when he talks?'

I recalled the clicking I'd picked up when I first met him.

'He wears dentures. I knocked his front teeth out,' she told me.

'But his father came and sorted it out for him?'

'Yes. Dad kicked Palm out too for a day or two, but then his father turned up. Money changed hands. Teena found out through Kern and she told me. My father's rich, but he's desperate for more money. He just can't seem to get enough.'

As we approached the house, I started to feel nervous. I had to make things right with Tyron. He had to know that he could trust me again.

He was waiting in the yard when we arrived. He and Kwin exchanged a nod, and then she went straight inside, giving me a squeeze on the arm before she left.

'I'm sorry for letting you down,' I said immediately. 'It won't happen again.'

I'd expected a lecture, or at least some sort of warning. But Tyron said nothing; simply flicked his eyes over me from head to foot. 'Get yourself cleaned up – I'll ask Teena to find you a change of clothes. Eat a good breakfast. It won't matter this time if you're late for the first session.'

I did exactly as he instructed, washing my face and hands before heading up to the bedroom to change. Then I went into the dining room, where I breakfasted alone, relishing every mouthful and helping myself to seconds.

Finally I entered the training room, as I had done on my first day, all those weeks ago.

The two other trainees had clearly not been warned about my return and seemed stunned to see me back. Palm's jaw almost hit the floor.

'Tyron's taken you back? I don't believe it!' he exclaimed.

I stared at him without comment and started to pull off my shoes and socks, ready for training. I'd not had a chance to prepare what I would say when I saw Palm again. On hearing his superior voice, my anger began to build; suddenly I could contain it no longer. Words burst from my mouth.

'No thanks to you!' I said. 'You couldn't wait to tell him, could you? Funny, you didn't mention you'd fought Kwin before as well. Does having false teeth make it hard to chew? I wonder.'

Palm glared at me, the flush rising up his cheeks, betraying his feelings. But he didn't reply, simply stomping off to the other side of the training floor.

Deinon gave me a dry smile. 'I'm glad you're back, Leif. It wouldn't have been fair if you'd not been given another chance.'

'Thanks, Deinon. I can't wait to get back to training.'

Soon Kern was putting us through our paces, and apart from a quick 'Welcome back,' he treated me as though I'd never been away.

I could have said other things that day, but as Palm said nothing more to me, I kept quiet too.

Whenever he replied to Kern or muttered something to Deinon, though, it was hard not to smile.

Now that my ears were tuned to it, I kept hearing the click of his dentures.

The Westmere Plaza

In the beginning was the wurde,
And the wurde was made flesh.
It was the biggest mistake we ever made.

Amabramsum: the Genthai Book of Wisdom

As the week progressed, I quickly became accustomed to the routine of my days under Tyron's roof.

After breakfast we spent the morning on practical skills under the supervision of Kern. It was hard work, and the hours spent dancing across the boards behind a lac gave me aches and twinges of pain in leg muscles I didn't know I had.

What gave me the greatest satisfaction was that I'd managed to find the throat-socket of the training lac with my blade on two more occasions, while Palm had failed to do so even once. He was getting increasingly frustrated.

I enjoyed practical work far more than the afternoon sessions, when I struggled to learn the basics of patterning in Nym. Tyron insisted that Palm, Deinon and I worked alone in one of the small studies adjacent to our bedroom. We were each summoned to an hour's private tuition with Kern. It was even worse on Thursdays, when Tyron taught the theory. I felt embarrassed by my mistakes and began to fear that I wasn't bright enough; I'd surely fail my month's trial.

The afternoons would always end with a run to help us develop both stamina and speed. Led by Kern, we would jog down towards the Wheel. After two steady circuits of that huge building, we sprinted the next two. Then, after five minutes to regain our breath, we would race each other – three fast circuits, finishing at the main entrance. It was a race that I won each afternoon. Kern pushed me hard, but I was faster. He always smiled and congratulated me. We'd developed a jokey relationship, and I had started to think of him almost as a big brother. Palm and I had not spoken to each other directly since I'd returned to training. And the fact that he was pushed into third place in our daily races did nothing to help us become friends. The only thing that spoiled my pleasure was that, with Palm coming third, Deinon was relegated to fourth.

After that it was a stroll back up to Tyron's house, looking forward to the biggest meal of the day.

'I'm starving,' said Deinon.

I was walking beside him; Palm was in front chatting to Kern.

'So am I, but the food's worth waiting for. Far better than what I ate back in Mypocine. There was never enough of it. The farmer I worked for didn't allow me to eat with his family. He brought a plate out to me in the barn where I slept. It was usually cold.'

'Sounds like you had a hard time.'

I nodded. 'The work was hard, but I did have a few

friends. I saw them at weekends when I went stick-fighting. How about you, Deinon?'

'I worked on a farm too, but it was my father's so at least I had a proper bed for the night. I've got two younger brothers. We all had to muck in together to help my father, working from dawn until dusk. This is better! But I have to succeed or I'll end up farming again.'

'What about your brothers?' I asked. 'Will they come to the city and train for the arena?'

Deinon shook his head sadly. 'My father can only afford to have one of us trained; he finds it really hard to keep up the payments. I'm the eldest, so it happens to be me. I've got to do well. I don't want to let him down.'

Every other evening, as part of our training programme, Tyron took us to the Wheel so that we could learn by watching the contests in Arena 13. One of the highlights was when I first saw Epson fight.

We'd settled into our seats just in time for the first contest of the evening. The combatants and their lacs were already in position.

Behind the single lac stood a man with white hair and a short beard; his bare arms were crisscrossed with old scars.

I had never seen anyone so old fighting in Arena 13. Long before their hair started to grey, most combatants were forced to retire, often through injury. It was something for young men – you needed to be in your prime. As your mobility and speed declined, fighting became much more difficult.

'That old codger won't last five minutes,' Palm sneered. 'He's more likely to die of old age before the contest even starts!'

'That's Epson.' Tyron's voice was filled with respect and he glared at Palm. 'He's been injured and hasn't fought since last season. But everybody knows him. Underestimate him at your peril, Palm! He's a veteran of Arena 13 and a legend amongst those who know what they're talking about. Perhaps he's not as strong and fast as he once was, but he's a canny fighter from both the min and the mag positions, which is very rare. Most combatants specialize in one or the other. My money would be on him. Look at all the scars on his arms.'

'Each scar marks a bout when he was beaten?' I asked. I was appalled that there were so many.

'Each scar represents an *honourable defeat*,' Tyron corrected me. 'But for every one of them there were at least fifty victories. They say he's to retire at the end of the season. He gets cramps in his legs now – a chronic condition; many older fighters get it – and there's a growing weakness in his back. But I wouldn't put it past him to spread negative rumours about himself in order to improve the odds; that way he'll get a better return when he backs himself to win. Now look at the young man he's facing. His name is Skule and he's ranked high on the Lists even though it's only his third season. He fights from Kronkt's stable – as you can tell by the eagle logo on the back of his jerkin. He's very popular with the women.'

I could see why. Skule had blond hair, a handsome face and a muscular body. I glanced around the gallery and noticed that there were more women than usual in attendance tonight. A few in the front row were leaning over the rail and calling his name in a bid to attract his attention. One young girl finally succeeded: he looked up, smiled and gave her a wave – at which she shrieked and buried her face in her hands.

'Skule's seriously good,' Palm said. 'We've watched him fight before. He won easily both times, didn't he?'

Tyron nodded. 'Yes, Skule will go far, but tonight I think he'll be in for a surprise.'

But I was more interested in Epson. Here was a man who'd had a long successful career in Arena 13.

'Whose stable does Epson belong to?' I asked; I'd noticed that he had no logo on the back of his jacket.

Palm was sitting on the other side of Tyron and I saw him smirk at my question. He obviously knew the answer, and was always delighted by any display of ignorance from me.

'Many like to fight from a stable like mine that offers good support to a fighter, but not every combatant follows that route,' Tyron explained. 'Epson maintains, owns and trains with his own lacs. Some combatants do so because it takes a long time to build up sufficient funds to get yourself into my position. Some, like Epson, choose not to fight from a stable anyway. He could have afforded it but prefers to work on his own. He'd rather fight than worry about training and managing other people.'

'I think I'd choose to do the same,' Deinon observed from my left.

Tyron smiled. 'It's something that everyone has to make up his own mind about. But for you boys, decisions like that are still in the future.'

Despite what he had said, I already knew what I wanted to do; I thought it unlikely that I'd change my mind. I lacked the ability to pattern to the highest level, so I could never become another Tyron. But I was fast and my reactions were excellent. I wanted to fight in the arena – to fight and win until I was the best min combatant in Arena 13.

After he'd blown the trumpet signalling that combat could begin, Pyncheon, the Chief Marshal, left the arena and the contest got underway. Skule crouched low behind his three lacs. His arms – like Epson's – were bare; far fewer scars were evident.

Suddenly Skule's feet drummed on the wooden boards using the sound-code, Ulum, to tell his lacs what to do.

Responding quickly, Skule's lacs began to move warily, the six blades glinting menacingly. Skule followed, dancing very close to the back of his central lac.

In response, Epson thumped the boards rhythmically himself, and then took one quick step backwards in unison with his own lac.

I heard a low murmur that quickly became a rising growl of anticipation. It was clear that Skule had already made a mistake: the crowd had spotted the over-commitment of the younger man.

Four pairs of blades flashed as Epson's lone lac whirled forward, thrusting its own blades – right, left and right again – into the throats of the three lacs that opposed it. And suddenly the tri-glad of Skule was an inert tangled heap upon the boards – almost, it seemed, before I heard the metallic thunder of its fall.

The speed of Epson's lac had been incredible, yet the older man had barely moved. My mouth dropped open, and a glance to my side told me that Deinon and Palm had had the same reaction. Epson was still crouching in the same position, a smile upon his face.

Without the protection of his three lacs, Skule's dance had come to a sudden halt; now the menacing form of Epson's single lac extended its blades towards him.

To a chorus of howls and shrieks of dismay from Skule's supporters, Epson's lac made a small precise cut to his upper arm – the ritual that marked the younger man's defeat. It was all over.

The doors were opened again, and attendants, directed by Pyncheon, removed the fallen lacs from the arena, while yellow tickets, the betting receipts of those who had bet on Skule, fluttered from disappointed hands.

Quickly people left their seats and there was a surge up the aisles towards the blue-sashed gambling agents, who'd now taken up positions close to the rear wall of the gallery.

'Epson hardly moved,' I said, still bemused by what had just taken place. 'It seemed an easy victory.'

'Indeed. A victory won before he even set foot in the arena,' Tyron said with a smile. 'Watch and learn, boy. That lac is patterned to perfection. Epson moved inside its mind and then told it exactly what to do. One step backwards, then attack. It's difficult for the combatant from the min position to win: his lac is outnumbered three to one. But the skilful and the brave *can* achieve it. A man like Epson does it again and again. A tri-glad needs to be perfectly coordinated, and sometimes it can go wrong – as you just saw. Not only that, the mag combatant can be tricked into making mistakes.'

I realized how much there was still to learn before I was ready to set foot in the arena.

*

At the end of my first full week of training back at Tyron's house I got a surprise.

Saturday was our one day off. We were free to do what we wanted. I would have preferred another day of training and was planning to get in some practice without Palm around.

But when I woke up that morning, Deinon was sitting on the end of his bed pulling on his socks. There was no sign of Palm.

'Morning.' Deinon smiled at me. 'Any plans for today?'

I shook my head. 'I thought I'd just have a wander around the city and then do some practice,' I told him.

'Have you seen the Westmere Plaza?' he asked.

'No – I don't even know what a plaza is! There certainly isn't one in Mypocine.'

'This whole district is called Westmere because of the nearby lake. A plaza is just a fancy name for a big flagged square, I think,' he told me. 'There's a market at one end, and shops and cafés at the other. I could show you round if you like . . .'

'That sounds good.' I felt like Deinon and I were starting to become friends – I wished I'd thought of inviting him to do something today.

'Shall we go straight after breakfast?'

Twenty minutes later we were out in the fresh air. There was a light breeze blowing and the sun was warm on my face. I'd been disappointed not to see Kwin at breakfast and I wondered where she'd be spending her Saturday. But I didn't want to appear too interested in her, and instead asked Deinon, 'What does Palm do on Saturdays?'

'Oh, his family come and collect him and take him out for a big meal. He's always boasting about the size of the steaks he wolfs down and the special sauce they're smothered in.'

That was typical of Palm. I didn't mind the fact that he'd been born into a wealthy family and had the best of everything. That was just the way things were – the luck of the draw. But I hated his air of superiority and constant bragging. However, now I made an effort to thrust him from my mind and concentrate on enjoying my day out.

'This is certainly the best part of Gindeen,' I observed. I'd spent my time in exile from Tyron's on the other side of town, never venturing this way for fear of bumping into Palm or Deinon – or even Tyron himself – so it was all new to me. We were still amongst the flagged walkways and big houses, some of which even had small gardens planted with shrubs and budding flowers.

'This is where the best artificers and the executives of the gambling houses live. Pyncheon has a house here, as do some of the richer merchants and farmers, for when they're in town. Right – here we are,' Deinon said as we turned a corner. 'What do you think of that?'

We were facing what I guessed was the plaza. I'd never seen anything like it: a vast paved square, its four sides planted with trees. To the west there were scores of market stalls covered by coloured canopies that rippled in the breeze. To the east stood a line of shops, along with cafés with tables outside. And the whole place thronged with groups and couples talking or strolling in the sunshine. They were all very smartly dressed – no doubt in their best clothes. All I had was the ill-fitting shirt and trousers supplied by Tyron.

'Let's go and get a drink,' suggested Deinon.

I felt the blood rush to my face. 'I'm sorry, but I don't have any money,' I told him.

'That's no problem. You can pay me back later. Or simply buy the drinks next time we come.'

'Then I'll need to get work of some sort. Is it possible to find a Saturday job here?'

'Tyron wouldn't want you working on Saturdays,' Deinon said. 'He thinks we should work hard all week and take that day to refresh ourselves. Besides, he'll give you money on the last Friday of each month. Each trainee receives a small allowance.'

'Tyron told me that, but I thought it would only be enough to cover basic things like clothes.'

'It's not a lot, but it'll run to a few drinks and snacks. The clothes you got when you started are free – as well as your first pair of Trig boots – but after that you pay. So you'll need to save some of it.'

Deinon led the way to what seemed the largest of the cafés and we sat down at a table in the warm sun, looking out at the throng of people gathered at the market stalls. Many tables around us were taken by young lads.

'The trainees come here,' Deinon explained. 'This café caters for them, and so the prices are a bit lower.'

'Do you know any of them?' I asked.

'I know some by name, but not to speak to. Most are in their second or third years. They don't usually deign to speak to first-year novices like us.'

'What about the first years who work for other artificers?'

'You won't see any of them here. For one thing they don't

get a day off. The one day they don't train, their masters use them like servants for cleaning and doing odd jobs. Tyron is different. He's a good artificer to work for. We're well looked after.'

After a few minutes a young waitress approached the table and took our order. She was wearing a blue knee-length dress and a cute little white hat with a matching blue ribbon. She looked very smart, as did all the young people seated around us. I knew I stuck out like a sore thumb. I would certainly have to save my allowance for some new clothes. After paying Deinon back, that would be my priority.

We both ordered apple juice. Deinon asked for buttered scones; the thought of them made my mouth water, but I pretended I wasn't hungry. I didn't want to owe Deinon more than was necessary. So I sipped my juice while he tucked into his scone.

I could no longer resist asking about Kwin – though I tried to make my question sound casual.

'What does Kwin do on Saturdays? She's not around much during the week either. Has she got a job somewhere?'

'During the week she works in Tyron's office, helping with the administration and ordering provisions and equipment. I'm not sure what she's doing today – often you find her sitting here. You see that guy at the table by the window . . . ? That's her boyfriend.'

My jaw dropped. The thought that she might have a boyfriend had never entered my head. She hadn't mentioned him. My heart sank in disappointment.

The Red Boots

The different types of djinni are more numerous than the stars. But of all these, most deadly is the rogue djinni, no longer subservient to the wurde that shaped him.

Amabramsum: the Genthai Book of Wisdom

I glanced across and realized that I'd seen the young man before. He'd called out to Kwin on the night she'd taken me to the Wheel – but she'd ignored him. I told Deinon and he nodded.

'Yes, they keep breaking up. She's a girl who knows her own mind, that's for sure! The only trouble is, she keeps changing it!'

Deinon took a sip of his juice and looked at me over the top of the glass as he did so. 'Palm is crazy about Kwin.'

I was shocked. 'I'd never have guessed!'

'He's wasting his time. Kwin and her boyfriend row a lot, but she always goes back to him. Besides, it wouldn't be a good idea for one of Tyron's trainees to get involved with his daughter, would it?'

I nodded carefully, hoping my feelings didn't show on my face. 'What happened when *you* fought her?' I asked, changing the subject.

Deinon laughed. 'She won the first two bouts so it didn't need to go to a decider. I was well and truly beaten. I just couldn't cope with her speed. Afterwards she said that I'd been boring. And she never knocked for me again! I don't mind, though. In a way, it was a relief. She's obsessed with fighting in the arena, even though she knows it's impossible. It makes her angry and bitter.'

We sat in silence for a few minutes, sipping our juice. I looked around the plaza and reflected that this was a far cry from the rougher areas of Gindeen, with their muddy roads and rotting boardwalks.

'Are you happy to be fighting from the min?' Deinon asked me suddenly.

I nodded. 'Yes, it's what I really want. I could never see myself fighting behind three lacs.'

'Fighting behind three – it offers a better chance of victory,' said Deinon. 'That would be my choice. You'd never have to face Hob! But you need a rich father to own three lacs; the min is a cheaper way to get started. I bet artificers like Tyron prefer it too. He's got a big stable and needs to provide the lacs for beginners like us. Even if I asked to fight behind three lacs, I don't think he'd let me.'

'So you're not happy?' I asked.

'I'll just have to make the best of it. Some min combatants do well. Take Kern, for example – he's got off to an amazing start this season, winning all ten of his early contests. Some say he'll be the Arena 13 champion this year. I just don't think I'll ever be good enough to succeed from the min. I'd like to become a patterner.'

'Are you good at patterning?' I asked, surprised. 'I find it really difficult.'

'I have to work hard at it, but I'm making steady progress. You don't often get praise from Tyron, but he said I'd made a very promising start to my studies.'

I smiled. 'Then maybe you will become a patterner one day. You could end up in Tyron's position – the most successful artificer in Gindeen with the largest stable of combatants!'

Deinon grinned at me happily. 'I'd never really thought of having my own stable, but I'll drink to that,' he said, draining the last of his juice. 'Do you want to see the lake? It's not far. First I'll go and find the waitress and pay.'

I smiled and thanked him again. I didn't like owing money, but I liked Deinon and that made his generosity easier to accept.

After he had settled the bill, we walked along the row of shops. Suddenly Deinon halted before a large window filled with goods for sale.

'This shop specializes in items for Arena 13,' he told me.

On display were the jackets, shorts and boots worn by combatants, as well as blades and the leather belts with their two scabbards.

'Most of this stuff is just replica, with the logos of the various stables; it's intended for fans. It's not the real thing: artificers like Tyron always use the city's best artists to paint their logos. But look over there . . .' Deinon pointed to the far side of the display. 'Those second-hand items are aimed at new combatants – those just starting out on a low budget without the support of a stable. The logos have been removed and most of the boots are worn at the heel – all but one special pair.'

He didn't need to tell me which one. All the boots were made of black or brown leather – all except one pair, which was red.

'You mean the red boots!' I exclaimed.

Deinon smiled. 'Yes – they look brand new, apart from the soles. On the night she first knocked for me, Kwin told me about those boots. She'd tried them on and they were a perfect fit, but Tyron wouldn't buy them for her. He told her that she's got enough crazy ideas spinning around inside her head and he wasn't going to indulge her any further. They're incredibly expensive. There's no way she can find that kind of money.

'Palm plans to buy those boots for her at the end of the season. His father has promised him a lot of money if he wins the TT. Not that it'll make any difference, of course. I don't think she'd even accept them from him.'

I didn't like the idea of Palm giving Kwin such a present and I hoped Deinon was right – that even if he tried, she would refuse it. I wished I could buy her those boots. It wouldn't change her feelings towards me – she already had a boyfriend – but it would make her happy. However, it was impossible and I thrust the thought out of my head.

We carried on to the end of the plaza, then continued through tree-lined streets to the grassy slope that led up to the lake. It was large and oval in shape, its calm waters reflecting the blue of the sky; rowing boats were tethered to a wooden jetty. The houses stopped here; beyond it I could see a wood. We could have been in the middle of nowhere, and suddenly, for the first time since arriving in Gindeen, I felt a sense of real peace.

Deinon and I walked clockwise around the lake in companionable silence, then settled down on the grass beside a small stream that was one of its two tributaries.

'Did you go to school in Mypocine?' Deinon asked me. 'I noticed one of your papers on Kern's desk – your handwriting is very neat. He's always complaining that mine is almost illegible.'

I'd not talked much about my life before arriving in Gindeen. 'Our farm was too far from the town,' I told him. 'My mother used to teach me.'

'She must have been a clever woman. Here there are Saturday schools that some of the farm kids attend. Our farm's quite close to Gindeen, so that's how I got my education. It was hard to keep up because there was lots of homework. I had to do mine after working a full day on the farm. Of course, Palm had a private tutor – only the best for him.'

I nodded. Everything had been easy for Palm. We sat in silence for a few moments, staring at the lake and enjoying the sunshine.

'You wouldn't think this was the same city,' I observed. 'The districts around the slaughterhouse and the Wheel are totally different.'

'Yes, this is where rich people live. I'd like to buy a house here one day,' Deinon mused. 'Anyway, do you fancy rowing out onto the lake for a bit? It's cheap and I'll pay.'

As we headed towards the jetty, I heard a shout. We were too far away for me to hear the words, but the tone told me that something was badly wrong.

A small crowd had gathered where the boats were moored; everyone was staring down at the water. As we approached, I shivered. The breeze had strengthened and all of a sudden it seemed colder.

'Oh no!' cried Deinon. He'd spotted what the people were staring at. A second later I caught up with him and, with a sick feeling in my stomach, saw a body floating face-down in the lake.

Close beside it a man was struggling to lift it out of the water, but it was too heavy for him.

'Help me!' he cried, but the crowd just stared; nobody made a move.

I wanted to help and was about to start running when Deinon raced ahead of me and splashed into the lake. I followed, the cold water making me gasp. The body was stiff and water-logged, making it really awkward, but somehow we dragged it up onto the bank. Then we rolled it over.

It was the body of a young woman – probably no more than twenty, her face a ghastly white. The man rolled her onto her stomach again, turned her head to one side and began pressing her back rhythmically as the crowd closed in to watch.

Water gushed from the girl's mouth in spurts, and I was filled with a sudden hope that he had brought her back to life. But she didn't respond any further, and finally he stopped and shook his head.

What had happened? Had she fallen from one of the boats? Or did her pale face mean that she had been in the water for some time?

I shivered again and glanced up as a cloud covered

the sun. Deinon caught my eye and shook his head sadly.

I heard gasps, and somebody screamed. Forcing my eyes back to the girl, I saw what had triggered the reaction: two deep purple wounds on her neck.

'She's been drained of blood,' Deinon whispered.

In a split second the crowd around the girl's body had dispersed, running down the slope towards the nearest houses and the plaza beyond them. As the man who'd been trying to resuscitate her passed by, I saw the panic in his eyes.

'We need to get out of here now!' Deinon snapped. He looked terrified as he stared up the slope towards the trees.

I looked at him questioningly.

'Hob killed her, and now the tassels will come for the body,' he explained.

'What? They'll come now – this minute?'

'Maybe now – certainly within the hour. They probably have a spy hiding up there in the trees. People have fled and the area is deserted. So they'll be here soon – you can be sure of that. Let's get away before it's too late!'

Without another word, he hurried off down the hill; I followed hot on his heels.

When we reached the first row of houses, I caught up with him and put my hand on his shoulder. 'Where are we going?'

'Back to Tyron's. It'll be safer there. Everybody will be heading home to lock and bar their doors. We need to do the same.'

'I'm going to stay,' I told him. 'I'd like to see what the tassels look like.'

Deinon's face showed instantly what he thought about this. 'It's dangerous, Leif. Far too risky. If they see you watching, they might take you too. The sensible thing is to get away from here.'

'That poor girl is dead!' I retorted, the anger building inside me and making my hands shake. 'I'd really like to stop them taking her body. I know we can't prevent them from doing that – there are too many of them – but I feel like a coward running away. I'm going to stay and see what our enemies look like. Do you see that clump of scrub and long grass . . .' I pointed to our left. 'I can hide there. I'll be out of sight and safe enough. Which way will they come – through the city or out of the trees?'

'Probably out of the trees,' Deinon answered. 'They some-times wander through the city streets, but only after dark.'

'Then I'll stay and watch – there's no need to put yourself in danger. You go back to Tyron's. I'll be OK.'

'If you're staying, Leif, then I'll stay too. You're new to the city and Tyron told me to keep an eye on you. I've never seen tassels in broad daylight before – I spotted a couple near the Wheel once, but they were some distance away. I want to see our enemies too!'

We headed over to the patch of scrub and settled down, hidden from anyone who came down the hill towards the lake.

'We should get a good view from here,' I said.

As the wait began, I felt curious but calm. My anger had subsided and I had no real sense of danger. Surely we'd be safe here?

But as time passed, my feelings gradually changed. I

began to worry. Tyron wouldn't approve of this. He'd say we were taking an unnecessary risk. I glanced back towards the nearest row of houses. The doors were closed and the curtains drawn. Everyone was safely inside but us. The people of the city knew all about the danger from the tassels. They wouldn't take any risks.

We waited and watched in silence, while more and more doubts whirled through my head. After about half an hour Deinon started to get restless.

He crawled closer. 'Tyron will be starting to get worried,' he whispered. 'News of this will have reached him; he'll be locking his own doors.'

Deinon was right. Tyron would expect us back by now. I didn't want to get on the wrong side of him again. I felt a few spots of rain on my face and I shivered with cold; my trouser legs were still soaking from our paddle in the lake. We'd have to head back soon.

'Let's just give it another ten minutes, then we'll go. Is that OK with you?' I asked.

Deinon nodded, and we continued to watch and wait. I felt certain that ten minutes had passed, but neither of us made a move to leave. It was drizzling now, the thin mist making our view less than perfect.

But I could see enough.

My heart lurched as the tassels appeared very suddenly, loping out of the trees like a pack of giant grey rats. I counted them quickly. There were at least a couple of dozen. The leader was big – maybe twice the size of a man – and ran on all fours. The others were of different sizes, some on all fours, most upright, but running with a strange gait that seemed far from human. They moved fast and silently in hooded grey gowns that trailed on the grass. If they came down the hill for us, I reflected, they'd catch us in seconds.

The tassels gathered around the body of the girl, but one on the edge of the pack suddenly lifted his head. His face was so gaunt that it was almost like a skull, the eyes hollow black pits. He seemed to be staring right at us.

My heart began to hammer with fear. Surely he couldn't see us? Maybe he could sense us in some other way? Unnoticed by the rest of the pack, he began to bound down the hill, directly towards our hiding place.

Deinon looked at me, eyes wide with fear, and started to rise, as if about to turn and run. I gripped his arm and shook my head. If we panicked and fled, the whole horde of tassels would chase us through the deserted streets. There would be nobody to help. We'd be hunted down and taken to Hob's citadel. We'd never be seen again.

The lone tassel halted close to the edge of the scrub. He was staring directly at us, but he didn't move. My heart was hammering so hard, I felt sure he must hear it. Suddenly the creature sniffed very loudly, as if sensing our presence, and gave a growl deep in his throat. Could he smell us? Maybe he was more sensitive than the others, who were only interested in the girl?

The tassel's face was partly in shadow, and at first I thought he had a beard, but then he took another step forward and I saw that his whole face was covered in hair.

He growled again, and I thought he was going to attack us, but then I heard a strange hooting cry from the other tassels.

The giant leader was scooping up the girl's body and carrying it back up the hill. The rest followed at his heels, and the tassel close to us, perhaps not wishing to be left behind, bounded away after them.

The moment of danger had passed, and soon the tassels had disappeared from view.

'What do they want her body for?' I asked Deinon, letting out a sigh of relief as I realized what a great risk we'd just taken.

Deinon shrugged. 'They'll take it to Hob, I suppose. He killed her; now she belongs to him. He probably drained her last night and left her floating on the edge of the reeds. It's happened before.'

'I'm sorry for getting you into that,' I said.

'It was my decision as well, Leif, so I'm to blame just as much. The tassels mostly hunt in the dark – we should have guessed that they don't simply rely on their eyes. That lone one couldn't see us, but he knew we were there. We got away with it – but another time we might not be so lucky. Let's hope that Tyron doesn't find out what we just did!'

We set off at a jog, while I mulled over what had just occurred. I couldn't understand this place; why this was allowed to happen in a city which had an armed force to protect its inhabitants.

'Why doesn't somebody do something about it?' I wondered. 'Hob might kill someone in the night undetected, but why are the tassels allowed to enter the city and take the body? It's the middle of the day – where are the Protector's Guard?'

'They would never interfere with Hob's business. And it's

a Saturday. Apart from a few left on duty, most of them will be in their barracks swilling ale like the pigs they are. It's the way things are here, Leif. Hob rules.'

'There were so many of those tassels,' I said. 'They were like a pack of wild animals.'

'Yes, they hunt in big packs,' said Deinon. 'There'd have been others watching from the trees.'

We walked back towards Tyron's house. The plaza was deserted and it was starting to rain hard. I was angered by what I'd just witnessed. Earlier we'd been sipping fruit juice in the sun; everybody had been enjoying themselves . . . And all the while, unbeknown to us, the body of a dead girl was floating in the lake, waiting to be found.

Hob and his servants could do whatever they pleased.

What a terrible place this was.

The Legend of Math

I began to feel myself to be the expression of a higher
   power, an aspect of Nym, the goddess of all
   pattern, movement and dance.
I was not merely dancing the patterns of the Trigladius.
In some way I had become those patterns.

The Testimony of Math

At supper I felt distracted. I couldn't get that poor girl's white face out of my mind, and I struggled to keep up with the conversation at the table. As usual, Palm was boasting, going on and on about the three lacs that Tyron was going to pattern for him. He never made eye-contact with me, but Deinon was listening with a polite expression on his face.

I could hear the conversation at the other end of the table, where Kern, Tyron, Teena and Kwin were discussing the dead girl. Only one thing lifted my mood a little: at one point I caught Kwin's eye, and she smiled at me. It was probably just a friendly smile, but my heart leaped with joy.

Then, at the end of the meal, Kern came over to speak to me. 'Tyron wants to see you up in his study in about five minutes. It's the room right at the top of the house. You can't miss it.'

My heart sank. Had he found out about Deinon and me and our encounter with the tassels? Kern must have read the dismay on my face because he gave me a kind smile and patted me on the shoulder. 'Don't worry, Leif. You're not in trouble – but don't keep him waiting!'

I climbed the stairs to Tyron's study. It was the first time I'd ever been up there. Despite Kern's words of reassurance I was very nervous. It would also be the first time I'd spoken properly to Tyron since he'd allowed me back.

I knocked lightly at the door, but there was no response. I was just about to knock again when Tyron opened the door.

'Come in, Leif, and sit there by the fire.'

I smiled and took the seat he'd indicated, glancing around the room. Panelled in dark, polished mahogany, it was furnished with leather chairs, and white wolf furs were laid upon the boards before the fire. This was clearly the den of a very wealthy man.

As I cast my eyes about the place thinking how different it was from my childhood home, something caught my eye. On the wall was a sealed glass case. It contained a simple shelf upon which, supported by heavy bookends carved in the shape of a wolf, stood six or seven volumes bound in soft brown leather. They looked very ancient.

Tyron walked across to a table in the far corner and poured himself a glass of red wine from a decanter. He returned carrying the glass and sat down in the chair opposite. He took a sip of wine and smiled at me.

The smile was reassuring; it made me feel more comfortable.

'Kern tells me that you're doing well. He says a lot of the

steps come easily to you, as if you are already familiar with them. Who taught you?'

I hesitated before answering.

'My father spent time in this city and knew the steps of the Trig. He taught me a few moves. As I said, I was a stick-fighter.'

'Did many of the lads lose their front teeth?'

'Some did. It was a risk we took.'

'I hope my daughter manages to keep hers,' growled Tyron. 'It'll be hard enough getting her married off as it is. I know that you and Kwin are friends, but that friendship brings some responsibility with it. Do you know what I mean?'

Was he about to warn me to keep away from his daughter? Was that why he'd summoned me to his study?

'Look, Kwin is wild. She takes chances and she's obsessed with Arena 13. I know she took the lead in arranging that stick-fight between you. No doubt she overcame your reservations and changed your mind. But you can change hers too. It works both ways. Try to talk a bit of sense into her from time to time . . . Will you try?'

I hadn't a clue how to do that, but I nodded and gave the answer I thought he wanted.

'Of course I'll do my best. Kwin has a mind of her own, but I'll try.'

'That's all I ask of you, Leif. Do you miss stick-fighting?'

I thought of the local boys back in Mypocine; we'd all been desperate to fight in Arena 13 one day. It had been a dream, something to sustain us while we scratched a living from the soil.

It was different for those farming close to Gindeen. Here the agricultural land was good; cattle grew fat and farmers rich by supplying beef and milk to the city. The lottery only provided five places a year. The large majority were purchased directly by wealthy fathers; they could afford to buy their sons training places with the best artificers. That was how Palm had got his place. That was how he would be able to maintain three lacs and fight behind a tri-glad.

'I like training for Arena 13 – it's far better than stick-fighting. I won't let you down again. You needn't worry about that.'

Tyron nodded, and I thought he was about to tell me to go back downstairs when suddenly he asked a question that took me by surprise.

'You know about Math?' His eyes were boring into mine.

I nodded, keeping my face expressionless.

'Do you know what happened to him?'

'Some of it.'

'Know what happened to Math and you'll understand Hob. What's wrong, boy? You've got a strange expression on your face.'

I changed the subject. 'Deinon and I were at the lake when they found the dead girl. It was horrible. I can't get it out of my mind.'

'So you know what this city is up against. That dead girl by the lake is just a part of Hob's tyranny. Now, I'm going to tell you what Math accomplished in Arena 13. It's something you need to know. If I begin at the beginning, we'll still be here at dawn,' he said, 'so I'll start at the end of Math's second year. By the end of that season he was ranked first in the Lists, and already the aficionados were saying he was the best who'd ever walked the boards.

'He was registered under the name Mathias, but every-one knew him as Math. He was in the stable of a man called Gunter, who at that time was just about the best artificer in Gindeen. Gunter the Great, they called him. They worked well together: Gunter had the brain for great patterning and Math had the speed to be a great fighter. Arena 13 hasn't seen the like of those two since, and maybe never will again. It was a true partnership.'

Tyron raised his glass and sipped deeply from the wine. He was staring into space as if seeing a ghost or something from the past. I shifted uncomfortably, had he just got me up here to tell me old stories?

'On the last night of Math's second season, Hob came to the Wheel, bringing with him a tri-glad. He offered the usual challenge, and a min combatant was honour-bound to respond.'

'Were you there?' I asked Tyron.

He nodded. 'I was one of the min combatants. I was standing so close to Math that I could have reached out and touched him.

'We gathered in the waiting room under the arena. Pyncheon, the Chief Marshal – he was a young man then, the youngest ever to hold that office – came in carrying the frosted glass lottery orb which contained the silver straws. The man who drew the short straw would be the one to fight Hob. There were nineteen straws that night – one for each min combatant who'd fought on that evening's Lists. Obviously I was nervous. Any one of us could have been chosen and it meant certain death.

'Epson – you've seen him fight – plucked the first straw.

Until all the straws had been drawn, it was impossible to tell which was the shortest, but Epson seemed safe. But then, suddenly, Math strode into the centre of the group and dashed the glass lottery orb from Pyncheon's hand. It fell to the ground and shattered into fragments, scattering the remaining straws amongst the shards of glass. Math knelt quickly and selected a straw.'

'The short straw,' I whispered.

Tyron stared at me for a moment before continuing. 'There was total silence in that room; even the Chief Marshal was glaring at him, but he didn't know what to say. "I hold the short straw, so the right of combat is mine," Math said.'

'Pyncheon wouldn't have liked that, would he?' I said. 'Math was breaking the rules in a big way!'

Tyron paused to sip his wine and gave a smile. 'Yes, he was breaking the rules all right – we all waited in a shocked silence. Nobody could guess how the Chief Marshal would react. But he simply bowed and accepted Math as the challenger. Math had already won a victory over Hob,' he explained. 'By breaking the orb and seizing the short straw, he'd ensured that Hob would be forced to face the very best opponent the Wheel had to offer – him. Hob wanted somebody to fight; Math had offered himself up. Pyncheon accepted that and told us all to get to our positions.

'That evening, we eighteen combatants up in the gallery watched in dismay as Hob's tri-glad entered the arena. The lacs wore black armour and moved with a speed and grace you wouldn't believe. Hob followed close behind them.'

'What did he look like?' I asked.

'When he fights in the arena, he looks much like a human

combatant,' Tyron answered. 'But he's bigger than most and his arms are exceptionally long – like the arms of a lac – and completely hairless. And he wears a bronze helmet that completely covers his head, right down to his chin. As his throat is open to a blade, nobody has ever thought to protest – and nobody would dare anyway.

'I couldn't believe my eyes when Math followed his own lac into the arena and took up combat position behind it. He was wearing a silver helmet shaped in the likeness of a wolf and held two blades. Until that moment, no human combatant had ever *carried* blades into Arena 13. They merely had a ceremonial function and were worn at the belt. And as for the helmet, why not? If Hob could do it, why shouldn't Math? Do you know why his helmet was shaped like a wolf's head?'

I nodded. 'Because he was Genthai . . .'

'Yes. He was *Genthai*.'

The word meant the People of the Wolf.

'We've a few fighting in the Trig now, but Math was the very first of his people to compete, changing his name so that he would be granted a licence. Of course, down south near Mypocine, you're not far from the Genthai tribal lands. You'll know all about how people can be prejudiced. Isn't that right, boy?'

I shrugged. 'A lot of trade goes on down there. There's probably more prejudice up here in Gindeen.'

Tyron looked at me keenly, and then went on, 'At first Math just waited. Even when Hob's tri-glad launched the first attack and there was the clash of blade against blade, he still didn't move.'

'Like Epson in that contest the other night?' I asked.

'Yes, exactly. But then Math's lac took two swift steps forward, pressing home its advantage, and Math stepped where it had stepped and crouched again, waiting. They attacked once more, but this time two of the tri-glad diverted his lac and the third surged in from the side, seeking his flesh. Math whirled round to meet it and lunged forward. His own lac half turned to protect him, but it was too late: he was already committed. He avoided the first of the blades, but the second struck him high on the temple, a blow that would have cleaved his skull in two—'

'The wolf helmet saved him,' I said. 'Where did he get it?'

Tyron ignored my question. I suspected that he was annoyed by my interruptions.

'Math was bent over, recovering from the blow to his head, but to our surprise he suddenly straightened up, thrusting his blade into the throat-socket of Hob's lac. The lac fell sideways and backwards, almost tugging the blade out of Math's hand. But he held onto it.

'It was astonishing. I could barely hear myself think, the noise from the crowd was so loud. A human combatant had felled a lac. This had never been done before. It was a first! It changed the way we think about fighting in the arena. Math showed what was possible and, although it's difficult to accomplish, it now happens once or twice each season.

'Of course, it wasn't over yet. Math withdrew behind his lac and kept very close to its back; patterned by the brilliant Gunter, it was able to deal with Hob's remaining two lacs. The fight was certainly over before the gong that would have called Hob and Math to fight in front of their defenders. Math had won, and everyone in the gallery went wild.

'Now we'd reached a very significant moment. Against Hob it was always a fight to the death, but until then it had always been the human combatant who had died. Sometimes they were badly wounded – claimed by Hob and taken up to his citadel, never to be seen again. But now the tables had been turned. A silence fell upon the arena.

'What would Math do? Would he dare to slay the djinni? Hob still had his own blades. Would he resist, or would he accept the defeat implied by the endoff of his lacs?

'We soon found out. Math went forward and Hob did not resist. So Math slit his throat cleanly, leaving the head attached. Hob fell to his knees, his long hairless arms flopping at his side, slumping forward onto his face. But all our eyes were drawn to the blood that gushed from his throat. It was crimson – far brighter than any blood shed by a man or animal. People talked about it for days.'

'So Math had won,' I gasped.

But Tyron shook his head grimly. 'Do you call that winning, Leif? One victory! Not by a long way. That was only *one* of his djinni bodies; one of his many selves. That was just the first bout.'

'So did Hob return to the arena the following night?' I asked. It seemed to me that Hob would have been eager for revenge.

'No, Hob came much later – the following season. This time the Chief Marshal didn't even bother with the lottery orb. His eyes locked upon Math's and, with a curt nod, Math put himself forward for combat. And it seemed to those who braved the gallery to watch that Hob was even more formidable this time.

'When attacking Math, no single lac risked its throat. Instead, they concentrated on his lac, pressing it hard so that it was a struggle to hold the centre of the arena. But Math fought with great discipline.

'This time the struggle lasted almost twenty minutes, Leif, with both combatants fighting in front, vulnerable to blades. But once again Math won. Once more, the bright red blood of Hob stained the boards of the arena.'

'How long did the contests go on?' I asked. 'Palm told me that Math beat Hob fifteen times.'

'Yes, it was exactly fifteen. It went on like that for weeks. But how long can something like that continue, boy? Something has to give.'

'What do you mean?' I asked.

'Think about it. How many selves was the djinni prepared to lose in the arena? And remember: Math only had *one* body and *one* life. It couldn't go on for ever, could it? It was midsummer's eve that proved decisive. All day long a storm had been brewing, and early in the evening the heavens were suddenly split asunder by a great fork of white lightning. The following crash of thunder seemed to threaten the end of the world. Soon the storm was raging overhead; it was as if the gods were throwing down thunderbolts.

'But that didn't worry the crowds who surged into the Wheel, heading for Arena 13. There were too many to fit into the gallery; they gathered excitedly about the Omphalos, on the floor above the arenas, desperate for news of Hob's arrival. And the gambling agents were having a rare old time, weren't they?

'There were bets placed on whether or not Hob would

appear; bets on exactly when the winning blow would be delivered; on the likelihood of Math repeating his feat of downing a lac with his own blade – or, indeed, the moment when Math himself might fall to Hob's tri-glad. There were even wagers on how Math would behave if defeated by Hob and taken live from the arena.

'This time the bout was very much in the balance. For a while it seemed as if Math must crumble before Hob's fierce onslaught, but then the gong sounded and both combatants stepped in front of their lacs.

'As you know, the combatants are usually more cautious at this point, but Math threw caution to the wind. With steps too quick for the inexperienced eye, blades flashing, he was right amongst the tri-glad of his foe.

'Some say that Math felled all three members of that tri-glad with his own blades; others that it was only one, and that his own long-armed lac reached over his shoulders and head to account for the other two. I was there, but it was too quick for the eye to see, and even to this day I'm not sure.

'Anyway, this victory brought about a change. From that day, Hob visited the arena less frequently; though each time he was defeated more easily. But as the odds offered by the gambling agents began to lengthen in Math's favour, people grew afraid. The fear grew into a dark unreasoning terror, and they began to leave the city.'

'How *many* selves does Hob have?' I asked. 'Do we know? How many would Math have had to defeat to win a final victory?'

'Hob is a djinni – the creation of the greatest artificers that ever lived; his technology is beyond the limits of our knowledge. We don't know how many selves are written into the wurdes that govern him so we can't know how many times we have to kill him to destroy him completely,' Tyron explained. 'As I said, people were fleeing the city. At first it was just the farmers and tradesmen returning early to their distant homes, but then Gindeen's own inhabitants began to leave.'

'But it doesn't make sense!' I blurted out, despite Tyron's warning. 'Math was winning, so why were they afraid?'

I expected him to be angry at the interruption, but he simply sighed and answered my question.

'They feared a defeated Hob more than a victorious one because he's a djinni, with all the dark powers of such a creature. It's dangerous to back him into a corner. What horrors might he unleash upon the city if he became desperate?

'It was Hob who finally broke the deadlock. He proposed that there should be one final contest to decide things. If defeated, he'd never visit Arena 13 again. In return, he demanded that Math spend the whole contest in front of his lac, while Hob himself would fight *behind* his tri-glad. It was an outrageous and unfair offer, but to everyone's relief, Math accepted. Now people were afraid; even his friends wanted the situation resolved.

'Nobody imagined that Math could win that fifteenth contest. Walking into Arena 13 that night, he must have felt totally alone.

'You see, two days before the fight, Gunter suddenly collapsed while eating a late supper. Some say he was poisoned.'

'Could Hob have done that?' I asked.

Tyron shrugged. 'He could certainly have arranged it, though it was never proved. But despite the odds against him, Math won that final contest – though it cost him dear. He was severely wounded and lost a lot of blood; his left leg was damaged beyond repair and he was left with a bad limp, so he was never able to fight in Arena 13 again. Imagine that! It had been his life, and now he'd lost it for ever.

'However, Hob failed to keep his word: he still visits the Wheel to issue a challenge, and it's still the end for some unfortunate min combatant. The Wheel Directorate suffers a considerable financial loss. That hits everybody in the pocket because combatants and artificers have to meet the tax that's levied to cover the deficit. So each pays according to his earnings; my bill is so large that it affects what I can afford to spend on lacs that year.

'Hob was the winner in the end. Math lost what he loved most – fighting in the arena. Some say that it was all for nothing, but I don't agree. Math and Gunter have inspired a whole generation of artificers and combatants. They showed us what is possible.

'So Math went back to live out the remainder of his days with the Genthai tribe. They say he died there, at peace, amongst his own people.'

Tyron raised the glass to his lips and drained the last of the wine. When he looked at me, his eyes were hard and unsmiling.

'But you and I know better, boy, don't we? We both know where the legend ends and the life of the man goes on. So tell me, Leif, son of Math: what makes a son disclaim his own father?'

The Cowardice of Math

Those who take the first steps rarely take the last.

Amabramsum: the Genthai Book of Wisdom

'How did you find out?' I asked.

'I suspected it the second time we met,' said Tyron, crossing the room to refill his glass from the decanter. 'It wasn't just the way you caught the blade I threw at you. It was the way you bowed afterwards – the set of your body; the moment's hesitation before the bow; then the dipping of your left shoulder slightly before the right. Do that in the arena, and anyone who saw your father fight will recognize you as his son.'

He returned to his seat and, after sipping wine from his glass, continued. 'It was exactly the same when you slid your blade into the throat-socket of the practice lac. You bowed afterwards. You have the same arrogance; the same self-belief. Both are vital qualities if you wish to achieve success in Arena 13.

'And, of course, if I look closely, I can see his face in yours. Once you know, it's clear enough. I wanted to be sure, so I sent someone to Mypocine to find out the truth. He talked to the farmer you worked for. He came back five days ago and confirmed what I'd suspected.'

My mind worked backwards. 'That's why you gave me another chance . . .'

'Yes. But that chance depends on you telling me the truth now.'

To tell the truth wasn't easy. I'd never told anybody the whole story before – I'd never even given a hint to anyone in this city. It was hard to force the words out, but it had to be done. My future with Tyron, my hope of fighting in Arena 13, depended upon it.

'Hob murdered my mother,' I told him. 'And my father just stood back and let it happen. Then he killed himself.'

'That's just the bones of the story. Either cover them with flesh or find yourself another artificer!' Tyron snapped, eyes hard as flint.

'My father didn't go back to his people – or if he did, he didn't stay long. He bought a small farm south of Mypocine. Soon afterwards he met my mother, Shola. She wasn't Genthai. I was born two years later. I was their only child.'

In spite of the bitterness I now felt, I couldn't help but smile at the memory of my childhood. My father had enjoyed farming, and I knew how much he loved me and my mother. We were happy; really happy. I often thought I'd never be as happy again.

Tyron pulled me back from my musings. 'And it was from him that you learned some steps from the Trig? He didn't keep his past a secret from you?'

'Yes and no. He showed me his blades with the wolf's-head handles, but he never talked much about his time fighting there. He never told me what you just have. I never dreamed he was so good until I saw the painting over Palm's bed and he told me it was of Math. Those fifteen victories over Hob came as a complete shock. My mother and I called him by his Genthai name, Lasar. He never told me that he had fought Hob.

'Then, when I was just eleven, it started. There'd been people dying even further south, but I never thought he'd visit our farm. It was horrible . . . It went on right through the summer and into the early autumn. He came every week, and always after dark. My mother would walk down the hill and wade across the stream to meet him in the wood. She couldn't help it, I know . . . He controlled her mind. At first they kept it from me and tried to pretend that nothing was wrong, but I soon figured it out when I saw my mother leaving the house alone late at night . . . Then I heard some of the things my parents said to each other: the name Hob came up over and over again. My mother cried. My father shouted. It became unbearable.

'I had no idea why Hob had chosen us, no idea who my father really was. I begged him to do something – anything. But he wouldn't even try. Instead, in his frustration, he used to smash his fists against the walls until they bled. He said he could do nothing or Hob would kill us all. So whatever he was in the arena, by then he'd changed. You talk of my father as if he was a hero, but I saw the other side of him. He was a coward who let my mother die.

'Each time she came back she was a little paler and weaker: Hob was taking more and more of her blood. Then, one night, she didn't come back at all. Just after dawn I followed my father down the hill. Her shoes were still on the near bank of the stream. Her body lay amongst the trees.'

My throat tightened and I sobbed, my whole body shaking.

'Take your time, Leif,' said Tyron. 'Take as much time as you need.'

It was a while before I could continue.

'My father cried for a long time, but then he became angrier than I'd ever seen him before. Until that moment he'd never so much as laid a finger on me; now he began to beat me, driving me away from the farm.

'I came back later; I hid and watched from a distance as he burned my mother's body. It was only when he set fire to the farmhouse that I realized what he intended. I ran down the hill but he was already dead. Through the doorway I saw his body lying there, covered in blood. Then the flames drove me back. There was nothing I could do.'

I saw it all again, and tears coursed down my cheeks. When I turned away in embarrassment, Tyron rested his hand briefly on my shoulder. Finally I managed to go on.

'A neighbour, Barrow, took me in – he'd a farm further down the valley. I stayed with him for three years – until I got that blue ticket. He worked me hard. Food and a roof over my head were my only wages. Apart from the sticks I used for fighting, all I owned were the clothes I stood up in.

'But Barrow did tell me that my father had fought in Arena 13 under the name Math – though he never told me how good he was.'

'You've faced more than most boys your age and come

through it, and for that you're to be congratulated, Leif,' said Tyron, his expression softer now. 'And now you're here, hoping to become a combatant in Arena 13 like your father was. Or is there more to it than that? Come on, boy, be honest with me. I want to hear you say it!'

'I *have* been honest. I've told no lies!' I shouted, emotion getting the better of me. 'No lies at all!'

'You can lie by omission,' Tyron told me, his voice very calm. 'Lie by leaving things unsaid. You've been less than open with me. So tell me: why are you here in this city? What do you *really* want to achieve?'

Despite his persistence, his expression was kind. My anger faded. I took a deep breath, and then the words I'd been holding within me for so long came out in a rush.

'One day I want to fight Hob in the arena. I want to kill him. That's why I'm here.'

Tyron sighed and drained his glass. 'I thought that might be your intention. Haven't you listened to a single thing I've said tonight? That's why I described exactly what happened to your father. Even if you won, Hob would only come back. He can fight over and over again – but you can only lose once and then you're finished; finished for ever!'

'Do you think I don't know that? Even after my father had retired from the arena, Hob pursued him and targeted my mother. He's vindictive and relentless – I've no illusions about what would happen to me afterwards if I lost. But it would be worth the risk,' I said. 'I'd like to kill him again and again. My father beat him fifteen times. I'll do the same – for as many times as it takes, until he has no selves left! I will make no deals with him. I'd never fight before my lac for a whole contest like my father did and let Hob be safe behind his. I'll destroy every last bit of him!'

Tyron shook his head wearily. 'Look, boy, I want you to promise me one thing. If you're ever chosen by the lottery orb to fight Hob, then so be it. It was meant to happen. But what your father did with the orb, deliberately selecting himself for combat . . . I'll have none of that. Do you understand?'

I nodded.

'Do you promise, then?'

'I promise.'

'Good. And there's one more thing. You kept the identity of your father from me, so for the time being at least, keep it from everyone else. I trust the man I sent back to Mypocine to keep quiet, but it'll get out eventually, and that'll make things much more difficult. You'll be under a lot of pressure. It's not just the expectation that you'll prove to be another Math . . . Your father had enemies as well as friends. Anyone that successful always makes enemies. So you might attract unwelcome attention.

'And your identity could affect the odds set by the gambling houses. You see, if you prove to be as good as I think you'll be, we might make quite a bit of money – but only if we have the advantage of surprise. Understand what I'm saying?'

I'd told Tyron things I had never revealed to anyone before, and I was tired and overwrought after our long talk. But I was only too happy to go along with his wishes. My heart was pounding with excitement. He had faith in me. I remembered what he had said – *as good as I think you'll be* – and was filled with elation.

When I nodded again, Tyron let out a long sigh. Then he leaned forward and rested his hand on my shoulder once more.

'I've a parting thought for you to mull over. The Math that I knew was the bravest man I've ever met. We trained together in Gunter's stable when we were boys. You're forgetting where you, his only child, come into all this. What if your mother insisted that Math did nothing because she was afraid for *you* – afraid that Hob would kill you? Then, after she was dead, he drove you away . . . and you're still alive. Hob gets to know everything eventually. Through you he would have found a way to punish Math even more. But your father killed himself and burned the farmhouse down so that all ties to him were gone. He set you free; gave you a chance of life. That's what I think, anyway.'

Money

Gunter was my teacher. I thought him far greater than
  I would ever be. Mine were just the dancing legs
  that served his nimble mind.
But then that changed.
In a vision, I saw Nym.

The Testimony of Math

Palm had been subdued since my return, but the following
morning he was back to his usual irritating, boastful self.
Every time I saw him I disliked him more. There was an
anger slowly building inside me.

'Tyron's promised to have my new tri-glad ready before
the end of the day,' he announced as we were getting dressed.
'I'll have three whole months to get ready for the trainee
tournament. That's more than enough time.'

He gave a self-satisfied smirk and waited for somebody
to say something. When nobody did, he sauntered over
to me. I was sitting on the edge of my bed pulling on
my socks.

'What about a bet?' he asked. 'Fancy a wager, just
between me and you?'

What was Palm up to? 'I've no money,' I told him.

'That doesn't matter. You'll earn money one day. You can owe me.'

'What's the bet?' I asked.

He smirked even more. 'Just this: that you won't win a single contest in the TT.'

I looked up and locked eyes with him, my anger growing. It was true that I wouldn't have much time to prepare. I could be drawn against a mag combatant like Palm, who'd already received months more training than I had. Alternatively, I might face another novice. My lottery ticket had won. Could I get lucky a second time? After all, the first phase of the competition was a league where you accumulated points. Only afterwards did it become a knock-out competition. So I was guaranteed two bouts. Surely I could win one of them . . .

'How much?' I asked.

'A thousand decs!'

It was a preposterous sum of money. As much as a trades-man earned in a year of hard work. You could almost buy a lac for that.

'The stake's too high,' I told him.

'Take it or leave it,' he said, giving me a patronizing look.

'I'll take it!' I snapped, desperate to wipe that expression off his face. But the one that followed was just as bad.

He looked as if he knew something that I didn't. 'You might be fast,' he said, 'but that won't count for much in Arena 13. It's not like stick-fighting, and nothing at all like the training floor. It's the lacs that decide a contest, and I'll have the best that money can buy. My father is rich; you don't even have a father. His money will pay for my lacs and Tyron's time. Tyron will be fully occupied getting my tri-glad up to scratch so he won't have much time left to attend to your needs. You've lost before you can even get started.'

I glanced at the painting of my father. Palm's had money; mine was dead. That was true. But my father was the greatest fighter the Arena had ever seen. I seemed to have inherited his speed and skill – but what would that count for against Palm's superior lacs?

'We'll see,' I retorted. 'You might be in for a surprise!'

My words sounded weak and hollow, and Palm just carried on smirking. I realized that I'd been manipulated into taking up a foolish bet that I would probably lose. This world was divided into the rich and the poor. I was clearly at a disadvantage here, but I was going to do my very best to prove Palm wrong.

Breakfast was usually quiet, but today, instead of just giving his usual curt nod towards our end of the table, Tyron came over and gave Palm a friendly pat on the shoulder.

'Your tri-glad will be ready by noon,' he told him. 'I'll come down and supervise your first session myself.'

This was what it meant to have a rich father. Instead of leaving it to Kern, Tyron was going to give his duties at the Wheel a miss and help Palm.

I watched that session, sitting on the bench next to Deinon while Tyron introduced Palm to his tri-glad and began the process of forging them into a fighting unit. Palm's face was a picture of delight and pride, and I couldn't really blame him. The three lacs were impressive. It wasn't just the fact that they were wearing brand-new armour that gleamed in the torchlight. They moved with a speed and fluency that matched anything that I'd seen in the arena. I looked on enviously.

After about an hour Tyron called a halt and put the tri-glad to sleep, telling Palm to join us on the bench. Then he called Deinon over.

'Now let's sort you out, boy,' he told him.

He went across to a bench on the far side of the room and pulled the cover off a lac. He spat onto a socket and eased it into its throat.

'Awake!' he commanded. 'Stand!'

Although Deinon's father wasn't wealthy enough to pay for a new lac, Tyron had provided for him generously. This one looked very good. However, I noticed that Deinon received only about twenty minutes of his time. Even so, Deinon was clearly happy, and by the end of that short session he was beaming all over his face. At one point he turned towards me and gave a thumbs up.

Then it was my turn. Tyron pulled the cover off another lac and gave it the usual first two commands: Awake; Stand.

The lac clambered off the bench and stood to attention before Tyron. 'Selfcheck!' he ordered, then turned to face me.

'Well, boy, this is your lac until I say otherwise. It'll do for now, so you'll be using it for the tournament.'

My eyes took in the scratches and dents to the armour, the deep gash in the helmet just above the eyes. This was the practice lac we'd all used in training. I struggled to hide my disappointment.

I heard a snort of derision behind me and glanced back to

see Palm struggling to contain his laughter. As I stared at him, he got himself under control, but he looked triumphant. The state of my lac proved that he had been right. I turned back to face the creature, and out of the corner of my eye I saw Tyron staring at me.

'Try to look a bit more enthusiastic,' he told me, shaking his head. 'There's an old saying – *Never look a gift horse in the mouth*.'

I nodded.

'Good. Then you'll know what I mean,' Tyron said. 'You're not paying for it, are you? All you have to do is put in a bit of legwork and get yourself ready for the arena.'

'But it's the practice lac,' I exclaimed, unable to hide my disappointment. 'It'll be too slow.'

'Not any longer. To look this gift horse in the mouth properly, you'd need to sift through the patterning. Had you the skill to read Nym and do that, you'd see that it's been changed and readied for combat.'

I nodded, but I must have looked doubtful because Tyron went over and drew a Trig blade from the nearest scabbard. He handed it to me.

'Actions speak louder than words, so I'll demonstrate the difference.'

He lifted the leather ball we'd used in training and smiled, turning to face the lac. 'Report!' he commanded.

'*Ready*,' rasped the lac.

'Combat Stance!' Tyron handed the lac the heavy leather orb.

'When you're ready, boy,' he went on, moving out of the way.

I moved closer to the lac and began the dance. Two steps to the left, two steps to the right.

This time I did a reverse diagonal to the right. I went backwards as fast as I could. Now that I was moving I felt a lot better. I would show Palm just how quick I was. As I danced, I felt my body start to do my thinking for me. When the lac came after me, I went straight at it with the blade, aiming for the throat-socket. I felt confident. I couldn't miss!

The next second I felt a tremendous blow to my head and found myself sitting on the training floor. I tried to speak, but my mind felt numb and no words came out. The Trig blade was on the floor, out of reach.

I heard Palm laughing out loud. When I glanced over, I saw tears of mirth rolling down his cheeks. Even Deinon was smiling.

Tyron hauled me to my feet. 'That was so fast, you never even saw it coming,' he said. 'Maybe that'll make you feel better.'

I felt bad because I'd been dumped on the floor, but at the same time it showed that my lac had the speed to cope with combat in the arena. I reflected that the laughter was deserved, and nodded contritely. 'I'm sorry,' I told Tyron. 'I was being foolish. Thanks for making my lac so fast.'

Palm could laugh for now, but maybe he wouldn't win his bet after all.

To my surprise, Tyron stayed with us for the rest of the morning. He gave us a lesson on patterning in Nym, mainly for my benefit. He said it would be revision for Palm and Deinon and demanded their full concentration.

Deinon seemed fine – he enjoyed patterning – but I could

tell by Palm's face that he wasn't happy. It wasn't just that he was bored. He clearly felt that he was above all this and was annoyed at having to endure it for my benefit.

By contrast, I was finally starting to understand much of what Tyron was saying. I would never become a good patterner, but I could now grasp the basic concepts. And the more bored Palm looked, the more I enjoyed his annoyance and discomfort.

'Each artificer uses Nym in a slightly different way,' Tyron was saying, 'but some wurdes are common to all. They can be called to bring pre-constructed sequences of patterns into play.

'Call one wurde and you call many. You see, Nym is what's called an "extensible language". Each patterner can enlarge it by creating and adding new wurdes to the dictionary. Wurdes are embedded within a larger wurde. So there are wurdes within wurdes. Call one, and others leap forth to do your bidding.

'And some of these wurdes are tools,' Tyron continued. 'One important one is called Newt. It's a specialized form of the wurde called Salamander and is used to explore the mind of a lac. It probes deep into the dark recesses of its memory, reporting what it finds. The mind of a lac is a tangled labyrinth, capable of ever greater complexity. Know its twists and turns, and you can add more of your own.'

Late the following afternoon, for the first time, I was allowed an hour alone on the training floor.

Privacy was essential: I was there to begin the slow process of using Ulum to develop an understanding with my lac. I would tell my lac what to do by drumming on the floor with my feet. I still didn't have any Trig boots, so for the time being, slaps with the soles of my feet would have to suffice.

Tyron had told me to keep it simple. I would work at this for years; sophistication would come with time.

My lac was dormant, lying on its back on a bench at the edge of the training floor. I walked up to it and gave the first command:

'Awake!'

It eyes flickered open and regarded me without blinking, and I felt a moment of trepidation. Lacs still made me feel nervous.

'Selfcheck!' I ordered.

Less than a second later the creature responded with its harsh, guttural voice.

'*Ready.*'

The lac had been prepared by Tyron, so its armour, including the throat-socket, was already in place. I just had to get it to its feet and begin.

'Stand!'

It obeyed immediately, clambering off the bench to stand before me, its red eyes glaring down at me. It seemed to be staring at me strangely, and that worried me. Lacs weren't supposed to be aware, but this one certainly seemed so. Was it thinking about me? I wondered. If so, what was going on in its head?

Now I had to tell it that we were going to develop and practise the sound-code, building a communication between us that would not be understood by anyone else. This wasn't strictly the case, because the Ulum put together by a novice was so simple that most spectators could work it out within minutes. It would take years to ensure that my instructions were truly hidden from observers.

'Enter Ulum Mode!' I commanded.

'*Mode Entered.*'

I had been told to begin with the basic manoeuvre, which was called 'Basic1'. It consisted of two steps to the left, two steps to the right, followed by a diagonal right reverse.

'Basic1 = First Signal,' I instructed.

I had already decided what my signal for that would be, so I gave two hard slaps of the boards with my bare left foot, followed by a short sharp slap with my right.

'*Understood,*' said the lac.

'Leave Mode!' I told it. Hopefully it would now respond under combat conditions.

'Combat Stance!'

The lac stepped forward onto the training floor as if facing an opponent, and I took up position to its rear. Then I slapped the boards with my feet to signal that basic manoeuvre.

My lac responded, taking the steps I had indicated. Unfortunately I was too busy concentrating on drumming with my feet, and it moved off too quickly for me to keep up. For a second I was exposed: in the arena I would have been cut to pieces. You needed to keep very close to your lac.

So I repeated the instruction and tried again. After five goes I was able to signal and then just about keep up. At this point I decided to add another signal. Two hard strikes with my right foot and a tap with my left meant the opposite, and I would finish with a diagonal left reversal.

I practised for about half an hour, dancing behind my lac until I was sweating with exertion. It was hard, slow, frustrating work, but I'd started to make a little progress. It was then that I heard three loud raps on the door. I was surprised: private time on the training floor was strictly limited and wasn't usually interrupted.

When I opened the door, I saw Kwin standing there. I was glad to see her. I smiled to myself. Three raps should have told me who it was.

'Want any help?' she asked.

'With Ulum?' I asked. 'I thought it was supposed to be private . . .'

'It is,' she answered with a warm smile, 'but it doesn't matter that much in the early stages of training. You're just trying to get some coordination with your lac – and let's face it, you're not going to face me in the arena. I could help, but it's up to you . . .'

I returned her smile. 'Come in, then,' I said. 'I need all the help I can get.'

The Commonality

Beware that which lies beneath,
For you shall reap what you sow.

Amabramdata: the Genthai Book of Prophecy

After five weeks I was really starting to get into a routine and enjoy my training.

By now Palm and I had settled into an uneasy state of silent hostility. We never spoke unless our training required it. But Deinon and I were getting on really well; I looked forward to our Saturday excursions in the city. Our friendship annoyed Palm and he seldom spoke to Deinon now.

During the week, the training was exhausting – I usually fell asleep as soon as my head touched the pillow.

However, on the Tuesday night of the sixth week I didn't even get the chance to undress before I heard three loud raps on the wall.

I hesitated. Last time I got kicked out for responding to that knock – though it would be good to chat to Kwin. She'd been helping with the sound-code training of my lac twice a week. I really liked being with her, but I didn't want to join her on another of her after-dark trips into the city. Still, I couldn't bring myself to ignore her knock. I decided to go and explain how I felt.

Palm scowled at me, but Deinon smiled. I nodded at him, opened the door to Kwin's room and stepped inside, closing it behind me. She was wearing her boots and her lips were painted red and black, as if for a visit to the Arena 13 gallery.

My heart sank.

'Tonight,' she announced, 'I'm going to show you something that my father never even talks about.'

I didn't like the sound of that. If Tyron never mentioned it, then he must have a good reason. It was something that would probably get me into trouble again.

'Does it mean I'll end up working in the slaughterhouse again?' I asked, giving Kwin a tired smile. I braced myself to tell her that I wouldn't be going. She wouldn't like it, so I intended to break the news gently.

She shook her head. 'If my father knew where you'd been, he wouldn't be happy, but there wouldn't be a serious problem.'

'That's what you told me last time – that he always does what you say. Look where that got me!'

'Look, trust me. This is different and it'll open your eyes. We're going to the Wheel again, but this time we're visiting the Commonality beneath the Wheel where lacs are kept by owners who can't afford to lease private quarters.'

'Sorry, but I daren't risk it, Kwin. Your father's given me another chance and I don't want to let him down.'

'Don't be silly, Leif! You know his rules – no stick-fighting and no alcohol. We won't be breaking them tonight. This is just to show you something that nobody else will. It'll give you another handle on how things work around here. Are you up for it or not?'

I was just about to say no and return to my room when she did something completely unexpected. She seized my hand and squeezed it; then, still holding my hand, she came very close and kissed me on the cheek. Our bodies were almost touching and I began to breathe more quickly.

It wasn't a kiss on the lips, but it was definitely more than just a motherly peck. As her lips brushed my cheek, she gently stroked the palm of my hand with her thumb, and I smelled lavender on her skin.

When she gripped my hand even tighter and tugged me along behind her, I didn't resist.

She walked beside me holding my hand as we made our way across the city, only dropping it when we reached the edge of the cinders outside the Wheel. We entered by the door that led down under the arenas.

This time there were few people about. A lone woman was pacing up and down outside, her arms folded across her body as if to ward off the chill air.

Soon we were descending stone steps, our feet echoing in the gloom. Down and down we went in a tight spiral, into increasing darkness, the wall torches less and less frequent.

'I thought it was dangerous down here . . .' I said. 'I thought you needed to be in a gang . . .'

I suddenly realized that I might have made a big mistake. Kwin's kissing me and holding my hand had snatched away my common sense.

'What's life without a bit of danger?' she called back over her shoulder.

The steps ended and Kwin hurried off along a tunnel. I followed, noticing something strange overhead. Growing on the roof of the tunnel was a cluster of fungi, its globular white fruit suspended from thick stalks.

'Hey, Kwin, what's that?' I asked.

She turned and looked where I was pointing.

'Can you eat it?' I wondered. 'It reminds me of a delicacy that grows on a high cliff just north of Mypocine – though that has red fruit rather than white. Climbers risk their lives to harvest it, but they make a lot of money selling it at the market.'

'Eat that and you'd be stone dead within a minute,' Kwin retorted. 'It's called "skeip" and it's extremely poisonous. At one time you only found it on the very lowest levels of the Commonality, but now it's spreading upwards. Some say that it feeds upon the blood that drips into these caverns from Arena 13. Superstitious nonsense, of course, but down here superstition breeds faster than scabby grey rats. One thing I know, though: you should never stand directly underneath it. When it's ripe, it sometimes drips poison.'

With a grim smile Kwin turned and continued until at last we reached a small open space; ahead of us I saw the entrances to three tunnels.

'Doesn't really matter which one we take,' said Kwin. 'These three all lead to the same place. The Commonality is a maze of caverns and tunnels that extends far beyond the perimeter of the Wheel, down into the very rock. When you're down here, always keep to the tunnels that are lit by torches. That means they're serviced regularly; if you get lost, it won't take long for someone to find you. Anyway, we'll take this one. It's a longer route, but I want to show you where the lacs are stored.'

Although the tunnel was lit, there were big gaps between the torches and parts of it were very gloomy. I reflected that being lost down here in the dark would indeed be terrifying.

Kwin was walking fast, drawing further and further ahead of me. What was the rush? I wondered. We reached a very dark section of tunnel, and suddenly I couldn't see her at all.

I halted. I could hear water dripping somewhere close, but there was no sound of footsteps ahead. Had she turned off down a side-tunnel while I'd simply gone straight on? For a moment I felt a twinge of panic and took a deep breath to calm myself.

Then there was a tap on my shoulder and my heart leaped up into my mouth. I turned round, sensing someone – or some*thing* – standing very close to me. For a moment I was terrified; then I smelled that lavender perfume and heard Kwin giggle.

I was angry. That wasn't my idea of a joke.

'Scared, were you?' she said softly. 'Maybe I should hold your hand again to make sure you don't get lost!'

She led me off into the dark, and as we walked along holding hands again, all the anger drained out of me.

Soon the tunnel began to narrow. Kwin squeezed my hand and smiled. 'We're coming to one of the dormitories now,' she said.

We passed through a small curved stone archway and I looked up, my mind reeling. For on each side I saw a matrix of stone cots lined with thin layers of straw – row after row, piled one above the other, extending from the floor to the high vaulted ceiling – hundreds of lacs could be accommodated here.

I'd spent time working with my lac and had overcome most of the fear and unease I'd experienced when I'd first seen the small lac dormitory in the Wheel. But now I was stunned by what I faced.

Most of the shelves were occupied, and I had glimpses of shaven heads, the yellowed soles of calloused feet, bellies and chests glistening with sweat, and slack mouths open to the stale air that stank of urine and wet dog. Not to mention the throat-slits, with their pink lips and disturbing hint of a deeper purple within.

There were so many of them – too many – and they were too close. The lacs were dormant now, placed in a deep trance for storage.

'It's not a pretty sight, is it?' Kwin said.

'There's something unsettling about seeing so many together like that,' I replied.

She nodded. 'It's something most of the spectators never get to see. It's a bit like the slaughterhouse: people tuck into a steak and enjoy it, but they don't want to think about the living animal that's slain and dismembered so that they can fill their bellies. This is what the lacs endure. They fight and train, but most of the time they sleep.'

I didn't feel comfortable until we were safely past the dormitory and heading down the tunnel again.

'How many dormitories are there?' I asked.

'Three more,' Kwin answered. 'The more successful artificers, like my father, have their own facilities on the level immediately below the arenas, but the majority keep their lacs down here. Most of these fight in Arenas 1 to 12. Then, of course, there are the feral lacs—'

'Feral?'

'I mean wild lacs – those without owners.'

'You're joking!'

The lacs used in Arena 13 were bought from the Trader for that purpose. Wild lacs beyond human control . . . that was something I'd never even imagined.

'You'll see. It's not much further.'

Kwin was making me nervous. Were there really feral lacs ahead or was it another of her jokes?

To my relief, we merely came to an iron grille across the entrance to a dark side-tunnel that sloped steeply downwards.

'Look at that,' Kwin said, pointing to a section of the grille. It had recently been repaired: the rest was rusty and much older.

'That tunnel has been sealed off – and for a very good reason. There are lacs down there – nobody knows how many – out of control and surviving in any way they can; probably by eating rats and each other. The dangerous sections are sealed off like this. The problem is, even Cyro doesn't know the location of all the tunnels. As I said, always keep to the ones that are well-lit.'

'Who's Cyro?' I asked.

'He's the official responsible for the Commonality, this whole underground zone. There are kitchens down here, training areas and even illegal combat zones. Cyro rules it all. I'll point him out to you in a few moments.'

She turned and led the way down another tunnel, and soon we emerged onto a ledge; below our feet was a big drop. We were looking down into a natural amphitheatre ringed with torches. So far we hadn't seen a soul, so I was astonished by the number of people gathered there. Several hundred were seated around an arena and there was a low buzz of conversation; it sounded like a drowsy hive of bees on a hot summer afternoon. The air was hot and humid, and very still; it smelled of stale sweat.

Towards the back, the seats were elevated; it was clear that the highest tier would offer the best view. The light wasn't good – this arena lacked the huge candelabrum of Arena 13, relying on perimeter torches, with the result that many of the seats were in shadow.

The arena itself was lit only by pairs of crossed torches, positioned high on the pillars at each corner. The edges were marked merely by a slight depression in the floor. Rather than bouncing off the walls, as in Arena 13 combat, it seemed to me that the combatants would keep stepping out.

'Look at the arena floor,' Kwin said, as if she knew what I was thinking. 'Look at the sand.'

The combat area was spread with a thick covering of sand, while there were further piles beside each pillar.

'The sand's there to soak up the blood,' said Kwin. 'Lacs fight each other down here; they wear no armour – they merely have the throat-socket. In theory victory is achieved by endoff in the manner of Arena 13 fighting, but usually the loser dies. It's a bloody business all right.'

'What prevents them from stepping out of the arena?' I asked.

'Just wait and see. It'll shock you.'

Suddenly the murmur of conversation rose in pitch and

echoed off the roof and walls of the cavern. A man stepped into the arena and raised his arms for silence. He was large, and his belly hung down over his broad leather belt.

'That's Cyro,' Kwin whispered. 'Come on – let's stay and watch the first contest. This whole business sickens me, but I think you should see it – then you'll realize how disgusting some things in this city are. That's one good thing I can say for my father. Despite his money-grubbing, he has nothing to do with what goes on down here.'

'If it's illegal, then why doesn't someone put a stop to it?' I asked.

'Because it's all about money,' Kwin said, her mouth turning down in distaste. 'Lacs die here every night, but nobody does anything about it because it's lucrative for everyone involved, the gambling houses in particular; Cyro also makes a profit that's even fatter than his belly. Only the lacs suffer, and down here, who cares about their needs?'

I stared at her in astonishment. This practice had clearly affected her deeply.

'But I thought they weren't conscious like us,' I said.

'That's what everyone says, but I don't believe it for a moment, do you?' Kwin asked.

I remembered the way my lac had looked at me – almost as if it was judging me.

'They might not be aware as we are,' Kwin continued, 'but surely everything that moves and breathes has some consciousness? And don't try to tell me that they can't feel pain. In Arena 13 they're protected by their armour, but down here they suffer serious injury.'

Cyro stepped out of the arena, and moments later, two

lacs stepped in to take up position facing each other, each wielding two long blades. I could see the metal bands circling their necks, holding the throat-socket in position. But apart from their loincloths – one wore blue and the other green – they were naked. They didn't even wear boots. I was seeing lac bodies standing upright and moving for the first time.

Their heads were completely hairless; indeed, they seemed to have no hair anywhere. Their skin had been oiled; it gleamed in the torchlight, and their backs, shoulders and arms were heavily muscled. The arms looked even longer without armour, but the legs were a surprise. They seemed almost too thin to support their bulky bodies. Then I realized that they were designed for speed.

Suddenly there was a swishing, rasping sound, and a circle of long blades, each over two feet high, their sharp edges facing inwards, sprang up out of the floor to mark the boundary of the arena.

Kwin was right. I *was* shocked. I realized what that would mean for bare flesh.

This signalled the beginning of the contest, and the two lacs started to circle each other warily.

All at once they exploded into action, whirling and slashing with their blades. I was astonished by their speed. This was much faster than anything I'd seen in Arena 13. Perhaps the rules of the Trig and their task of defending human combatants there slowed them down.

I almost missed the blade that sliced into the upper arm of the lac wearing the blue loincloth; blood sprayed upwards, drawing excited cheers and shouts from the audience.

The next second the cut lac struck back, ripping open the chest of its green-clad opponent, which staggered and almost fell.

They backed away and circled each other again, their blood dripping onto the sand.

Again they came together hard in a whirl of stabbing and slashing. Blades found their targets again and again. Blood splattered and fell, glittering like red rain in the torchlight.

It was terrible to watch. They were cutting each other to pieces. I just wanted it to be over.

But the ending was even worse.

The lac in blue was pushed back towards the edge of the arena. There was no wall to stop it, and it wasn't near any of the four pillars. It was forced to step backwards into the blades. It twisted against them, its legs cut to ribbons, then fell onto the blades as the other lac slashed at it again and again.

The spectators were on their feet now, shouting and stamping in appreciation of the carnage. Their voices rose in a great roar that resounded through the cavern. But above that could be heard a terrible sound – the shrill, agonized shrieks of the lac as it died on the blades.

Kwin turned away, bent over, and I heard her retching. I had been nauseated by the spectacle too, and the moment I smelled her vomit I was sick myself, my stomach churning in rapid, painful spasms.

When I'd finished, we looked at each without speaking, then withdrew back into the tunnel. Kwin was walking even faster than before.

'That has to be stopped!' I told her angrily, but she didn't comment. 'Where are we going now?' I asked.

'To the stick-fighting,' she replied. 'Oh, don't worry. My father bans you from taking part, not from watching.'

Ten minutes later we were descending into a small cave where a contest was already underway. There were few spectators, probably no more than fifty or so, which was fortunate because the cave was quite small, with a low ceiling. It was hot and claustrophobic.

I could see only one blue-sashed gambling agent there; he was leaning against the wall with a bored expression on his face. The rules seemed to be the same as they had been back home in Mypocine. There was no clearly defined arena, and the fighting raged backwards and forwards, using the full limits of the available space, pushing into the crowd, which expanded and contracted accordingly.

But I saw that they were fighting one against one, something we'd rarely done. In Mypocine it was usually one against three.

We stood a little way back and I studied the fighters. It soon became obvious that there could only be one winner. Maybe that's why the tout looked so bored. One fighter was clearly playing with his opponent, using the contest to display his skills. He was tall and muscular, with dark hair, and I felt sure I'd seen him somewhere before.

'Who's that?' I asked.

'That's Jon,' Kwin replied. 'He's an Arena 13 combatant. He fights from the min in Wode's stable. He's in his third year; doing quite well – though he'll never be as good as

Kern. But this is what he's really good at. Stick-fighting. He's the best stick-fighter in the city.'

Kwin's final sentence was a jolt, and I felt something stir within me. It was like a challenge. How good was he really? I wondered. Maybe I was better. But I certainly couldn't even dream of fighting him.

'He's allowed to do both?'

'Of course he is. Wode doesn't mind. That's just my father's rule. A lot of the younger combatants come down here to fight. Stick-fighting is fine. The Wheel Directorate doesn't interfere. It's better than fighting with knives. That's what they used to do before they introduced the ban. Many young lads were killed every year at this very spot.'

The contest ended suddenly, when Jon stepped through his opponent's guard and backhanded him across the left temple. There was little force in the blow, showing greater restraint than I'd ever seen in Mypocine. The stick didn't even draw blood.

Jon bowed to his opponent and it was over. The spectators surged towards him and clapped him on the back. He was clearly very popular, but while he was being congratulated, his eyes were searching the crowd, as if looking for somebody. The next moment he smiled and started to move directly towards us.

His grin seemed to be aimed at me, and I was puzzled, but soon I realized that he was looking at Kwin. And then I recognized him. I had seen the man twice before, the second time when Deinon had pointed him out at the plaza café.

It was Kwin's boyfriend.

They hugged each other, and when Jon stepped back a

little, his right arm still draped across Kwin's shoulders, I noticed how her body leaned in towards him, their eyes locked together as if there was nobody else around. I felt a sudden stab of jealousy.

Why had she held my hand? I asked myself. Was she playing with me? Was she just a tease? Or maybe it was her way of showing friendship. After all, the kiss she'd given me had been on the cheek – not on the lips.

'Jon, this is Leif,' Kwin said at last. 'He's my father's novice.'

It was true. As the latest recruit to Tyron's stable I was officially the 'novice', but I didn't like the word.

'Any friend of Kwin's is a friend of mine,' Jon said in his deep voice. I remembered it from my first visit to the Wheel. Then, he'd looked sad and hurt; now he was beaming, as if everything was right with the world and he was the happiest person in it.

I nodded and tried to smile, but I found it difficult.

'It's a pity you're working for Kwin's father,' Jon said. 'She's been telling me a lot about you. She thinks you could give me a real fight.'

'I agree,' I told him, 'but he's already kicked me out once so I daren't risk it.'

'I know all about that too,' he said with a grin. 'Anyway, Leif, would you excuse us for a moment? I need a few words in private with Kwin. We won't be long.'

I felt hurt but knew I was being foolish: I'd built up that kiss into something it wasn't. I was about to walk away, but Jon kept his arm around Kwin's shoulders and guided her past the crowd, down a side-tunnel and out of sight.

As I waited for them to return, I watched another two contests, but I wasn't concentrating. I didn't like Kwin being with Jon. It was nothing personal: I had nothing against him. I just didn't like the idea of Kwin being with anyone.

Kwin came back alone; she didn't look happy.

'Come on, let's go,' she snapped, and led the way back up to the surface by a quicker route.

Soon we were weaving our way through the dark streets of the city, Kwin striding along at a furious pace.

'What's wrong?' I asked.

'Nothing! Don't ask. It's private!' she said shortly.

I was annoyed by her tone. It was obvious that she'd quarrelled with Jon.

'Look, I don't want to intrude into your private business, but don't take your problems out on me!' I retorted angrily.

She didn't reply, and when we reached her bedroom, we didn't even say goodnight.

Then I was back in my own room, finding it impossible to get to sleep.

The Tassels

The tassels are like the fringed knots on the hem of
    Hob's cloak.
Each one is dipped in poison.
We will feed them to their master.

Amabramdata: the Genthai Book of Prophecy

I knocked on the door of Tyron's office in the administration building – the room where we'd first met. I'd asked for an appointment and he was expecting me. My month's trial had ended a couple of weeks previously, and he hadn't yet told me whether I'd passed or not.

Was he going to keep me on as his trainee?

He nodded towards the leather seat, and I sat down facing him across the big desk. My mouth was dry. I'd done my best – but would it be good enough? I wondered.

'You asked to see me, so what can I do for you?' Tyron said with a smile.

'I'm here for two things,' I told him: 'firstly, to ask you if I've passed my probationary period, and secondly to give you the answer to the question I posed on my first day of training. I asked you why we didn't fight in Arena 13 just man against man. I asked you why we needed the lacs. You told me to try and work it out for myself . . .'

'So go ahead, Leif. Tell me the answer you've arrived at.'

'I've arrived at no one clear answer. I've thought of several reasons, but most of them are just speculation,' I told him.

'Then speculate, Leif. Let me hear your thoughts.'

I had thought long and hard about what I was going to tell him. So I took a deep breath and began.

'I think the way we fight is mostly to do with tradition and the generation of wealth. If people do things one way long enough and it works, they just carry on. Arena 13 combat is an industry. It provides work for artificers, combatants and those who service them. The gambling houses create more jobs and wealth. But I think that Trigladius combat – three swords – goes back much further: to things that happened before the defeat of man and the building of the Barrier. Back then, something happened – maybe some form of combat or entertainment – and that's what Arena 13 commemorates. But what we do now may be only a poor shadow of what went on then.'

I looked at Tyron and saw that his face was impassive.

'And there may also be evidence in Genthai lore which my father told me about. When I get the chance, I plan to go and visit them, and maybe I can find out some more about their rituals.'

Tyron shrugged. 'You've clearly thought about your answer, Leif,' he said with a smile. 'It's as good as what most people can come up with. I think about it a lot myself. One day I hope to find out more, so I look forward to hearing what you discover from the Genthai.'

He paused and smiled at me. 'Apart from the stick-fighting,

you've got off to a very good start. You've passed your month's trial. Well done!'

Tyron reached down, picked up a parcel from behind his desk and tossed it over. 'Open it,' he commanded.

It was a pair of Trig boots. They were of excellent quality and gave off the pleasing smell of new leather. Now I had boots of my own – there'd be no more training in bare feet. It would improve my performance, and was another step towards achieving my ambition to fight in Arena 13.

'They're the best boots you can buy,' he said, 'but they'll take a bit of wearing in. Expect a few blisters at first. You've a lot of hard work ahead of you, but I know you won't disappoint me.'

It was a Saturday afternoon and I was sitting with Deinon at a table outside our usual café on the plaza. It had been a week of sudden showers and the flags were damp. Clouds were piled ominously on the horizon and a strong wind made the trees writhe. There were fewer people about than usual.

We were sipping juice and chatting. It was my turn to pay: I had money in my pocket and I was starting to save up. It was then that I saw Kwin coming towards us across the plaza with her boyfriend, Jon.

Ever since our visit to the Commonality, she had avoided my eyes at the breakfast table, and even when we'd passed each other in the house. I couldn't understand why she was behaving like this. After all, I'd done nothing wrong. But pride wouldn't allow me to make the first move. I felt wronged. I thought she should apologize, even though I knew she wouldn't.

They passed quite close to our table, and I felt certain that she must have seen us, but she didn't even glance in our direction. However, Jon smiled and nodded, and I gave him a wave. They sat down together a few tables away.

'Have you and Kwin had some sort of argument?' Deinon asked. 'I hope you don't mind me asking, but I couldn't help noticing that she keeps ignoring you. I thought you were good friends.'

I shrugged. 'She had an argument with her boyfriend, I think, and then she started behaving oddly with me. She snapped at me and I told her off. She didn't like it and hasn't spoken to me since. She'd been helping me with my sound-code on the practice floor, but that's stopped too.'

'Girls can be strange sometimes. Who can understand them?' Deinon shook his head.

'Well, I certainly don't.'

'Maybe you should be the one to break the ice,' he suggested.

'How?' I wondered.

'Just say you're sorry.'

'But I don't think I've done anything wrong.'

'Sorry is just a word. You can say it. Then everything will be OK.'

'You make it sound easy, Deinon.'

'It is. She probably wants to say sorry too, but her pride won't let her. You can be bigger than that. There are a couple of labourers on my father's farm who haven't spoken for over thirty years, yet people say they were once good friends. That's how long their argument has lasted. I bet they can't even remember what they rowed about. If one of them had said sorry, they'd still be friends today.'

On our way home we passed the shop that sold Trig paraphernalia, and I smiled as I noticed that the red boots were still displayed in the window.

I never got a chance to take the initiative and say I was sorry. The long silence between us ended that very night with three loud knocks on the wall; knocks which, unusually, came very late at night, waking me from a deep sleep.

I ignored Kwin's summons. I knew I wasn't being invited into her room for an apology. She always wanted something. The first time she'd wanted to find out what the new trainee was like. The second time she'd wanted to fight and beat me. The third time – what was that for? Did she simply want an excuse to go to the stick-fighting and see Jon?

The three raps were repeated, but I didn't move. I heard a hiss from Palm, no doubt angered both by the disturbance and by the fact that Kwin was summoning me.

She knocked again. Three really loud knocks on the wall.

'Remember what we talked about this afternoon?' Deinon called out of the darkness. 'This is your chance, Leif.'

So I climbed out of bed and angrily pulled on my shirt, trousers, socks and boots. My mood had changed since talking to Deinon. I wasn't going to be the one to say sorry. I would go and see what Kwin wanted one last time, then tell her never to knock for me again. I would be cold. I would be like ice.

However, once I saw her, my resolve began to melt. Her eyes were swollen and red from crying. She was wearing trousers and Trig boots, her lips painted in her usual fashion, but she was also wrapped in a blanket and I noticed that she was trembling from head to toe.

What was this about? Part of me thought it might be some sort of trick – a ruse to get me to do what she wanted. But there were tears trickling from her eyes now. This was real.

'Leif, you've got to help me,' she said. 'You're the only one who can.'

'What's wrong?' I asked, dreading the answer. I knew it had to be something really bad.

'It's Jon,' she said. 'The tassels have him. Soon it'll be too late. Before dawn they'll take him to Hob.'

I tried to make sense of what she was saying. How could that be possible?

'I don't understand,' I told her. 'How's Jon got involved with the tassels in the first place? Did they come into the city?'

I remembered how they'd loped down the grassy slope to snatch the body of the dead girl. Had they gone into the Commonality after dark? But why had Jon been taken?

'He went to them,' Kwin explained. 'It was a challenge with a big bet involved – big, big money. Had he won, Jon would have been set up for life, able to buy any lac he wanted. But he lost to the tassel champion. It should still have been all right – there were other backers from the city in on the bet. But now they've refused to pay up. It means that Jon's life is forfeit. The tassels will give him to Hob.'

I couldn't see what I was supposed to do. It seemed like something that should be reported to the Wheel Directorate or someone else in authority. The tassels were no better than outlaws. This was even worse than what had happened at the lake. How could they be allowed to get away with it?

'Have you told your father?' I asked Kwin.

She shook her head and the tears streamed down her face.

'Tell him,' I said. 'Surely he'll be able to do something . . .'

'He can't do anything. Nobody can. The tassels are Hob's servants and nobody dares interfere in Hob's business. If I tell him, he'll stop us trying to help. There's only one way we can help Jon.'

'How can I help? The only money I have is what your father gave me.'

'Someone has to fight the tassel champion again. It's like stick-fighting in some ways, but it's blade against blade. That's why you're the only one who can help me. You haven't taken the oath yet and you're fast enough to win.'

'You want *me* to fight?' I asked, finding it hard to believe what I was hearing.

Kwin nodded.

'What if I lose?'

'Don't worry, I've already agreed the terms, but it's got to happen tonight. If you win, Jon goes free. If you lose, I'll be forfeit, not you.'

I couldn't believe what I was hearing. 'That's stupid. If anything happened to you, I wouldn't just be kicked out – your father would kill me.'

'It's happened already, Leif. I've made the deal. If I don't go back with you now, I'll die anyway . . .'

What did she mean? What was I being dragged into?

I stood there, trying to understand what had happened,

while Kwin eased the blanket off her shoulders and dropped it on the bed. She was wearing a short sleeveless jerkin, and I saw a long fresh cut on her left shoulder. Although it wasn't deep, it looked swollen and angry, and yellow-green at the edges.

'The tassel champion uses poisoned blades; they're dipped in skeip berries. There's an antidote, but I'll only be given it if I return immediately. Without it, I'll be dead before morning.'

My throat constricted with emotion. I couldn't bear to think of anything happening to Kwin. Seeing her hurt like that affected me more than I could have believed possible. My body began to tremble and I couldn't trust myself to speak.

But then the feeling passed, to be replaced by a wave of cold fury that swept down me from head to toe. Nobody would hurt Kwin while I was around. I couldn't walk away from this, no matter what it cost me.

'Of course, I've had to sweeten the wager with money,' Kwin continued.

A small canvas bag was attached to her belt. It had been hidden by the blanket. She patted it with her right hand.

'It's gold. It belongs to my father. If we get it back before dawn, he'll never know it was missing. So, will you help?'

My mind twisted hither and thither, trying to find a solution. Of course I would fight to protect Kwin, but was there another way?

'Couldn't you just get your father to pay off the first wager? Surely he'd do that rather than let you put yourself in danger . . .'

'My father's rich, but even he doesn't have that kind of money. Those who defaulted are big players – bankers from the gambling houses who were supposed to share the bulk of the cost if Jon lost. But now they won't pay up. It's part of the struggle between Hob and some of the money men in this city. They aren't all in Hob's pocket, and they're not prepared to pay the price of losing this time. What Jon stood to gain is nothing set against what they'd have won.'

I began to pace back and forth beside the bed, trying to think.

'You can win, Leif. Trust me. You're faster than the tassel champion. I know you can do it,' Kwin told me.

'What about Jon? He lost. So could I.'

'He was not at his best,' she said. 'It was the oath, you see. He'd sworn not to use blades outside the arena. Breaking it made him feel guilty. He was defeated before he even started. Inside his head he'd already lost the fight. We'd been arguing about it for days.'

'Arguing? You mean *you* wanted him to fight and he didn't?'

Kwin shook her head. 'No! Of course not – just the reverse. I never wanted him to get involved at all. Then, when I found out how bad he felt about breaking his oath, I did my best to persuade him to withdraw from the contest. But he wouldn't listen. He never listens to a word I say. That's why we're always arguing. But he doesn't deserve to die for his mistake. Nobody deserves to be given to Hob. So please, Leif. Please help him.'

I frowned, but I was determined now. 'I'll fight,' I told her.

It was either that or watch her die.

*

We crossed the city, heading north; soon we'd left the last of its dwellings behind and were climbing a muddy track towards the camp of the tassels.

There was a crescent moon shining through a break in the cloud, and by its faint silver light I could just see the spires of Hob's citadel rising above the brow of the hill. I glanced back down at the rooftops of Gindeen, homes filled with ordinary families.

A sad, dilapidated dwelling loomed up ahead of us. Its windows were broken and the front door hung ajar at a crazy angle. A hooded figure came out into the moonlight and beckoned to us, and we left the track. The rough grass was uneven, and I kept stumbling over large tussocks. Once I stubbed my toe on a rock, and when I grunted with pain, laughter cackled somewhere close behind.

So there were two of them, I realized, one in front and one behind. Two? I was deceiving myself. This was where they lived. This place was crawling with them. Then I saw the hooded tassels waiting silently, gathered in the darkness on the bare, bleak hillside.

There must have been two or three hundred of them. The arena was a patch of open ground with a slight slope, but it was dry, and covered with fine cinders that crunched underfoot.

I was just wondering whether I'd be expected to fight in darkness when a torch suddenly flared to my left. Within moments a dozen torches were alight, each held by a tassel.

Faces watched me; some were hooded, while I could see

others in all their hideousness, the features barely human and twisted with cruelty.

Not all the tassels stood upright. Some seemed to shrink away from the torches. These were small and oddly shaped, and crouched on all fours.

The creatures parted at our approach, but then closed ranks behind us, sealing us within a circle.

There was a saying that was used by city-dwellers: *He who sups with a tassel must use a long spoon.*

Well, it would be impossible to follow the advice this time.

A tall cowled figure waited for us at the centre. His face was in darkness, and when he spoke, his voice was filled with a mixture of authority and contempt.

'Is this the one?' he asked Kwin, inclining his face towards me.

Kwin nodded. 'He was a stick-fighter in Mypocine, but he has no blades of his own.'

'Have you brought the money?'

Kwin handed him the canvas bag. He opened it and poured the coins into his palm before counting them carefully.

Then he nodded, and a tassel came forward carrying a small jar. Kwin went towards him and he dipped his fingers into its contents and began to rub a dark ointment into the cut on her shoulder – the antidote to the skeip poison. Kwin sucked in her breath sharply and grimaced with pain.

I gripped her hand and she squeezed back. Her eyes were filled with tears.

'I'm OK, Leif. The pain will pass in a moment.'

Then the tall tassel gestured to the two on his left. 'Get them ready,' he commanded.

As he walked away, a tassel came towards me with a short length of rope. To my astonishment, he knelt at my feet and began to tie one end of the rope to my right ankle.

'What's this?' I demanded of Kwin.

'They tie our legs together,' she told me. 'Your right leg to my right leg. The rope's just long enough to let me get behind you. You're my lac. I'm the target. If he cuts me, we've lost. That's how I got the cut on my shoulder.'

Fighting by Instinct

Above all avoid a fall. It brings the risk of injury or
death.

The Manual of Trigladius Combat

'You didn't say anything about this!' I accused Kwin,
staring down at the rope. 'You didn't tell me I'd have to fight
like this!'

I was angry. What else had Kwin failed to tell me? By
now the tassel was attaching the other end of the rope to
her ankle.

'It's my problem. Don't worry, I'll match you step
for step.'

'Will he be defending someone?' I said, nodding towards
the tassel.

Kwin shook her head.

'How do we win?' I asked.

'Make it impossible for him to continue.'

There was a cold flatness to Kwin's voice when she
said that; she was clearly trying not to think about what
might happen. I think she saw the dismay on my face,
because she gripped my left arm tightly and put her lips close
to my ear.

'Give him half a chance and that's what he'll do to you!' she hissed. 'If he stops you, he can cut me. It's as simple as that.'

'Will the blades be poisoned?'

'His will. Yours won't. But the poison's slow-acting – nothing to worry about now. It's just something the tassels use to make sure opponents don't default on a bet. Get cut and, win or lose, as long as you keep to their terms you'll get the antidote.'

A blanket was laid on the ground and unrolled. Upon it lay about a dozen blades. No two were alike. I took my time, weighing each one carefully and testing its grip. They were all too heavy.

'You'd be better off with Jon's blades,' Kwin said, but when she asked for them, the answer was no.

So I made the best of it, choosing the two lightest. The lighter of the two I gripped in my right hand. It would have to do.

My anger at Kwin was suddenly replaced by fear. I was scared. This was nothing like stick-fighting: I'd be hobbled by the rope. We could fall, go down in a tangle, and then we'd be cut.

Once I was armed, the crowd of tassels drew back to mark the edges of the arena, an oval set across the slope. Then our opponent came down to face us. He was very tall and stripped to the waist, his body glistening with grease. It was indeed the same tassel who'd been in command earlier.

The fight began disastrously. He came in fast, and despite Kwin's promise to match me step for step, our legs became entangled in the rope and we went down hard. We scrambled for our lives, rolling over and over across the cinders while the tassel's blades arced downwards savagely. Somehow we survived and got back to our feet.

The tassel's speed unnerved me. All we could do was retreat desperately, while he scuttled across the cinders like an insect. But it was his greased and glistening upper body that posed the greater threat. It bent from the waist as if his bones were soft and pliable. Either that or he was double-jointed, allowing his long arms to strike from unusual angles.

We were gradually being driven back down the hill. I was already puffing hard, the air rasping in my throat, sweat pouring down my face, my palms damp, which made it hard to grip my blades properly.

I made a couple of lunges towards the tassel, but they were slow and cumbersome, and he never hesitated in his remorseless advance. Only his body moved back fractionally, just to take him out of range of my blade tips.

I could hear the tassels jeering and hooting behind us. I knew what would happen if we were forced back amongst them; the same things that happened in Mypocine. Someone would grip your sleeve in the dark. Feet would try to trip you. Or you might even be seized and hurled forward towards the waiting stick of your opponent.

And here it was blades . . .

By now I was terrified. My heart was hammering in my chest. Something inside me was already defeated. I was scared for Kwin and Jon, knowing that their lives would be forfeit. But I was afraid for myself as well. I remembered what Kwin had said:

Make it impossible for him to continue.

That was what the tassel was trying to do to me. Blades could kill. Blades could also disable. Even if I survived, my life might never be the same again.

It was then that it happened.

For some reason I halted, stopping our retreat. I took a deep breath and waited there, my blades extended before me, and the tassel halted too. His eyes were staring hard into mine, but he wasn't moving.

A silence seemed to have fallen over everything. And then I heard Kwin's feet crunching on the cinders behind me.

Two firm crunches with her left foot, followed by a short, quick, lighter tap with her right. She was indicating the basic manoeuvre, using the sound-code we had developed together: two steps to the left, two steps to the right, followed by a diagonal right reversal.

She was so close, I could feel the heat of her breath on the back of my neck. Like a lac, I obeyed, and we danced slowly across the cinders, left then right, executing the patterns of the Trig, signalled by the Ulum we had practised together; it seemed so long ago now.

The tassel didn't like it. I could see the doubt in his eyes. When we began the retreat, he did not follow.

It didn't matter. We attacked anyway, moving forward along the same diagonal, attacking with speed and coordination. And for the first time we moved like one creature, our steps in unison.

The tassel gave ground, and we went after him. And we were very, very fast. We flowed rather than moved, gliding forwards, our feet hardly seeming to touch the cinders.

Now my hands obeyed my brain, striking effortlessly,

with quick arcs that had the tassel bending back from the waist. My third strike almost cut him, and only the speed of his legs saved him. They were still scuttling over the cinders, but now they carried him backwards as we drove him up the slope.

Kwin didn't need to use Ulum again, which was fortunate. The time we had spent rehearsing the sound patterns together had been relatively short and our repertoire was limited. Yet it had served its purpose, shocking me out of my fear, giving me time to think and catch my breath.

Now, my confidence growing, I moved on to the next stage, where I was fighting by instinct and no thought was required. Each movement I made was spontaneous. I was a stick-fighter again, trusting to my body, the speed and skill devolved to my arms and legs while my mind was detached from what was happening, a cool observer calculating strategy, noting the weaknesses of my opponent.

And I wasn't alone. Kwin matched me step for step. Even when we moved she was so close I could still feel her hot breath on my neck. It was almost as if I could hear her heart beating, thudding to the same fast rhythm as my own, as if we shared one system of circulation, her arteries and veins joined to mine.

It was exhilarating, and I actually began to enjoy it. But the end was approaching rapidly.

The first chance I had was a slim one, but Kwin probably didn't even spot it. She didn't notice because she didn't know what I was capable of. When we'd fought, she'd tested me hard, but I knew that I could raise my performance to another level, which I'd reached perhaps only once or twice in combat. And now, under the pressure of fighting the tassel, facing all the dark consequences of defeat, I'd reached that place again.

The second opportunity was obvious, and when I let it go, Kwin reacted immediately.

'Finish him! Finish him now!' she hissed into my ear.

But I couldn't do it. This was nothing like fighting with sticks. To finish it, I had to cut him with my blades. I had to cut him so badly that he couldn't continue. Somehow the tassel must have sensed what was going on inside my head. Or maybe he realized that I'd missed my chance. Whatever it was, he was suddenly fighting with renewed energy and ferocity; once more we began to give ground, forced backwards down the slope.

In the end I did finish it. I won because the result of losing was too terrible to face.

The tassel had committed himself, taken that extra step, his body bending forward from the waist, his blade scything towards my throat.

He was fast, but I was faster, and I stepped inside his guard, thrusting with my right blade, feeling the rope at my ankle grow taut as Kwin hesitated fractionally. She reacted just in time to avoid bringing us down onto the cinders; in time to allow me to follow through.

But I didn't cut the tassel. I turned the heavy handle of the blade towards him and drove it hard into his mouth, breaking his teeth.

I used the blade in my left hand in a similar fashion, like a club, striking his right temple. He was unconscious before he hit the ground.

I thought I'd won, but I was wrong. The tassels waited expectantly. The oval became a circle as they began to close in.

'You still haven't finished it,' Kwin said. 'When he's back on his feet, he'll carry on!'

I knew then what was expected of me. The tassel was on his back, his throat open to my blade. That was one way to finish it. Another option was to cut his hamstrings so that he couldn't walk.

I couldn't do either. I couldn't cut him like that in cold blood.

But I did make a cut.

As if in a nightmare, I made it without thinking. I cut the rope that bound me to Kwin. Immediately she buried her face in her hands and gave a cry of despair.

Only then did I realize the enormity of what I'd done. By cutting the rope that bound us before slaying or maiming my opponent, I'd ended the contest.

But I'd also forfeited it.

I'd lost.

Now the lives of Kwin and Jon belonged to Hob.

Genthai

We are the People of the Wolf.
Our god is called Thangandar
And none shall stand against us.

Amabramdata: the Genthai Book of Prophecy

The tassels formed a tight circle about us. I sensed the weight of them, a living barrier. We had no hope of escape. Within moments, Jon had been pushed into that small, claustrophobic space to join us.

Immediately Kwin hugged him and started to cry. He stroked her back and whispered into her ear. But then one of the tassels gave them a rough push, and we were driven up the hill. They didn't bother to bind us. Every hand held a blade or a spear.

Now they began to extinguish the torches until we were walking in darkness. I suspected that the tassels could see very well in the dark. I couldn't see a thing, but I felt the casual blows from the tassels. Twice my left shoulder was thumped hard. Weapons prodded my back, feet kicked at the backs of my legs. Apart from that the tassels were silent, and that somehow made them all the more menacing.

We were still climbing, and it was clear that we were

being taken to Hob's citadel. I didn't know exactly what would happen to us there, but we would certainly meet our death – or maybe something worse than death. Sometimes defeated combatants had been taken alive. They never came back, so what happened to them?

Or would the djinni take our minds and return our bodies? I remembered the girl I'd seen eating offal in the slaughter-house, reduced to that desperate animal state. Would that be our fate?

For all Kwin's assurances, I knew that because I'd cut the rope I would now suffer the same fate as her and Jon.

Ahead of me, Jon and Kwin had their arms wrapped around each other. After all I'd risked, she still preferred him to me. She'd just used me to try and save him, I thought angrily. They could comfort each other, while I was about to die alone. I felt hurt and abandoned.

I took a deep breath and tried to stop feeling sorry for myself. What did anything matter now? All three of us were done for. I stared down at the ground, my mind numb, not thinking about it any more.

The moon was obscured by dark clouds, and for perhaps ten minutes we climbed through the darkness, until the massive outer walls and twisted spires of Hob's citadel began to rear up before us, blacker than the night sky.

The moon came out briefly, illuminating the walls. They were constructed of enormous blocks of stone, of a type I didn't recognize; stones that sparkled, distorting the moon-light as though through a prism, transmuting it into a new subtle shade of bronze.

Moments later we were plunged into darkness again, but

I'd already glanced about me and noted that the majority of the tassels had dispersed across the hillside, leaving perhaps forty as a guard.

We approached the citadel, until finally I could just make out the massive bronze gates. But then I heard something else; something that made the hairs on the back of my neck stand on end.

Three massive shapes stood between us and the gates. At first I thought they might be emissaries of Hob. I heard the snort of a beast and a metallic jingling sound, and at that moment the crescent moon appeared from behind a cloud to conjure an apparition and light it to gleaming silver before my startled gaze.

Directly ahead I saw three horsemen dressed in chain mail, two great swords attached to the saddle of each. But what horses! Never had I seen such creatures. These were not the bulky, squat beasts used to draw barges or pull wagons. They were sleek thoroughbreds, fine and high-stepping, with arched necks and legs made for speed.

To my astonishment, the riders looked like Genthai. They had dark skin, aquiline noses, high cheekbones and long hair. One had a thick moustache that obscured his mouth. But I'd never seen Genthai quite like this.

Then I noticed something else. Their faces were painted with long thin lines; patterns of curves and whorls that followed the contours of their features.

These were no foresters, nor did they resemble those sad, bedraggled figures that traded and sometimes begged on the outskirts of Mypocine. These were warriors.

The man in the centre of the three drew his sword and

urged his horse forward as our guard readied their weapons. Some of the tassels wielded short blades; others had spears, huge hooked scimitars, or long poles to which cruel double-edged blades had been bound with twine. But when the Genthai charged towards us, the tassels scattered. I was knocked to my knees and I looked up as the hooves thundered by, close to my head.

It was a short and unequal struggle: the six blades flashed and cut until the air was filled with screams. The tassels fled howling and hooting into the night. Some went down the hill; a few managed to crawl into the narrow tunnels on either side of the large bronze gates.

Within seconds, apart from a few scattered bleeding bodies, there wasn't a tassel to be seen. I rose to my feet and went to stand beside Kwin and Jon. The Genthai were riding back up the hillside towards us, the one with the moustache pointing his sword at the bronze gates of the citadel.

They passed quite close by, but never even glanced in our direction. The leader rode up to the great gates and hammered upon them with the hilt of his sword.

Again and again he thundered out his challenge. Then he shouted into the night, his words booming and echoing back from the high walls.

'Come out and fight with Genthai!' he challenged. 'Come out and face men!'

But there was no reply. The stone walls loomed high above our heads, glistening with a bronze fire in the pale moonlight. But no one came to answer. Nothing replied to their summons.

Again their leader hammered on the door, thundering out

a challenge. 'We're here, Hob! Come out and face us! Come out and fight us, if you dare!'

But again there was no reply.

'Hob fears us!' one of them cried out. 'We should break down the door!'

But their leader, the man with the moustache, disagreed, and his voice was filled with authority. 'Not tonight, brother. Be patient. Our time will come soon enough.'

With that, he turned his mount and led them back down the hill, halting directly in front of me.

'You fought well, brother,' he said softly, his teeth just visible below the fringes of his moustache. 'We watched you.'

I didn't reply, but I felt my mouth widen into a smile. His next words drove that smile from my face.

'But a true warrior would have slain that creature. You have much to learn.'

He turned, gesturing for us to follow, and we walked after the three horsemen down the slope towards Gindeen. What they were doing didn't need to be explained. The Genthai were providing an escort, guarding us against any tassels still lurking in the darkness.

None of us spoke. Kwin and Jon had their arms around each other. She was still crying softly.

When we approached the first houses, the three men brought their mounts to a halt, while Kwin and Jon continued ahead, arms still interlocked.

I raised my hand in salute, a gesture of thanks, and began to follow them, but the leader called out to me.

'Wait, brother,' he said.

I turned and took a few steps up the slope to stand before

him. He'd used the word 'brother' for a second time. On the first occasion I'd thought little of it, assuming it was just a common term of address, but the second time the tone of his voice told me that he recognized my Genthai blood.

Then I realized something. Those marks on his face weren't painted on after all. They were tattoos. Those whorls and lines gave him a fierce, dangerous look.

'What do they call you?' he asked.

My reply flew from my lips unbidden. 'I am Leif, son of Mathias.' I'd spoken quickly – it was too late to bite back my words.

I glanced down the hill, worried that Kwin and Jon might have heard, but they were some distance away now and seemed totally absorbed in each other.

'Mathias? Do you mean *the* Mathias who fought Hob in the city arena? The one whose true Genthai name was Lasar?'

I nodded.

'He was a brave man, and skilful,' said the rider, 'but he chose the wrong path. Don't make the same mistake. Come with us now and fight for your people.'

'Fight who?' I asked.

'First we must take back this land from the traitor who calls himself the Protector,' the Genthai warrior replied, 'and cleanse it of abominations such Hob. That done, we will ride forward beyond the Barrier to defeat those who confined us here.'

My jaw dropped open in astonishment. What he said was impossible. Even if the Genthai had sufficient warriors to defeat the Protector, what chance did they have against those who lay in wait beyond the Great Barrier? But he spoke calmly, his words filled with certainty. It was no boast, but a statement of intent. Something he really believed could be accomplished.

'I'm sorry,' I said. 'I still have something to do here in the city. Something I've sworn to accomplish.'

I hoped that he wouldn't question me further. Would he laugh if I told him that I intended to defeat and slay Hob in the arena? I'd already said more than I should.

'These things will happen in your lifetime. Do you wish to be a part of what we do?'

'When my task here is done, I'd be happy to join you.'

'First, do what you must. Then journey south, deep into the forest. My name is Konnit. When challenged, ask for me. Soon I will become the leader of my people. Then the things I have spoken of will come to pass.'

With those words, Konnit wheeled his horse round and led the others back up the hill. I continued down the slope after Kwin and Jon. There was no sign of them, so I made my way to Tyron's house, my head whirling.

I knew that the ruler of the Genthai was female. The tribe was matriarchal – it had always been ruled by women. So how could a man lead them?

Kwin was a dark shadow lurking on the path beside the house. Jon had already gone. She took out her key and opened the back door, trying to make as little noise as possible. I half expected Tyron to be waiting for us inside, but the house was silent and dark.

Once back in her room, Kwin wasted no time in opening the connecting door.

'Get a good night's sleep,' she whispered. 'There'll be big trouble tomorrow. The tassels kept my father's money, so I'll have to tell him what happened. He'd find out soon enough anyway, so it's better coming from me. I'll try to leave you out of it as far as I can. But whatever happens, he won't dismiss you again, I promise you that.'

I nodded and forced a smile onto my face. What was that promise worth? After all, she had been unable to save me from her father's anger last time.

Back in the bedroom, I undressed and climbed into bed. In spite of all Kwin's reassurances, I had no illusions about the next day. I expected to take some of the blame; probably enough to finish me as Tyron's trainee.

I felt bitter and angry. By noon tomorrow I could be on the road south again, my dream over. But at least now I had somewhere to go. I would head for the Genthai lands.

A servant came for me just before dawn. I was ordered to dress quickly and go downstairs. Tyron was waiting for me, his face grim. He gestured towards the back door and I followed him out into the darkness, shivering in the chill air.

Anger flared within me when I remembered what I'd been dragged into the previous night: every muscle in my body felt sore and stiff. The exertions of fighting the tassel had caught up with me. I hadn't been cut, but I shivered at the thought of what might have happened. I could have been maimed or killed.

I expected to find a bundle of my belongings waiting for me in the yard, but Tyron strode off across the city, and I hurried after him. The sky was becoming lighter and it soon became obvious that we were heading for the administration building. One of Tyron's servants was waiting at a side door.

'Well?' Tyron asked impatiently.

'He's agreed, sir. But because of the inconvenience of the early hour, he demands twice the money you offered. He's waiting for you now.'

Tyron nodded curtly and we left the man by the door. Soon we were walking along a corridor that I recognized, the one I had used to reach Tyron's office. At this hour it was deserted.

I wanted to question Tyron and find out how much Kwin had told him, but I sensed his mood and held my tongue. This was a time to keep quiet.

We continued to the very end, where we came to a large door. The plaque fastened to the wall beside it stated that this was the office of the Chief Marshal. Tyron knocked at the door and a voice inside bade us enter.

Pyncheon was standing behind his desk, and to my surprise he was wearing the red sash of the Wheel Directorate, formally dressed as if presiding over Arena 13.

On the desk a large book lay open, and next to it was a sphere of frosted glass with holes in its upper surface. I realized that this was the lottery orb, which was used when a combatant had to be selected to face Hob. My father must have smashed a similar one out of the Chief Marshal's hand when he'd insisted on fighting Hob.

'Name?' Pyncheon asked, staring at me hard.

Before I could speak, Tyron answered for me. 'Leif, son of Tyron.'

The Chief Marshal wrote my name down in the big book,

adding it to the bottom of the List. At first I was puzzled as to why Tyron had given me his name. Then I remembered that he wanted to keep my real name secret so as to improve the odds offered by the gambling houses.

'Put your hand on the orb and take the oath,' Pyncheon commanded. 'Repeat these words after me.'

I obeyed, listening carefully to what he said before repeating his words.

'I, Leif, son of Tyron, do solemnly swear never to wield a blade outside the jurisdiction of the Wheel Directorate.'

'Right, boy, remove your hand from the orb. You are bound now. Break the oath and you'll never fight in Arena 13 again. Do you understand?'

I nodded; then money changed hands, and soon we were walking back across the city, Tyron's servant following at our heels.

'Does this mean you're going to keep me on?' I asked fearfully.

Tyron nodded. He seemed deep in thought.

'You do know what happened last night?' I went on.

He looked sideways at me and cursed under his breath. 'Of course I do! It took me almost an hour to prise the full story out of that stubborn daughter of mine. Why do you think I brought you here at this ungodly hour?' he snapped. 'Why do you think I've just spent more of my money, when last night cost me dearly enough?'

'I'm sorry,' I said.

'It's my foolish daughter who should be sorry. Kwin could have got you all killed – or worse. Anyway, what's done is done. You've taken the oath at the first opportunity, and that's for a reason. Soon the whole city will know what happened last night and you'll get other offers to fight with blades. Offers that would have been difficult to refuse. Now you can say no. You can refuse with honour because you're bound by the oath.

'At least they don't know your real name yet. That's why you took the oath using mine. That brief ceremony back there also doubled as a registration. You're now officially on the Lists of Arena 13 combatants. Lots of artificers have combatants who fight under their name, so it won't be remarked upon. It buys us some time. Time to get back some of the money I've lost.'

There was no sign of Kwin at breakfast and, to my surprise, instead of giving us his routine nod of acknowledgement, Tyron came over to our end of the table.

'This morning the usual training schedule is suspended,' he said. 'Palm and Deinon – you'll spend the day being tutored by Kern to improve your patterning. That's because the training floor will be in use. I'll be working alone with Leif.'

The expression on Palm's face was almost worth everything I'd gone through last night.

Right after breakfast, I went down to the training floor to join Tyron.

'Well, boy, let's get to work on that lac of yours,' he said. 'I don't want you looking too good too soon; usually I like my trainees to lose badly at the beginning. That's the first lesson you have to learn. Know how to lose and the winning becomes much easier.'

He smiled grimly. 'But I know about that bet between you and Palm. I do talk to my younger daughter, you know, and she's worried that you'll start off your career with a massive debt to pay back. Well, in the time available, I can only do so much. If you were to meet Palm in the first round, you'd lose. His tri-glad is just too good. But let's see how lucky you really are. Let's see what the lottery throws up this time.'

Within a few hours Tyron had transformed my partnership with the lac. I would devise a signal for a particular sequence of steps, and Tyron would translate it into Nym, embedding the response within the lac's brain. Then we would practise the Ulum signal and the subsequent coordinated move over and over again. By the end of the second afternoon session I was moving behind it with a new confidence.

Occasionally I noticed the lac staring at me. It was a strange sensation to be watched like that.

'It keeps looking at me,' I told Tyron.

He gave me one of his rare smiles. 'Well, that's good, Leif. It's got more awareness than some of its kind. They vary in that respect. The fact that it's looking at you means it finds you interesting. You've got its attention. It'll fight all the better for it.'

'That's fine. I just hope that it's not looking at me because it's hungry and thinks I might make a tasty meal!'

'I don't think you need to worry on that score,' Tyron answered with a smile. 'There have been a few isolated cases of cannibalism by lacs, but it was down to incompetent patterning. I think I'm good enough at my craft to keep you off the menu!'

*

That night, when I went back up to our room, I got a shock. Carpenters had been at work. The door that led to Kwin's room had been boarded up.

I hadn't seen her all day. She hadn't even been present at the evening meal. No doubt she was still suffering the effects of Tyron's anger and was confined to her room.

Palm nodded towards where Kwin's door had been and shook his head. 'It won't be the same now,' he said.

I stared at him in astonishment. He was actually talking to me.

'Still, I'm only here until the end of the season,' he went on, giving me a sly smile. 'Then I'll move to new quarters. And there's just one thing left for me to do before I leave. Win that tournament!'

The Trainee Tournament

Death changes everything.

Amabramsum: the Genthai Book of Wisdom

Summer in Gindeen was short – barely five months, which was also the length of the Trig season. After this the transient workers would leave the city and journey back to their winter homes in the provinces.

But this final month was the most exciting of all for first-year trainees, for the beginning saw the competition when we would get the chance to fight in Arena 13.

The TT began at noon, when we were herded into the green room under Arena 13 to witness the draw.

I had only visited it once before, and then the large oblong room had been empty. When Tyron had shown it to me, I'd been surprised to see its colour. Combatants took seats against the walls while they waited for their turn to fight. In the centre was a large table covered with a coarse brown cloth. But the floor was fitted with a shabby brown carpet and the walls and ceiling were painted a dull brown.

'Why do they call it the green room?' I'd asked.

'Nobody knows, boy. The reason is lost in the mists of time. But get used to it because that's its name.'

Now the room was full, with every seat taken by the boys who were to fight in the tournament. I was already dressed for combat, wearing a sleeveless leather jerkin, which had been lent to me by Tyron. It was slightly too big, but it conformed to the rules of the Trigladius, and on its back was the wolf logo of Tyron's stable. I felt proud to be wearing it.

My bare arms made me realize that, even though our contests would be fought by beginners, they would still be the real thing. Most of the Arena 13 rules would apply. My arms were bared for the blade.

When Pyncheon lifted the lottery orb from the table, it gleamed brightly, reflecting the candlelight, and you could feel the excitement in the air. The glass orb contained straws inscribed with our names. It was opaque, and those names only became visible when drawn by Pyncheon. Mag straws were coloured red. Min straws were blue.

Pyncheon set it down at the edge of the table and prepared to draw the first red straw. Each time he drew a mag combatant, it was followed by his min opponent.

There was a gasp as he called out the name on the first straw. It was Palm, and because he was the clear favourite to win the tournament, each min combatant in the room was holding his breath, desperately hoping that he wouldn't be drawn next.

When the next name was called, I let out a sigh of relief. I'd avoided him!

Palm, who now had a huge grin on his face, would be fighting Deinon.

I turned to him, grimacing. 'Bad luck!' I whispered.

He just shrugged, not seeming particularly upset at the prospect of fighting in a contest he'd no hope of winning.

It seemed a bit of a coincidence, but I'd been told that it wasn't uncommon for two combatants from the same stable to be drawn against each other. Still, it wouldn't please Tyron. With over thirty trainees in the draw, each artificer hoped that those from his own stable would progress as far as possible. Rivalries began even at this level: afterwards the gambling houses did their sums carefully, ranking the stables for the whole of Gindeen to see.

Of course, there were wheels within wheels; pride could be sacrificed to another end. Tyron had already told me that in one respect it was good for a promising trainee to begin badly. It increased the odds against him and meant that in the future money could be won by those in the know.

I listened to the names being drawn; at last my straw was held up and my name read aloud by Pyncheon while my heart thudded with excitement.

'Leif, son of Tyron!'

My opponent was Marfik, a novice who fought for an artificer called Wode, who had one of the largest stables of combatants in Gindeen. So at least I'd half a chance. To my knowledge, I'd never even seen Marfik before.

I turned to Deinon again. 'Which one is Marfik?' I whispered.

He nodded across the room towards a tall red-haired youth, who had left his chair to lean back against the wall with his eyes closed. He looked utterly relaxed while my stomach was churning with anxiety.

'He's only been in training for a few months,' said Deinon,

keeping his voice low, 'and his father's farm is quite small. Wode will have provided him with a utility tri-glad, nothing special. You'll be in with a chance.'

'Sorry you drew Palm,' I said.

Deinon smiled. 'I'm OK with that, Leif – it takes the pressure off me. I'll do my best, but I've no hope of winning. Nobody can blame me if I lose to Palm.'

'I'm going up to the gallery to watch you fight,' I told him. 'Good luck, Deinon!'

Combatants fought in the order in which they'd been drawn from the lottery orb. This meant that Deinon would fight first. I was due to fight in the eighth contest. I had plenty of time to watch Deinon fight Palm, then return to the green room and compose myself.

The gallery was only half full. The TT was naturally of great interest to the contestants, their trainers and the gambling agents, who were there to assess the capabilities of future combatants in Arena 13. But apart from the aficionados and a few enthusiastic fans, the general public was not attracted by the spectacle of uncertain novices fighting under rules which had been modified to protect them.

The truth was, the spectators liked to see blood and the occasional death – that's why the red tickets were so popular. The rules of the Trainee Tournament made this far less likely.

The first important rule change was that no gong would sound to signal that combatants must fight in front of their lacs. Here each contest would be fought entirely behind the lacs, which was of course much safer.

The second concerned the ritual cut made to the arm of

the defeated combatant. In full Arena 13 combat, lac blades were coated with a substance called *kransin*, which intensified the pain of the cut. I had watched several combatants accept that ritual cut without even flinching and never guessed at the agony they were suffering. According to Tyron, this was why the spectators grew quiet at that moment. They were watching carefully to judge the bravery of the loser. Sometimes a small cry was uttered or the face twisted in pain.

So there would be no kransin coating the blades and no red tickets – which meant that we only had a small audience.

But despite these modifications to the rules, that day there was indeed a death in the arena.

The front row was taken up with artificers and those trainees who weren't fighting in the first few contests. I sat down next to Tyron just in time to see Palm and his tri-glad enter the arena from the mag door. He had a smug smile on his face as he looked up towards the gallery. Suddenly a girl called out his name, and there were a few shrieks of appreciation that made him grin like an idiot.

I realized that with his good looks Palm would attract a lot of fans. He certainly looked the part, and his gleaming lacs were clearly expensive – the best that money could buy, and patterned by Tyron, the best artificer in the city.

Moments later Deinon entered from the min door. He looked nervous: he was frowning and staring down at his boots rather than up at us.

Pyncheon strode between the combatants and their lacs and gave a short speech to mark the start of the contest. I barely listened to what he said. I was watching poor Deinon and feeling sorry for him. Down in the green room he'd put on a brave face, saying that it didn't matter because nobody expected him to win. But I knew that it *did* matter. If only Deinon could pull something special out of the hat and beat him!

The Chief Marshal was coming to the end of his speech. 'What we shall see here, over the next three days, is the future of Arena 13. Some of these combatants will go on to make their names, mastering the skills of the Trigladius to bring fresh honour to this arena. We wish them long and successful careers. Let the tournament begin.'

As soon as he'd left the arena, the shrill sound of his trumpet cut the air, the two doors rumbled shut and the contest was underway. The lacs of Palm and Deinon clashed together, blades flashing while the two boys danced at their backs.

My heart was in my mouth, but Deinon was doing well. Palm's tri-glad was actually in retreat!

But then a blade was buried in the throat-socket of Deinon's lac, and the metallic crash of its fall filled the arena, quickly followed by cheers, applause and shrieks of delight from the girls supporting Palm.

It was endoff. The contest had lasted less than thirty seconds.

'Poor Deinon,' I said sadly, watching him accept the ritual cut to his upper arm. He had a slight smile on his face and didn't flinch.

'He did what he could – there was never the slightest hope of him beating Palm,' Tyron said. 'He has another contest tomorrow, and he'll have a better chance then. But it doesn't really matter whether Deinon is a successful combatant in this arena or not. He's a very clever lad and has the makings of a patterner. He'll begin by patterning lacs for the other arenas, but within five years he'll be working with those that fight in Arena 13 without ever having to step inside it. Mark my words, Leif, one day Deinon will be an artificer with his own stable of fighters. So don't you feel sorry for him. Concentrate on what *you* have to do.'

I nodded and started to rise from my seat, but Tyron shook his head. 'You might as well watch another contest. It'll do you more good than biting your nails down there.'

So I settled back in my seat, pleased that Tyron thought so highly of Deinon. I'd tell him what had been said later. It would cheer him up after that defeat.

'This should be worth watching,' said Tyron. 'The boy behind the tri-glad is called Scripio – he's from the same stable as the one you're listed to fight. Wode tells me that he's the most able trainee that he's ever had. He's fighting Cassio, who's also a promising young combatant from this year's crop. So watch closely – you might learn something.'

The contest was evenly matched and lasted for about fifteen minutes. It wasn't particularly exciting because both combatants were very cautious. No risks were taken and the spectators were mostly silent, occasionally breaking into applause at some display of skill that I couldn't yet appreciate.

Tyron watched the struggle intently, but I had to force myself to concentrate. My stomach kept filling with butter-flies in anticipation of my own first appearance in Arena 13.

With my thoughts elsewhere, I missed what happened at the end. I should have been watching more closely. It seemed to me that the single lac of Cassio, the min combatant, had surged forward in the first real display of aggression. It engaged violently with the tri-glad of Scripio, which fell back hastily. One of these lacs stumbled into Scripio, and both human and lac went down in a tangle of limbs.

I wondered why Cassio wasn't pressing home his advantage. Instead, he stepped back, a look of horror on his face. No blade had found the throat-socket of the fallen lac to call endoff, and it quickly scrambled to its feet.

For a moment the arena was totally silent, but then, from behind and to our left, someone began to cry, wailing in anguish. I stared down into the arena, trying to make sense of what had happened.

The fallen boy did not rise. His eyes were open and staring, his head lying at an impossible angle. His neck was broken.

Poor Scripio was dead.

By the time Palm and Deinon returned to the gallery, the body had been removed from the arena, but they'd already heard the news and sat down with shocked expressions on their faces. The spectators were quiet – apart from a few of the girls, who sobbed or sat with their faces buried in their hands. It had been a terrible accident and it made me realize just how dangerous Arena 13 was. In spite of the change of rules, a boy had died.

Nobody made a move to leave, and I wondered how long we would sit there. I was shocked and needed to get out into the fresh air. I kept seeing Scripio lying on the arena floor with his neck at that terrible angle.

At last the Chief Marshal entered and looked up at the gallery.

'Our condolences to the family and friends of poor Scripio,' he said, his voice quiet but easily heard in the intense silence. 'A boy of great promise has been taken from us. The tournament is suspended for twenty-four hours.'

As he left the arena, people began to rise from their seats. We followed Tyron home in silence.

Because of the threat from Hob's tassels, Scripio's body was burned that very evening, and a service held in one of the few small churches in Gindeen. The family wanted it to be private, so none of the dead boy's friends and colleagues was able to attend.

'These things happen,' Tyron told us back at the house. 'Each time you set foot in Arena 13 you place your life on the line. But we just have to get on with it. There's still time for your usual theory lessons before supper. Keep busy – that's the best way to take your mind off things. The tournament will begin tomorrow afternoon. I suggest you get an early night.'

When I entered Kern's study, to my surprise I saw that he was not alone. His son was sitting on his knee, scribbling energetically on a piece of paper.

'Sorry about this,' he said, patting the boy on the head. 'Teena's feeling a bit off colour so I'm looking after little Robbie.'

I smiled and took my seat. The child looked up at me with wide eyes. He was curly-haired and fair like his mother rather than dark like Kern. He was big for a two-year-old.

'Robbie, say hello to Leif,' Kern told him.

'Hello,' the child said, and then went back to his drawing.

'How are you feeling?' Kern asked.

'It was a shock. I thought the TT was safe.'

'Nothing is safe in that arena,' he told me. 'It must be terrible for the boy's family. It's upset Teena – she's always thinking about our own son, worrying about the future. Sometimes it makes her quite ill. She says Robbie's first word was *Mama*, his second *Dada* and his third *endoff*. She's joking, of course, but she has a point.'

Kern was smiling, but I saw the concern in his eyes. He'd never opened up about his family life before. The death in the arena had clearly affected him deeply.

'The trouble is,' he continued, 'it's in our blood; it's the family business. Tyron fought in the arena, and if he'd had a son, *he* would have fought too. Instead it's me – the son-in-law. It's natural that Robbie should follow in that tradition. For Teena's sake I just hope that he turns out to be a brilliant patterner like his granddad and eventually makes his living that way.'

Little Robbie was still busy drawing, his face screwed up with intense concentration. He paused and started to suck the end of his pencil.

'Well, any questions before we examine a few new wurdes?'

This was the way Kern started off his lessons, so I always had a question ready.

'I know that *gladius* means a sword, but I still don't see why they call the form of fighting in Arena 13 the *Tri*gladius. There aren't three swords. Each lac has two blades, and there are four lacs – that makes eight altogether, plus the weapons of the human fighters.'

'You're not the first newcomer to make such an

observation, Leif. But the name comes from the fact that the min combatant faces three lacs that seek to cut his flesh. *They* represent the three swords.'

'I suppose that makes sense . . .'

'What have you drawn?' asked Kern, turning back to his child. 'Let me see. Shall we show Leif your drawing?'

He picked it up and showed it to me. 'Maybe he'll be an artist,' he said with a smile, kissing the top of the boy's head.

The 'drawing' was just a crisscross scribble of pencil lines.

'Well, maybe not!' Kern said with a grin.

Arena 13

Learn how to lose so that later you may learn how
to win.

Amabramsum: the Genthai Book of Wisdom

The following afternoon I was back in the green room,
nervously awaiting my turn to fight.

For what seemed like an age I sat with the others in
silence. I'd never imagined it would be like this, with combatants sharing the same room before they went up to fight.
And was it as quiet as this for the senior combatants? Or did
they sometimes exchange angry remarks?

I knew that there were some bitter rivalries in the Trig –
though of course, the scabbards at the belt of each contestant
were empty. Nobody was allowed to carry a blade into the
changing rooms or the green room.

I wondered how yesterday's terrible accident had affected
the contestants' mood. The boy's death had dampened my
excitement at finally getting to fight in Arena 13. I'd already
witnessed a death in the arena – that grudge match I'd seen
on my first visit – but the accidental death of Scripio had
made me realize just how dangerous the Trig could be.

At last it was my turn. I followed a grim-faced marshal

along a passage until we came to the min door. I was surprised to see Tyron waiting there, but grateful that he'd taken the trouble to come down and wish me luck. He held out the blades he'd lent me and I sheathed them quickly, taking up position behind my lac, which had already been brought up to wait before the door to Arena 13.

Tyron patted me on the shoulder. 'Just do your best, boy,' he said. 'If you do that and lose, then nobody can blame you.'

When the door rumbled open, I followed my lac into Arena 13, where my opponent and his tri-glad were already waiting. It was a strange feeling to be standing there; I was shaking with nerves.

There was no going back now.

I glanced up towards the gallery. Here, the great cande-labrum shed a bright circle of light; beyond it, in relative darkness, the spectators were anonymous shapes. I could hear their applause, but it was restrained and polite, with none of the shouting and foot-stamping that greeted the contests that I'd witnessed from the gallery. It reminded me that we were just young trainees; they didn't expect too much of us.

The Chief Marshal entered the arena and we bowed to him. He withdrew to stand just beyond the mag door. An assistant handed him his trumpet, and he blew a shrill blast.

Then both doors rumbled shut and the tri-glad began to advance towards my lac, which stood unmoving. I hadn't heard my opponent's Ulum. Maybe he'd drummed out instructions while the trumpet was sounding?

I found myself signalling the routine opening. Two

steps to the left, two to the right, then a reverse diagonal to the right. I was just reacting conventionally to the attack, rather than initiating some significant move of my own. But that's what I'd decided on before entering the arena. It was the recommended manoeuvre for a min combatant facing a challenger of unknown ability.

The tri-glad came in fast, six blades threatening, while Marfik danced close to the back of his central lac, seemingly relaxed and comfortable while my mouth was dry with nerves. Under pressure, we were forced back towards the min wall.

The tri-glad surged forward and I didn't react quickly enough. My lac stepped back, bumping into me and knocking the wind out of my lungs. I stumbled and felt a stab of fear, remembering how Scripio had died. I dropped to one knee, afraid that my lac would fall on me with the full weight of its armour-clad body.

But it held its ground just long enough, allowing me to scramble to my feet. I took a deep breath, attempting to calm myself.

Think! Think! I told myself as we were forced back against the wall.

I made a quick signal with my right boot, and we moved rapidly to the right, my back bouncing off the wall.

It was one of Kern's favourite moves, one that he taught during the training sessions. I'd practised it carefully, but still fell a long way short of his expertise. Nevertheless, the manoeuvre brought us clear of the menacing arc of blades and back into the centre of the arena before the tri-glad could complete its turn.

Executing that move successfully made me feel better. My confidence was returning.

Then things improved even further. My lac struck: it stepped towards its nearest opponent, right arm stabbing forward, and, to my surprise, buried its blade to the hilt in the lac's throat-socket.

Marfik's lac fell backwards and hit the boards with a loud metallic sound. I'd already taken my first step towards victory!

Of course, it had little to do with me; so far I'd been ordinary. It was the skilful patterning of Tyron that was responsible. Now I needed to keep a cool head and concentrate. The inert body of the lac was an obstacle that would remain there until the end of the contest; I had to use it to my advantage.

What I planned was not an attractive way to achieve victory. I'd seen it used in Arena 13 before, provoking a chorus of catcalls and boos from the crowd. But the tactic was simple. All I had to do was keep circling, using the fallen lac as a barrier. This meant that only one of the tri-glad's remaining lacs could attack us at any one time – unless they both moved away from Marfik in a pincer movement, leaving him alone and dangerously exposed.

That was exactly what happened. I kept signalling right and left, playing a game of cat and mouse that, in a senior contest, could have gone on for some time. There were brief clashes of blades, but that was all.

It couldn't last long. Marfik was a novice like myself, and when the mutters of disapproval from above turned to howls of derision, he took it personally and launched a lac from the left in a desperate attack.

By now I was totally relaxed. My nerves had disappeared. I knew that I'd as good as won. I'd already seen my lac in action and was confident that Tyron had done an excellent job. It was ready and it reacted quickly. Marfik's second lac went down in a tangle of arms and legs.

Then we became the hunters and it was Marfik's turn to signal the retreat. Moments later we had him cornered, his back against the wall. When his final lac had been brought down, he stood waiting, his eyes filled with fear.

I watched my lac approach him, lifting the blade in its left hand. I knew how Marfik felt. As the defeated combatant, he had to accept the ritual cut to his upper arm. It was done quickly, and a thin red line of blood appeared.

Afterwards he smiled in relief, and there was a muted round of applause from above, acknowledging my victory. I'd won my first Arena 13 contest, but the crowd were grudging in their praise.

Still, what did it matter? I'd also won my bet against Palm. Not only had I avoided a big debt, but now he would have to pay me. I suddenly realized that I could afford a good quality lac of my own.

The gambling houses had made Palm the favourite. It was all based on complicated statistics and the gathering of data. They knew what each patterner was capable of, and the relative quality of the lacs. They were very good at predicting the outcome of a contest.

As Kern had explained in one of our lessons, they adjusted the odds so that it was difficult for a punter to win significant amounts, the profits of the gambling houses were guaranteed. And you didn't need to be a mathematical genius to work out that Palm was the likely champion – he had the best artificer patterning his tri-glad and the best lacs his father could buy.

The tournament proceeded. Normally the loser was eliminated after each bout, but as it was generally the mag combatant who won, there was a device ensuring that a min faced a mag in the final contest; it was a points system which ensured that not every winning mag would get through to the next round. It depended on how quickly they won. It was in the interest of every mag contestant to do *more* than just win. He had to get the bout over as quickly as possible to earn the points that would allow him to continue in the TT.

That helped me to win my second contest: my opponent, desperate for points, was in too much of a rush to finish me off. He became careless and I won again.

However, in my third bout, the first of the knock-out stages, I was outclassed and defeated within three minutes. Still, my overall performance in the tournament filled me with elation. I had won twice when one victory would have sufficed.

Not only had I progressed far enough to help Tyron's stable's position in the rankings; I had also earned a reputation as a somewhat pedestrian combatant. So Tyron had won twice over. We would get good odds when I fought in the future.

And the gambling houses showed that even they sometimes got it wrong.

In the final contest of the TT, Palm lost.

It cost them a lot of money, and they had to pay

out large sums to those who had taken a real gamble by betting against Palm. It was the biggest shock of the tournament.

Deinon and I were walking across the plaza. It was a sunny Saturday afternoon but the breeze was a little chilly. Autumn was approaching and already the sun was losing some of its warmth.

Deinon was in a good mood. He'd won his second contest and was still high on the afterglow of that victory.

'What will you do at the end of the season, Leif?' he asked me.

'I'll go south, but further than Mypocine,' I replied. 'I want to visit the Genthai lands and see where my father was born.'

'That sounds exciting,' he told me. 'Far better than what I face – a cold winter working on the farm.'

I had told Deinon that my father was Genthai, but hadn't, of course, revealed that he was Math.

'Did your father tell you much about his people?' Deinon asked now.

'Not much – only bits about their beliefs. They worship a new god called Thangandar, a wolf deity, but they also have ancestor gods called Maori, who are supposed to live on a long white cloud.'

'How do the Genthai make a living?' Deinon asked. 'Some come to Gindeen to trade. They sell wood carvings.'

'Those Genthai aren't part of the main tribe. There are some like that who live in shacks on the edge of Mypocine. They're poor – they drink too much and gamble away what little money they make. But the tribes in the southern forest are different. They keep to the old ways, hunting and fishing. They're warriors too.'

'Warriors? Who do they fight?'

I thought about what the Genthai called Konnit had said to me after driving away the tassels and hammering on the great gates of Hob's citadel:

We must take back this land from the traitor who calls himself the Protector and cleanse it of abominations such as Hob. That done, we will ride forward beyond the Barrier to defeat those who confined us here.

They were preparing for future battles they surely couldn't hope to win. But I didn't tell Deinon that.

'They probably fight each other,' I said. 'Anyway, that's part of what I want to find out.'

We walked on in silence, and then Deinon changed the subject.

'I see that Kwin's speaking to you again,' he said.

I nodded. 'Just about,' I replied. 'She nods and smiles when we pass each other, but hasn't offered much in the way of conversation.'

'You'd think she'd be more grateful after the way you risked your life like that to fight the tassel. But it's always hard to work out what's going on inside Kwin's head.'

We reached the long row of shops and paused outside the one that sold Trig paraphernalia. I saw that the red boots were still there.

'It took Palm down a peg or two, losing in the final,' Deinon said. 'But he didn't deserve to win, did he? He grew reckless. All the other victories went to his head – he kept glancing up at those shrieking girls. Has he paid out on the bet yet?'

'He gave me a banker's draft last night – handed it over without a word. I thanked him but he just turned and walked away.'

'He's bitter about what happened,' Deinon commented. 'Don't forget, he lost twice over. He had to pay you and, because he didn't win the tournament, his parents won't give him the money to buy those boots for Kwin.'

We both stared at the red boots.

'She'll get the boots eventually,' Deinon observed with a smile. 'She'll win her father round. She always gets her own way in the end.'

Hob

All djinn are the wurde made flesh.

The Manual of Nym

It was the last night of the season. I found it hard to believe that it had passed so quickly.

I was sitting in the Arena 13 gallery. This was a special occasion. Kern had fought a brilliant campaign. If he managed to win tonight's contest, he'd finish first in the rankings.

So, in expectation of a celebration, Tyron had acquired seats in the front row for himself, Teena, Kwin and his first-year trainees, but as yet he hadn't arrived.

I was wearing my best clothes, bought for occasions such as this; at my belt hung two Trig blades provided by Tyron. Now that I was on the Lists, it was my right to do so. They were good blades, but I couldn't help noticing the ones at Palm's belt. They had handles embellished with silver, each embedded with a large ruby.

I was sitting next to Kwin. We'd hardly spoken since the night I'd fought the tassel. She hadn't exactly ignored me, but she'd kept her distance, just giving me cursory smiles. I decided to try to break the ice. But when I turned towards her, she spoke first.

'Congratulations,' she said. 'You fought really well in the tournament. My father said you were "canny", and that's real praise from him. What are you going to do with all that money you won from Palm?'

'Put it towards the cost of a really good lac, I suppose.'

'There'll be no need for that,' Kwin said with a smile. 'My father'll take care of all your needs. I've never seen him so enthusiastic about a new trainee.'

'He doesn't always show it to me,' I said, frowning. That was certainly true. On a day-to-day basis Tyron was grudging with his praise. He always seemed more interested in Palm's welfare.

'He keeps a lot to himself, but trust me, he thinks a lot of your ability,' Kwin told me. 'I could understand it if you'd a rich father like Palm. He must have special plans for you. I can't believe that he's even registered you under his own name!'

'He said that was common practice . . .'

'That's true for *most* artificers, but you're the first that *he's* ever registered in that way.'

This was really good to hear. It made me think that Tyron had faith in me in spite of all the trouble I'd been involved in. Maybe it was more than just trying to keep the identity of my father a secret.

'How's Jon?' I asked.

'Doing all right, but he's worried that he might lose his licence. As yet, nobody's brought any charges against him, but what he did is common knowledge and they might do so at any time. If he has any enemies, he'll find out soon enough.'

'What would he do if that happened?'

Kwin shrugged. 'We haven't talked about it. I don't see him now, anyway. We've broken up. My father keeps me in the house most of the time – except when I'm working in his office. I'm not allowed out after dark – apart from special occasions like this.'

'I'm sorry,' I said.

But inside I wasn't sorry at all. Oh, I knew it was hard for Kwin, not being allowed to leave the house: I knew how much she liked to go and visit the Wheel after dark. But my heart soared at the news that her relationship with Jon was over. Could I dare to hope that I had a chance now?

'There's no need to be sorry,' Kwin told me. 'It's not your fault. Jon shouldn't have got involved like he did. Anyway, things will soon improve. I know my father. He starts off being really strict, but he always relents in the end. I'll soon wear him down!' she added with a smile.

A silence descended between us, while I struggled to find something cheerful to say. Down in the arena the two doors were still closed, but it wouldn't be long before the bout started. Tyron still hadn't appeared, and I was just starting to worry that he might miss Kern's contest, which was early on the evening's Lists.

Suddenly, without warning, the torches flickered, and then we were plunged into total darkness. Cries of dismay and distress went up from the spectators around us.

Another flicker, and the lights – both on the walls and on the candelabrum in the centre – were burning again as if nothing had happened.

I looked up: the torches were now giving out a steady light, but even as I watched, they began to flicker once more, as if fanned by a cold breath – even though the air was absolutely still. There was no obvious explanation for what was happening.

We were plunged again into pitch darkness, and screams and wails rent the air; then, as the lights came back on, spectators began to rise from their seats and scramble into the aisles in their hurry to escape. A sense of panic and terror spread through the gallery as they surged towards the door at the back.

'What is it?' I asked Kwin. She didn't answer. In any case, it was a stupid question. I'd already guessed what it meant – the worst thing that could possibly happen.

Hob had arrived to issue a challenge.

'Kern! What about Kern?' Teena asked, leaning across towards us. Her eyes were wide and her mouth had opened in dismay.

'There are twenty-seven min combatants on the Lists tonight, so the odds are against him being chosen,' Kwin told her sister. 'I promise you it won't be him . . .'

I turned and looked around the gallery. Moments earlier the place had been full to capacity – about two thousand people had been sitting there – but now barely a few score remained.

I didn't speak. My heart was racing because I knew what was happening. Below the arena, the min combatants would be gathered in the green room. The Chief Marshal would be approaching them with the lottery orb.

The one who must fight Hob was now being chosen.

With a deep rumble the two doors began to open simultaneously, and Hob's tri-glad entered the arena. The three lacs wore armour as black as ebony, but were neither more nor less human in form than those I was familiar with. Then a fourth combatant followed them in.

For the first time I set eyes on Hob.

I felt a surge of anger and my whole body began to tremble. This was the creature who'd killed my mother and caused the death of my father. To be so close to him, unable to do anything, was almost unbearable.

From the neck down, he looked no different from any other Arena 13 combatant, though he wore the bronze helmet Tyron had told me about. The face-plate had no human features, but there was a wide black slit where eyes would normally be located on a human face.

It was at that moment that the min combatant entered the arena from the door directly beneath us. With a shock I saw the silver emblem of the wolf emblazoned on the back of his leather jerkin.

Teena gave a little cry and buried her face in her hands, bowing down until her head rested on the safety rail.

Against all the odds it had happened: Kern's straw had been drawn from the lottery orb to fight Hob.

I glanced across at Palm and Deinon; they were both staring down into the arena, shock evident on their faces. Deinon looked at Teena, opening his mouth as if about to say something; then he seemed to think better of it and turned away.

Kwin leaned forward and put her hand on Teena's shoulder. Deep sobs were shaking her sister's body.

The rules appeared to have changed. The Chief Marshal entered Arena 13 only briefly to nod to the two combatants, and there was no trumpet blast to mark the precise moment when combat should begin.

The doors closed with a shudder, and there was a delay while the combatants prepared for battle, taking up positions and manoeuvring as they gathered themselves for the first attack.

It was about to begin.

Kern was advancing slowly towards his opponents, dancing very close to the back of his lac. His face was rigid with concentration rather than fear. He shuffled left, then right, and began to drum with his heels to signal the pattern of attack.

I couldn't follow every detail of that sequence of signals, but I'd watched him training often enough to get the general idea. Kern was going on the offensive. It was the way he usually fought. Tyron called it 'controlled aggression'. There was nothing reckless about it; this was what had got him to the top of the Trig rankings.

It was impossible to judge how Hob felt, for his head was completely covered by the helmet. Was he cold and expressionless? I wondered. Or was he smiling in anticipation of victory?

I didn't like the idea of him wearing a helmet while Kern had none. My father had been right to wear his wolf helmet. Why hadn't others challenged by Hob done the same? Was it forbidden now?

Kern's first attack was skilful, and there was a rasp of metal upon metal as his lac's blade just failed to locate the throat-socket of the nearest of Hob's tri-glad; but then, in turn, Kern came under pressure and was forced back against the arena wall, his lac trying desperately to shield him from the blades that arced towards his body.

Using the wooden wall to his advantage, deploying his favourite trick, Kern bounced off it rhythmically, working his way along while his lac, although pressed hard now by the combined power of its adversaries, struggled to shield him.

Once more, Kern moved onto the offensive; for a while he held the centre of the arena. He was good, and that night he fought better than ever, raising himself to new heights. At one point he even drove Hob and his tri-glad back towards the far corner – there seemed a real chance that he might win.

The small crowd began to whoop and cheer, and then drum with their boots on the floor of the gallery in appreciation. Kern was a very poplar combatant. Everyone had expected him to finish the season as champion. They believed in him. He was the best they had, and they willed him on to victory over the hated Hob.

The struggle was fast and furious, but gradually Hob began to dominate until, once more, Kern was forced back.

Then the gong sounded. I couldn't believe that five minutes had passed already. Now both combatants had to fight in front of their lacs.

They halted, disengaged and took up the new positions.

Now the crowd fell quiet; I could sense their anxiety. Hob was fast and deadly, more formidable than a lac. Kern would face him blade against blade. The long arms of his own lac would reach forward over his shoulders in an attempt to protect him, but would it be enough?

Hob attacked ferociously and Kern retreated.

Teena covered her face with her hands, unable to watch. Deinon was biting his nails.

'Get away from the wall, you fool. Get away from the wall!' cried Tyron as he lowered himself into the seat next to Teena. He was breathing hard.

Tyron's words seemed harsh. It was obvious that Kern was desperately trying to get clear of the wall but was being prevented by the sheer ferocity of Hob's assault. His back was pressed against the armoured chest of his lac. He had nowhere to go. Hob was right in his face and the tri-glad was pressing in from each side.

But I knew that Tyron loved Kern as his own son – it was simply his fear for him that had forced those words from his mouth.

Teena lifted her head from the rail and leaned towards her father, who held both her hands in his. She was gazing down into the arena as if hypnotized by what was taking place.

Suddenly, horribly, shockingly, it was over.

Kern's lac went down, a blade hammered into its throat-socket.

Kern staggered sideways, looking dazed. He had already been cut by Hob. There was blood on his face, and a darker stain slowly spread down his right side, leaking from inside the leather jerkin. Even as I watched, another of Hob's blades buried itself in his flesh.

I felt sick to my stomach. This couldn't be happening. It was too cruel. He was being slain in front of his wife and there was nothing anybody could do to save him.

He swayed, but he didn't fall – even though it was clear that he was seriously – probably fatally – wounded. Under the normal rules of engagement, the combatant and his tri-glad would have moved back the moment blood had been drawn. Lacs were designed to do just that – unless that pattern was overridden by the dictates of a grudge match – or the different rules that seemed to apply here. They moved back now, but for Kern it was already too late.

He was defeated and, dead or alive, he belonged to Hob.

We watched in shock as he left Arena 13. The whole gallery was silent. He went bravely, limping ahead of Hob and his lacs, trying to stay on his feet, his face twisted with pain and resignation. There was a trail of blood behind him, and at the entrance to the mag door he paused and staggered.

I thought he was going to collapse, but he turned to the gallery. He was looking up at Teena; seeing the distant face of his wife for the last time.

Teena screamed out his name, the anguish in her voice terrible in the silence. Then Kern went through the door and was lost to our sight.

We left the gallery immediately. Tyron and Kwin gripped Teena's arms fiercely as they half lifted, half dragged her up the steps. The spectators remained in their seats to allow us through the door. They watched us in silence, their faces showing a whole range of emotions: pity, anger, sorrow, regret and dismay.

Teena's body was rigid and she was trembling from head to foot. Back at Tyron's house, his servants, ever swift and efficient, moved to help. A doctor was sent for and Teena was wrapped in blankets and placed close to the fire. She was shivering now; the first wave of hysteria had passed, to leave her lucid and calm.

'Help him, Father,' she pleaded quietly. 'Please help him! I know you can do it.'

Tyron shook his head and paced the room like a caged animal.

'Buy Kern back. Please . . . if you gave Hob enough money . . .'

Still Tyron paced, and more precious irrecoverable minutes ticked by.

'Let me offer myself in his place. Please, Father.'

The doctor came in and they had to hold Teena down while he forced the potion he'd brought past her lips. When she was unconscious, two servants carried her up to her bedroom, Kwin following behind. Only then did Tyron cease pacing the room. He became very calm and the decisive look that I knew so well came into his eyes.

'Go to bed now!' he snapped, glaring towards the doorway, where I was waiting with Palm and Deinon.

But when I turned to go, Tyron called after me.

'Not you, Leif! You come with me.'

I followed him through to the back of the house, then down into the cellar. There was a small metal door embedded in the stone. I'd noticed it before but had never thought much about it. When Tyron opened it, I realized that it was a safe.

He took a bag from the vault and handed it to me. It was heavy – far bigger than the one Kwin had given to the tassels.

'It's gold,' Tyron said. 'The only coin Hob understands.'

We walked out into the cold night air, Tyron leading the way towards a tall wooden wagon; a team of six horses stood before it, already harnessed.

He was going to visit Hob – and he had chosen me to accompany him. I felt honoured, but nervous as well. Why me?

Tyron climbed up and seized the reins. But before we moved off, he turned towards me.

'Do you know where we're going?' he asked.

I nodded.

'You don't have to come. If you're afraid, go back into the house.'

'I'm not afraid,' I said.

'That's because you weren't born in this city. If you knew more about Hob, then you'd be afraid. You know what he did to your mother, but that's only a fraction of what he's capable of. That's one reason why I'm taking you with me. I want you to understand what you're up against. And there's another reason. It's because you're here and I trust you. I trust you as I trusted your father. Nobody should go alone into Hob's citadel. So I want somebody with me whom I can rely on.'

'Are we in danger up there?' I asked, pointing up the hill.

'Not tonight. Not if you keep your head and do exactly what you're told.'

'Will he listen? Will he give Kern back?'

'He might,' Tyron answered grimly. 'But I suspect that poor Kern was dying before he even left the arena. No, we're not going up there in the hope of returning Kern's body to Teena, although there's almost nothing I wouldn't give to be able to do just that. We're going up there for something else . . .'

'Something else?' I asked.

'Yes,' Tyron said grimly. 'I hope to buy back Kern's soul.'

Whom Do You Love?

To begin a war is easy,
But some wars are without end.

Amabramsum: the Genthai Book of Wisdom

The moon had already risen and was almost full, though it was still hidden behind the hill, so the sky was very dark, with only a cold and very distant sprinkling of stars.

Images kept running through my mind. Over and over again I saw the dying Kern turning and looking up towards Teena for the last time. At that vivid memory I sobbed deep in my throat. Tyron gave me a quick glance, but said nothing. I struggled to get the picture out of my head and concentrate on the world about me.

Gradually the track between the wooden dwellings grew steeper and the horses began to slow. I knew that Tyron preferred horses to oxen: generally they were faster, but when the gradient increased, they began to strain against the harness and the sweat poured off their flanks. There was little doubt that oxen would have been more suited to a task such as this.

As we left Gindeen, the dwellings grew sparser, and those few we passed had an abandoned, dilapidated appearance.

Tonight, however, there was no sign of tassels on the bare, dark slope. Somewhere over the next rise stood those thirteen spires, but we were moving towards a citadel whose defences extended far beyond its grey stone walls.

I felt both nervous and curious about what lay ahead. I wanted to ask Tyron about Hob. Only one thing stopped me – the strange reference he'd made to Kern's soul. It made me afraid to enquire further – as if the answers might reveal a different Tyron to the one I respected and admired: a superstitious stranger I barely knew.

How could you buy back a man's soul? I wondered.

As we moved higher, the air cooled and, from nowhere, a thick mist swirled before us, coiling like serpents with a single determined aim: to form an impenetrable wall of whiteness. It was as if we'd penetrated low cloud – though I'd seen no hint of cloud previously, and on a night in late summer, with the air still warm, the thick white blanket that had enveloped us without warning could surely not be natural.

Then, as suddenly as it had descended, the mist was below us, a white collar circling the hillside; above it, the whole landscape was bathed in moonlight, and the great walls and thirteen twisted spires of Hob's citadel reared up like a dark beast before us.

Tyron brought the horses to a halt and, with a curt order – 'Bring the bag!' – jumped to the ground.

The money bag, although merely sealed with cord, was attached to a long loop of security chain. Once clear of the wagon, I slung it around my neck. It was heavy and I struggled to keep up with Tyron, who strode off along the outside of what soon proved to be a curved wall. But for the fact that it was stone rather than wood, we might have been circling the outer rim of the Wheel.

At intervals along the wall were a number of small dark openings, barely large enough to admit a man. Each one went down at a steep angle and the grass around them was churned into mud, as if they were used frequently by tassels. The night when the three Genthai warriors had come to our aid, I'd seen some of the tassels escape, slithering away into tunnels such as these. We passed the large gates against which those Genthai had hammered, but without even glancing at it, Tyron continued along the wall.

At last we came to a great curved archway. No gate barred our way, and Tyron turned into it without hesitation, crossing a small flagged courtyard to enter a dark tunnel. There was no glimmer of light ahead, and if it hadn't been for the sound of Tyron's footsteps clattering on the stone flags, I would have turned back.

To visit this dark citadel at all seemed like folly, but to come in the dead of night seemed reckless beyond belief. But then I thought of Kern, the reason we'd come to this forbidding place, and tried to banish my own fears from my mind. I had to trust that Tyron knew what he was doing and that good would come of it.

One thing was now certain beyond any doubt: Tyron knew exactly where he was going. He'd visited Hob's citadel before.

We emerged from the darkness of the tunnel into a great space illuminated by hundreds of flickering candles. Some were fastened to the walls, others embedded in huge iron candelabra standing on the floor. Despite their light, the walls towered so high above us that the ceiling was lost in gloom. To both right and left stood rows of pillars, beyond which lay sinister shadows, with the hint of other pillars beyond them.

The floor was constructed of marble, with an intricate design of intertwining fantastical creatures; it was a complex glittering mosaic formed of vivid reds, yellows and rich royal purples. Tyron walked swiftly forward, and then I saw that, at the far end of the room, three steps led up to an elevated platform bearing a huge throne.

As I stared at it, the hairs on the back of my neck began to rise.

That throne was occupied . . .

At first I thought that the seated figure was a giant, maybe three or even four times the size of a man. But as we drew nearer, I realized that it was just an illusion created by the size of the hall and the positioning of the pillars.

It was certainly very effective, no doubt calculated to inspire awe in anyone who approached that throne. And as we crossed the hall, I sensed that I was being watched from either side; a feeling that was reinforced by a disturbing noise, so faint it was almost inaudible, of whisperings and mutterings.

I gazed quickly left and right, searching amongst the pillars, but there was no sign of anyone other than the figure seated upon the throne.

Why were there no servants in attendance? And was this indeed Hob, my enemy, or was it some mere keeper of an anteroom with something even greater beyond it, as yet unseen?

My question was immediately answered for, to my dismay, Tyron suddenly cast himself first upon his knees and then upon his face before the throne. He lay prone for many seconds while I tried to adjust to what I was seeing.

Could this really be Tyron, the greatest artificer in all Gindeen? Tyron, who was respected the length and breadth of the city? I stared up at the throne, trying to understand what could have caused him to behave in such a way. It was then that Hob slowly turned his head in my direction and his eyes locked onto mine.

He no longer wore the bronze helmet. Was this indeed the creature who had just slain Kern in the arena? I wondered.

He had the shape of a man, and his clothes were dark and nothing out of the ordinary, but his arms were long like a lac's. He wore a short, full-sleeved jacket of good quality leather, and his trousers were sewn by a first-rate tailor, and across the back of his throne lay a cloak with long tassels, each ending in a black bead. It was from this that his servants got their name.

But then I noticed his boots – boots made for fighting in Arena 13, light and trim, laced to a point high on the ankle. Tyron had once told me that, about ten years previously, it had been fashionable in the city for aficionados to wear such boots in imitation of the combatants they supported. But this was no longer the case; apart from Kwin and some stick-fighters, only true combatants now wore that type of boot outside the arena.

The boots looked new, but they were splattered with small dark stains. I shivered as I realized that it was blood from Arena 13.

It was Kern's blood.

As Hob continued to stare at me, my knees began to shake. At first it was only a slight trembling, but for some reason I took a step backwards and the tremor began to grow, my legs becoming weaker until they threatened to give way beneath me. Another second and I'd have fallen; however, just in time, Hob's gaze was directed back at Tyron, who'd come to his feet.

'Lord,' said Tyron, 'I am here to beg a great favour.'

Hob gave a barely perceptible nod, as if indicating permission for Tyron to continue. Free of his gaze, I was able to examine him once more.

His head was slightly larger than normal and completely hairless. There wasn't even a hint of facial hair. The nose was large and hooked, so that he looked like one of the large predatory eagles that soared over the Southern Mountains in spring.

'Lord, the youth that you defeated in the arena tonight was the husband of my daughter,' Tyron continued. 'Would you allow me to buy his remains?'

At the word 'remains', I grew cold. He was talking about Kern, who'd recently been so full of life and hope, so happy with his wife and child, so proud of his rapidly developing skill in the Trig.

There was a long pause before Hob spoke. Rather than answering Tyron's question, he asked one of his own.

'Is your elder daughter well?'

'Yes, Lord,' Tyron replied. 'She is in good health. But I fear that what has happened will destroy her sanity, unless you will be gracious.'

'How much have you brought?' Hob asked.

Tyron turned and waved me forward, so I unslung the chain from my neck and placed the bag on the marble floor at his side. Tyron immediately knelt before it, untied the string and pulled out a handful of gold coins, allowing them to fall through his fingers somewhat theatrically, to cascade in a golden shower back into the bag.

'This is but a deposit, Lord. Twice this I will give you for the remains of Kern.'

'Would this include his soul?' Hob asked.

There was a long silence. At last, with his eyes fixed upon the floor, Tyron gave the merest of nods.

'Then we have a bargain,' the djinni said. 'For double what you place before me, you may have the remains as agreed. You may take them now, but the full price must be with me before the new moon.'

A hooded figure emerged from the pillars to our left: one of the tassels carrying a large black wooden box. He halted before the throne and bowed to Hob, setting the box down before Tyron. After another bow to his master, he withdrew into the shadows behind the pillars.

Hob gestured, and Tyron immediately fell to his knees before the box. Although it had no visible hinges or clasps, he quickly raised its lid and pulled down the front panel, as if he was familiar with such devices.

I could only gaze in horror upon what was now clearly visible within the box.

It was the head of Kern.

Bile rose in my throat, and I struggled to hold down the contents of my stomach.

There was a worse horror to come, for it was clear that the head still lived. It was supported upon a tangle of fibrous tissue that resembled roots or fungi, and the face was horribly animated, twitching as if in spasm. But the features suddenly settled, and the eyes opened and looked directly at Tyron. A moment later their gaze fell upon me, and I knew beyond a shadow of a doubt that the head was conscious. That Kern, even in this appalling condition, was still alive and aware, still able to recognize us.

Tears were running down my cheeks now. Why should such a terrible thing have been allowed to happen to Kern? I remembered the patient teacher; I saw him holding his wife's hand and smiling into her eyes; kissing the child on his knee.

Kern's mouth started to move. No sound emerged, but a pink froth formed upon the lips. Tyron placed a hand very gently upon the head, as might a father upon the head of his child.

I watched, filled with sadness and horror. Now, turning back to look at Hob, I saw again my mother's shoes lying in the long grass by the river bank. I saw her dead body drained of blood. I saw the angry eyes of my father as he used his fists on me, driving me away. I saw our house burning and smelled the charred flesh of my parents.

I had left Tyron's house as I had entered it, dressed for the gallery and, like Tyron, still wore two blades at my belt. Now my urge to kill Hob was so overpowering that before I even realized what I was doing, I had drawn my blades and taken three steps towards the throne.

Hob didn't respond, but time itself seemed to freeze, and

slowly, very slowly, I became aware of the enormity of what I'd done.

The drawing of the blades had been an instinctive response, born of deep emotions that now boiled up into my throat, robbing me of speech. Something within me sought to end the life of the sinister creature on the throne, the blood-drinking djinni who had done such unspeakable things.

But now it was not only emotion that took away my ability to talk. Hob's eyes were regarding me, and never had I seen such eyes. The whites were unusually large, the small dark iris sitting above the centre of each orb. I'd heard the expression 'wall-eyed wrath' used to describe staring rage. There was something of that here, but if this was anger being directed at me, it was of a type I'd never encountered before.

For the eyes were cold and gazed unblinkingly, like a great predatory fish from the darkest depths of the ocean, unfeeling and without pity, at a mote of life that had fallen into its domain. There was no emotion behind those eyes, no compassion. They were windows through which something utterly alien peered out upon the world of humans, and I struggled to break free of a great weight that was dragging me down into unspeakable depths of darkness.

Out of the corner of my eye I saw Tyron staring at me; a sequence of emotions flickered across his face, but they were impossible to read. I'd caused more trouble. I should have controlled my feelings. He would be angry.

He'd said I was somebody he could rely on, and now I'd let him down.

Suddenly Tyron was on his knees again, prostrate before the throne, and as he spoke, he began to beat his forehead rhythmically against the marble floor.

It was hard to make sense of his gabbled words, but it was clear that Tyron was now begging for my life. I stood there like a fool, unable to speak or even move, until at last he came to his feet, approached me and, seizing my hands, guided my blades back into their scabbards.

Now he had his arm around me like a father and, with a sudden shock, I saw that he was weeping. Finally he seemed to gather himself and spoke more slowly and carefully.

'The boy is young and hot-headed, Lord. I should not have brought him here. He knows not what he does. But I will teach him. Just allow me time, Lord. You will see how he can change.'

'Perhaps,' Hob acknowledged, 'but before I decide what is to be done, I would ask a question.'

He directed his cold gaze upon me again. 'Whom do you love, boy?' he asked slowly.

It was a strange question. I didn't want to answer, but knew that, if I refused, I'd never leave that place alive. And I also knew that, within these walls, there waited more terrible things than death.

I tried to answer, but was filled with confusion. I had no father or mother to love now. Hob had been responsible for their deaths. Deinon was my friend, but as far as emotions went, Kwin was the person I'd felt closest to since arriving in the city. I was strongly attracted to her, but my feelings couldn't be described as love. In any case, she'd once had feelings for Jon, and since discovering that, I'd tried to distance myself from her. And although I thought of Tyron as my friend and guardian, I did not love him as I had once loved my father.

So there was only one answer I could give.

'I love no one,' I replied.

For the first time Hob smiled. 'You may take two souls with you, Tyron,' he said. 'But the price will be doubled and the whole must still be paid before the moon wanes to new.'

Tyron began to babble out words of gratitude, but Hob silenced him with a gesture of his hand. He was looking at me again.

'You have dared to threaten me, boy, and for that a price must be paid. You must be punished. One day, in the fullness of time, you will change,' Hob said. 'You will learn to have for others the emotion that man calls love. One by one, as you grow older, the number of those you love will grow, and the depth of that love will grow too. Then, one by one, I will take from you those you love. Piece by piece, I will take from you all that you hold dear until only you remain. Only then will I kill you. Only then will I devour your soul.'

Again, my hands seemed to have a life of their own: they moved to draw the blades a second time. But Tyron had already lifted the wooden box and had wrapped his other arm about me with a grip of iron; he was turning and forcing me across the marble floor towards the door at the far end of the hall.

Once we reached the wagon, Tyron seized the reins and urged the horses back down the hill, while I sat beside him, lost for words. The horror of Kern's condition was a great weight that lay upon my soul like a coffin of lead.

But the ordeal wasn't yet over. I realized that Tyron was not taking the track that led directly back into the city. Soon we were on a wooded slope, pressed on either side by young trees. Here, Tyron stopped the wagon, seized the box and leaped down onto the grass.

I followed, hardly knowing what to expect. We were in a small clearing, and the moon was just visible between the trees, its faint white light casting spectral shadows across the grass.

I stared at Tyron, expecting him to be livid with anger at what I had done. He had said he trusted me, but I had let my emotions get the better of me. I had let him down again. However, he looked sad and close to tears.

Tyron set the box down on the ground between us and opened it quickly. In the shadows, Kern's features were not clearly visible, but I could see the eyes rolling in their sockets.

I watched Tyron lay a hand gently upon Kern's forehead, his fingers covering the eyes, and murmur simply, 'Peace . . .'

There was the glint of a blade and, with two swift strokes, Tyron severed the fibrous tissue beneath the head. He pressed the eyelids shut and sighed. Then he went back into the wagon, returning moments later with a spade.

He handed it to me. 'Dig it deep,' he commanded.

So I began. At one point I glanced back at him; he was sitting cross-legged before the box. All around us there was utter silence – apart from the sound of Tyron weeping.

At one point I leaned back on my spade and asked if the hole was deep enough.

'We need it deeper than that, boy. Twice as deep,' he replied.

When it was done, Tyron placed the open box in the hole. The head was still now. Mercifully, all life seemed to have left it. Tyron then went back to the wagon and returned moments later with a can of thick lubricating oil. He doused the contents of the hole liberally, and then ignited it.

There was a *whoosh*, a sheet of flame, and then a nauseating smell of burning flesh. Twice more he doused that hole. Twice more he sent flames searing upwards into the night sky.

'We can't take any chances,' Tyron told me. 'You wouldn't believe what Hob's capable of.'

Then, without further explanation, he took the spade and began to fill the hole with earth. Finally he shook his head sorrowfully and stamped the earth down hard with his feet.

We returned in silence. My mind was numb.

Dignity

Our master Caesar is in the tent, where the maps are
   spread.
His eyes fixed upon nothing, a hand under his head.
Like a long-legged fly upon the stream,
His mind moves upon silence.

The Compendium of Ancient Tales and Ballads

Once inside the house, I muttered a goodnight and headed
for my sleeping quarters. I assumed that Tyron would want
to be alone with his family, but to my surprise he beckoned
to me.

Obediently I followed him upstairs to his study, expecting to receive a dressing down. A fire was blazing in the
hearth, and without a word Tyron pointed to a seat before it.
I sat down, and was left alone for half an hour or so.

Tyron returned carrying a decanter of dark red wine and
two glasses. He placed all three items upon the table, and I
was astounded to see him fill both glasses to the brim. He
brought them over and sat down before handing one to me.

'Teena's in a deep sleep,' he said. 'The doctor plans to
keep her that way for at least twenty-four hours.'

'What will you tell her?' I asked.

'As little as possible,' Tyron said gruffly. 'I'll tell her that I obtained the remains and cremated them. I'll tell her that Kern is at peace.'

'Why didn't we get the rest of the body?' I asked.

'Because the tassels are cannibals,' he replied.

I shuddered and looked down in horror. That must have been why they'd come for the body of the girl by the lake. We sat in silence for a long time before I could bring myself to drink.

I sipped at the wine tentatively. It had a bitter taste, but it slipped down my throat smoothly, giving an instant sensation of warmth.

'This house is one of the safest places in the city,' Tyron said. 'It has stout reinforced doors, and several of my servants can handle themselves and fight with weapons. The tassels rarely enter the wealthier parts of Gindeen. That incident by the lake was unusual. They prefer the dark streets close to the Wheel. But if Hob does get it into his mind to come after you, there's nothing I can do.'

'Am I in danger?' I asked. 'From what he said, it's the future I should worry about.'

'True, but Hob isn't to be trusted in anything he does or says. In time he may forget. And then again, he might not. The most dangerous time may be the next few days. We might be wise to postpone your entry to Arena 13 for at least a year; the season after next or maybe even later than that.'

Tyron's words stunned me. Usually second-year trainees fought a few contests matched against each other. The best were sometimes even pitched against those with high rankings, who had many years of experience behind them. It was part of the learning process. I'd been counting down the days to the end of my first year, looking forward to fighting in Arena 13 again.

'Why?' I asked.

'Trust me,' Tyron said. 'It's best if you keep a low profile. The very first time you fight for real, Hob may visit the arena looking for you. And strange things can happen with that lottery orb. However, I may be able to negotiate with him to leave you alone for a while so that you can develop your skills in the arena. It would cost me, but it's a possibility.'

'Can we do nothing without fearing Hob?' I asked Tyron, my voice full of bitterness. 'Can there be no peace or dignity?'

I saw Tyron flinch at the word 'dignity' as if I'd struck him. I glanced at his forehead and, even in the low light, noticed the bruise where it had struck the marble floor of that throne-room.

'*Dignity?* You want *dignity*, boy?' he demanded angrily. 'Well, there's precious little dignity to be had right now. It'll be a great many years yet before we can afford dignity. You weren't much impressed, I take it, with my behaviour tonight? Well, I had to pay for two souls; if you'd stayed calm, I need have paid for only one.

'It's cost me my profits for almost a whole season. But it's not the first time I've climbed that hill. Not the first time I've handed hard-earned gold over to Hob. Not the first time I've burned and buried flesh to keep it from him. What's gold anyway, when weighed against the torment of a man?'

I was stunned by this outpouring of emotion. I guessed that there was much more here than Tyron was saying; things I didn't yet see.

'Do you think I wanted to bow and scrape before that creature? Why do you think I did it? Tell me!' Tyron demanded.

'For Kern and for me,' I answered lamely.

'Yes, for poor Kern, and for you, and also for something else. You don't yet see how powerful and dangerous Hob is. Without his sufferance, I wouldn't be where I am today. Even now, he could break me, had he a mind to. So I bow and scrape and put away that thing you call dignity. I do it because something's growing here. Something centred upon this house and upon what I and others do in the Trig.

'You see, we're getting better, boy. Slowly but surely we're getting better. We're climbing that long stairway back to dignity. Once men ruled the whole of this world and there was no Barrier of mist and fear to confine us in this cursed place called Midgard – that's what the ancient books say.'

He gestured towards the bookshelf and shook his head.

'Who knows if we're fit to rule ourselves, never mind this world . . . ? But I'll tell you this: if we don't rule, then others will. Dark things like Hob. And even darker things from beyond the Barrier – creatures that support that so-called Protector of ours and keep us in our place, making us shut our doors against the night, fearful for the safety of our womenfolk and children.'

I was staring at the floor now, beginning to see what had happened in Hob's lair in a new light.

'Drink your wine, boy, but don't get used to it. As my trainee, this one glass is all I'll allow you. I want you to remember this moment when you sat sipping wine with old

Tyron and he told you the truth about what he's trying to do; a truth that even my own daughter isn't aware of. She thinks I'm a money-grubber, and in some respects she's perfectly right. Money is important to me, but I need it for a *reason*. I need it to buy lacs from the Trader, the best quality lacs possible. I need it to buy wurdes; wurdes that might one day transform the best of my lacs into something else.

'You see, boy, despite what happened to poor Kern, we're still here. We're still alive. And you *will* fight in Arena 13. You're just going to need a little more patience, that's all. How would you like to fight behind a fully sentient lac?'

I looked up at Tyron, hardly able to believe what I was hearing. I stared into his eyes and saw that he was completely sincere.

'Do you know what that would mean?' he asked. 'There'd be no more drumming on the boards to a mind-dead lac. It would be fully conscious. It would know the patterns as well as you, appreciating all the permutations. You could use Ulum together. Such a lac might take the initiative and signal to *you*! You could speak to it. Give it tactical commands verbally.

'Imagine your speed and instincts allied with such a lac. The time might come when we'd welcome a visit from Hob. Remember Gunter and your father – remember what they achieved . . . Well, let's see what Tyron and Leif can do together!'

'Could you really pattern full sentience into a lac?' I asked.

'Does the snow melt in spring? Does the wolf howl at the moon?' Tyron asked with a smile. 'I'm close, Leif. Very close. Maybe not this year and maybe not the next, but very, very close. That's why I beat my head on the ground: so as to keep it on my shoulders.'

He pointed at his forehead. 'I was trained by Gunter – Gunter the Great – who was the best artificer Gindeen's ever seen. Your father was the best Arena 13 combatant he ever trained, and I was Gunter's best trainee patterner. It's a clever head, this, even if I do say so myself. I wish there was another as clever living in this city now. With my head and your legs we might well do something one day, and I don't just mean in Arena 13.'

Tyron sipped his wine, and in the silence I tried to work out what he meant.

'Remember what Hob said to you?' he continued. 'Piece by piece . . .'

'Maybe they were just threats . . .'

'Aye, they were threats all right – threats he's vindictive enough to carry out. But he has a limited number of selves. Oh, they can be replaced, but it takes time. That's how he can be destroyed; that's what we'll do to him. Piece by piece we'll weaken him. Your poor father must have been so close, so very close. Hob was desperate. That's why he challenged him to fight in the arena in front of his lac for the whole contest.'

'You mean, if he'd carried on, eventually he might have faced Hob for the last time? Defeated the last of his selves?'

'Maybe . . .' Tyron answered slowly. 'But remember, people were fleeing the city in terror. With his back against the wall, who knows what Hob might have done? There are ancient weapons called atomics, capable of burning a city and slaying thousands. Who knows what a rogue djinni like Hob has stored in the vaults of that citadel? No, there's another way; one that could take him by surprise.

'First, we could weaken him in the arena. That would be *your* job. Then, when we have him where we want him, we could attack him in his lair. He wouldn't expect that. It might just work, especially if we used sentient lacs to lead the attack.'

My mouth opened in astonishment. What he was saying sounded incredible. From anyone else's lips it would have been just a fantasy, a dream offering refuge from the harsh reality of life in the city. But Tyron meant every word and I believed he was capable of doing exactly what he said.

He smiled. 'So, work at your craft and try to make your brain catch up with those legs of yours. The Trader visits the Sea Gate early in the spring. I'll take you with me. It'll give you a better idea of what I'm trying to do.'

I nodded, drained the last of my wine and set the empty glass down on the table.

Tyron refilled his own glass but ignored mine. Five minutes later I was in bed, but I didn't sleep well. I couldn't get the events in the arena and the visit to Hob's citadel out of my head. I kept seeing Kern looking up to meet Teena's eyes for the last time. Then I saw his head lying in that box.

The Memorial Service

This is the time of waiting.
This is the time when women rule.
But soon it will be over.
The moon shall dim while the sun grows bright.
Then Thangandar shall return to lead us to victory
over the cursed djinn.

Amabramdata: the Genthai Book of Prophecy

Gindeen was mostly a godless city, with few places of worship, none of them large enough to hold more than a couple of dozen people.

So the memorial service for Kern was held in Arena 13. He had been very popular, both with spectators and with fellow combatants; the gallery was full to capacity. Everyone sat in silence, waiting for Pyncheon to make his appearance and begin the proceedings. The sashes worn that day were all black, and the women were dressed in purple and grey, the traditional colours of mourning, their lips unpainted.

I sat in the front row with Deinon and Palm on my left; immediately to my right was Tyron, and Teena was seated between him and Kwin.

Before we left the house, Tyron had given stern

instructions, mostly directed against Kwin – though his eyes did settle upon me briefly. Anyone could speak at the service, but we must not use the occasion to attack Hob. To speak out in that way would bring disaster down upon the whole family.

The great candelabrum descended, filling the arena with flickering yellow light, and the mag door slowly rumbled open. Pyncheon, wearing a black sash and holding the ceremonial staff of office, walked slowly to the centre of the arena and looked up at the gallery.

'We are gathered here to celebrate Kern's life and mark his death!' he cried out, his words echoing back from the walls of the gallery. 'He died bravely, just as he lived. He was also a combatant of great skill. He would have gone on to become one of the greatest fighters this arena has ever seen. Who else would speak of Kern?'

In reply, a number of hands were raised in the gallery. Pyncheon rapped three times with his staff on the floor and then pointed it at a young man to our right.

'Crassius will speak!' he called out.

Crassius was one of Tyron's min combatants; he had just completed his three years of training. I had only met him once as he was now based in the Wheel. He was ginger-haired and freckled, and as he came to his feet he blushed bright red at the prospect of speaking before such a large gathering.

'As well as being a skilled combatant, Kern was also a great teacher,' he began. 'He was kind and patient, and I owe him much. He filled me with confidence when I had none. He made me believe that I had the ability to succeed. I came to this city alone and without friends. Kern and his wife, Teena, befriended me. Teena, I am sorry for your loss. We all share your grief, but yours must be greater than anyone's.'

As he sat down, a tear tricked down Teena's cheek, but she smiled across at Crassius and then raised her hand.

She rose to her feet, but it was some time before she could speak, and I feared that she was asking too much of herself. But then she took a deep breath and began.

'I loved Kern, I love him now and I'll love him for ever. I miss him terribly. But the greatest loss of all is that suffered by our child, who will never know him. I will remember Kern and I will tell his son that he had a great man for a father.'

After that Tyron spoke with great formality, and was followed by another dozen contributors – mostly combatants, apart from Wode, an artificer friend of Tyron's, and a representative of the largest of the gambling houses.

But nobody in that gathering was saying what should have been said. Nobody expressed outrage at what had been done to Kern. The defeat was acceptable – something that happened routinely in this arena. Death too was to be expected. After all, the fight between the Wheel's combatant and Hob was the equivalent of a grudge match; it was a fight to the death.

No, it was what had happened afterwards that appalled me; rage surged through me in waves so that my whole body shook. Hob and his tassels were permitted to take a defeated adversary alive or dead from the arena. Somewhere in the dark recesses of that thirteen-spired citadel the head was severed from the body and kept alive while the body was eaten by the tassels.

How could that be tolerated?

How could what was so despicable remain unchallenged?

'Is there anyone else who would like to add to what has been said?' Pyncheon demanded.

There was a silence; then I noticed a movement to my right. Kwin was raising her hand.

A female was not permitted to set foot in the arena, but could speak from the gallery. No other woman but Teena had made a contribution so far, but now Kwin wanted to have her say. I felt a surge of elation, but I could see the dismay on Tyron's face.

Pyncheon rapped with his staff and then pointed at Kwin, naming her as the next speaker.

She began to rise, fury twisting her features.

'No!' said Tyron, reaching across Teena to restrain his daughter. But she tore herself free and got to her feet.

Suddenly Teena reached up and grasped her hand. 'Please,' she said quietly. 'Please don't do this.'

The two sisters stared at each other for a moment, and then Kwin nodded, bowing to her sister's will. I think only Teena, the widow of poor Kern, could have stopped her that day. Kwin certainly wouldn't have listened to her father.

'I loved Kern as I would my own brother,' she said, her voice clear and sharp. 'He was fierce in combat but a kind and gentle man in private. Memories make us what we are; they shape our consciousness; they give direction to our lives. I will cherish my memories of Kern.'

As Kwin sat down, she added something very softly so that only we could hear: 'And I will live to avenge his death!'

A short concluding address from Pyncheon followed, and then the memorial service was over.

After the evening meal Tyron asked me to stay behind in the dining room.

'I just want a little chat,' he told me.

So I waited while Palm and Deinon went up to our room to pack; both were going home the next day.

'What happens during the next three months or so is your decision, boy,' Tyron told me. 'Most trainees return to their families, but as you don't have that option you're more than welcome to stay here.'

'Thanks for that offer,' I told him. 'But I've decided to travel south to visit the Genthai domain. I want to see how my father's people live.'

'That's a good idea, Leif. I think we all need to return to our roots. I know someone who is about to head south. If you're prepared to wait here for a couple of days, I should be able to arrange a ride on a wagon for you – at least as far as Mypocine. After that it'll be up to you. But you must be back at least three clear months before the next season starts to begin training. Is that clear? Our work goes on.'

I nodded, and Tyron shook my hand and without another word left the dining room.

When I went upstairs, both of my roommates were getting their things together. The painting of Math had already been removed from the wall. Deinon turned round and smiled at me. 'I'll say goodbye now, Leif. I'm off early tomorrow before breakfast. My father's picking me up.'

'I'm staying here for a couple more days before I go back

to Mypocine,' I told him. 'Tyron's fixing me up with a ride back. See you when pre-season training begins. Have a good break until then.'

Out of the corner of my eye I saw Palm watching us. I thought he was going to make some sarcastic remark or ask why I was going back to Mypocine when I had no family to return to, but he held his tongue. So I thought I might as well be polite.

I turned to him. 'Have a nice break too, Palm,' I said. 'This'll be your last night in this room, won't it?'

He nodded. 'Yes, I started training before the end of last season, so I've been here well over a year. It's time to move on. My quarters will be in the Wheel next year. But no doubt we'll see each other again. One day we'll meet in the arena!'

There was a challenge in his voice: he was clearly looking forward to beating me in Arena 13. I merely smiled back at him.

Yes, no doubt I would face him in the arena one day. And despite that formidable tri-glad of his, I was determined to win. But I'd be happy to see the back of him. I'd miss the painting – although the artist hadn't managed a good likeness of my father's face.

The next two days were too quiet. The house seemed to have lost its bustling sense of purpose. Teena kept to her room, Tyron and Kwin spent the time at his office in the administration building, and Palm and Deinon were gone. I was at a loose end. I tried to work on my patterning but couldn't concentrate. So I did a lot of walking around the city.

Late in the afternoon of the second day, I found myself

strolling across the plaza. My feet knew where they were going. They stopped in front of the shop that sold Trig paraphernalia.

That evening, I managed to catch Kwin alone after the meal. 'This is for you,' I said, my heart beating fast. I wasn't sure how she would react.

'What is it?' she asked, staring at me as she accepted the parcel dubiously, turning it over in her hands.

'It's just a present,' I said. 'It's something to thank you for showing me the city when I first arrived.'

'I don't deserve to be thanked for that,' Kwin said. 'First I got you sacked and then I almost got you killed.'

She tore open the parcel and just stared at the red boots. 'I can't accept these!' she snapped. There was real anger in her voice.

'Why not?' I asked, my heart sinking. 'Deinon told me you really liked them.'

'They're too expensive, Leif. They've cost you too much.' Her eyes widened and a solitary tear trickled down her left cheek. Then she walked away without even thanking me.

I felt a little hurt – but at least, I reflected, she hadn't thrown them back at me. She had kept the boots.

Early the following morning I was waiting at the gate for the wagon that was to take me as far south as Mypocine. I'd taken my leave of everyone at breakfast, so I was surprised when a figure emerged from the side door and came towards me.

It was Kwin.

'Have a safe journey, Leif,' she bade me with a smile. 'I

wish I was coming with you. It would be good to visit the Genthai lands.'

'I wish you could come too,' I told her. 'It would be really good to have a companion.'

'I did ask, but my father turned purple – I thought he was having a fit!' she laughed. 'Maybe one day we will go there together.'

'Yes, I'd like that very much.'

I heard the rumble of the approaching wagon.

Kwin suddenly came close. Her eyes were serious, and she gently kissed me on the cheek. 'Thank you for the boots, Leif. They're the best present anyone's ever given me.'

Then she turned and ran back into the house.

I stared after her in astonishment. Was it just a sisterly sort of kiss, or was it something more?

Dwelling on this I threw my bag into the back of the wagon before climbing up beside the driver.

I would miss Kwin, and I was looking forward to returning to Tyron's house to begin my pre-season training. But I was also filled with a sense of adventure. I would visit Mypocine to see Peter and my other friends, but then I would head further south. I was looking forward to visiting the Genthai.

I wanted to see what my father's people were like.

THE MIDGARD GLOSSARY

This glossary has been compiled from the following primary sources:

> *The Manual of Nym*
> *The Testimony of Math*
> *The Manual of Trigladius Combat*
> *Amabramsum: the Genthai Book of Wisdom*
> *Amabramdata: the Genthai Book of Prophecy*
> *The Compendium of Ancient Tales and Ballads*

Aficionados

These are the devotees of the Trigladius; spectators whose knowledge of the proceedings – of the positions adopted by lacs and their tactical manoeuvres – is often greater than that of some combatants. Some specialize in the history of the Trigladius and can remember classic encounters of long ago by recalling, step by step, the patterns that led to victory.

Amabramdata

This is *The Genthai Book of Prophecy*. Although this holy book is written by a multitude of Genthai authors, it is believed that it represents the voice of their god, Thangandar.

Amabramsum

This is the name of *The Genthai Book of Wisdom*. It contains observations on djinn, Midgard and the world before the fall of the ur-humans. This is the collective wisdom of Genthai scribes. It is not a holy book.

Arena 13

This is another name for the Trigladius Arena. Once it was compulsory for human combatants in this arena to have the number 13 tattooed upon their foreheads. When this rule was rescinded, it remained fashionable for many years, but the custom is now dying out.

Artificers

These are adepts skilled in patterning the wurdes of Nym. The first artificers were ur-human and they developed their power to its height in the Secondary Epoch of Empire. Asscka, the most advanced form of djinn, are now the greatest artificers, having total control of Nym and the ability to shape themselves. The poorest artificers are barbarian humans, who pattern lacs who lack sentience. They build into them the steps of the dance that informs Trigladius combat in Arena 13.

Asgard

In Norse mythology, this signifies the Place Where the Gods Dwell. Some inhabitants of Midgard use this name to signify the place beyond the Barrier.

Barrier

The Great Barrier is the zone of mist, darkness and fear that encircles Midgard, preventing entry or exit. Those who approach too closely either never come back or return insane. The Trader passes through the Barrier unharmed, but he makes the journey by sea.

Chief Marshal

This official is the highest authority within the Wheel, with many assistant marshals to enforce his decisions. The main focus of his attention is Arena 13, where he supervises combat. Although his function in that arena is largely ceremonial, in the case of any dispute his decision is absolute and there can be no appeal.

Commonality

This is the name given to the underground zone beneath the Wheel where lacs are stored by owners who cannot afford to lease private quarters.

Cyro

He is the official responsible for the Commonality, the large underground zone below the Wheel. With the help of a small army of assistants, he supervises the storage of lacs, the kitchens, the training areas and the combat zones. Cyro rules his domain with absolute authority and nobody interferes in his activities, some of which are highly illegal.

Djinn

A djinni is the wurde made flesh. The different types of

djinn are more numerous than the visible stars. They range from low singletons, who may hardly be higher than base simulacra, to high djinn known as asscka, who may now generate selves almost beyond counting. Almost all djinn are subordinate in some way – some major, some minor – to the patterns of the ur-humans who first gave their progenitors shape. But of all these, most deadly of all is the djinni who is no longer subservient in any way to the wurdes that shaped him. Originally they were created by the military to serve the Human Empire.

Endoff

This is the close-down function called when a blade is inserted into the throat-slit of a lac, which becomes temporarily inoperative. For the min combatant, it signals the end of the contest. All that remains is the ritual cut to the arm of the defeated human combatant.

Extensibility

This is a characteristic of Nym which allows a patterner to add new wurdes and features or modify existing ones. The language can be increased by those who have the skill to do so.

False flesh

False flesh is the derogatory term first used by ur-humans to describe the flesh hosts of any djinni born of the shatek and the wurde. When the war between djinn and ur-humans intensified, the former adopted the term in defiance and proved, victory by victory, its superiority in every way to ur-human flesh.

FORTH

This computer language was created by a programmer called Charles H. Moore. It became the main source from which Nym was eventually developed.

Gambling house

The gambling agents (sometimes known as 'touts') accept wagers on behalf of the three large gambling houses which underpin the economy of Midgard. From their profits fees are paid to combatants who fight from the mag position. Only min combatants are allowed to bet upon themselves – but only to win.

Bets offered to Arena 13 gallery spectators are often very complex. Many aficionados attempt to predict the actual time of a victory and use accumulators, where winnings are placed upon the outcome of succeeding contests. Red tickets are sold, and these bets are made on the likelihood of a contestant suffering injury or death.

Gindeen

This is the only city of Midgard, although there are some small towns and hamlets. Gindeen consists largely of wooden buildings, with roads that are just mud tracks. Its main landmarks are the Wheel, the large cube-shaped slaughterhouse, and the citadel of Hob, which casts its shadow over the city.

Hob

It is believed that Hob is a rogue djinni who remained within the Barrier when barbarian humans were sealed within it. He preys upon humans, taking their blood and sometimes their minds. He occasionally fights within Arena 13 from the mag position.

Humans

Humans are the ur-race of creatures that created the language called Nym, thus constructing the first djinn and preparing the way for those that would supersede them. Outside the wurde, they are termed ur-humans, whereas their fallen and debased descendants are called barbarian humans. These latter are closest in form to the type of singletons known as lacs, though without their strength, speed and coordination. Their strength comes from their ability to cooperate and combine strength for a common purpose. It may also spring from the fear of death, having only one self which can easily be snuffed out in battle.

Index

This is the catalogue of lacs, souls bound within false flesh and wurdes offered by the Trader on his twice-yearly visits to Midgard. The Index exists only within the mind of the Trader and there is no written record of its contents.

Kransin

This is a substance used to coat the blades of lacs for contests in Arena 13. It is a combined coagulant and an intensifier of pain. Thus the ritual cut suffered by the loser is agonizing. That pain must be faced with courage, as the spectators watching from the gallery judge how the losing combatant conducts himself.

Lottery orbs

These objects are made out of crystal or glass. One is used to select the five winners of the annual blue-ticket draw. These are then given free training to fight in Arena 13. Another smaller orb is used when Hob visits the Wheel 13 to issue a challenge. The min combatants draw straws. The one who selects the shortest must fight Hob. That orb is also used to select the pairing of combatants in the Trainee Tournament.

Midgard

From Norse mythology, it means the Place Where Men Dwell or the Battlefield of Men. It is the zone allocated to the barbarian humans, the survivors of the fallen empire.

Newt

Newt is an analytical wurde-tool used by an artificer to explore a wurde-matrix and, if necessary, penetrate defences set up by the original creator of that system. It is far more sophisticated than either **poke** or **peek**.

Maori

These are the ancestor gods of the Genthai, who are believed to live in the sky on a long white cloud.

Nym

Nym evolved from a primitive patterning language called FORTH. It is the language that enabled the creation of the first djinn. All djinn are the wurde made flesh.

Omphalos

This is the centre post of the Wheel. Cut from a tree of great girth, it is considered by some to be the very centre of Midgard and the hub of the Wolf Wheel.

Other

The 'Other' is the term used by djinn for those not numbered amongst its own selves. Only by protocol can djinn achieve cooperation. Only by combat can they know their position.

Overseer

This is the title given to the man elected by the gambling houses and financial institutions of Midgard. He oversees all gambling and the issue of tickets for that purpose. He chairs meetings and adjudicates when there is conflict.

Peek

This is a basic Nym wurde-tool which is used to read elements of patterns and how they are linked.

Poke

This is a basic Nym wurde-tool which is used to insert other wurdes or primitives into a pattern.

Primitives

Primitives are the building blocks from which a wurde is constructed.

Protector, the

The Protector is the ruler of Midgard. He was placed in

that role by the djinn from beyond the Barrier and is answerable to them. His role is to keep order, and for this he has an armed guard of several thousand men who mainly confine themselves to the city of Gindeen and the surrounding area.

Some believe that the Protector is the same one who was appointed when the Human Empire fell and the remnants were placed within the Barrier. He has the appearance of a middle-aged man, but there is speculation about his provenance; some believe that he is a djinni.

Protocol

Protocol is the name for the rituals, both physical and of the wurde, by means of which djinn coexist without constant bloodletting. Protocol, once completed successfully, is known as a handshake.

Shape-shifters

This is a category to which all high djinn belong. To change the form of a self takes time, ranging from hours to weeks depending upon the degree of change required. Preceding this process, high intakes of food are necessary, the most useful being blood taken directly from living creatures. The more usual method of shape-shifting is through use of the wurde and the shatek to generate selves for particular tasks.

Self

A self is a sentient component of a djinni; it is a host of false flesh born of a shatek.

Stack

The stack is a defensive tri-glad tactic in which the human combatant is sandwiched between two defending lacs which rotate like a wheel according to the dictates of combat.

The stack is also the term for a sequence of Nym code to which a patterner might add or subtract. New code is always placed at the summit of a stack.

Tassels

This is the name given to those who dwell on the fringes of Hob's citadel and sometimes within it, serving his needs. Some have been grotesquely modified by Hob and are no longer fully human. These have enhanced powers, such as extreme strength and speed, plus the ability to see in the dark and locate the position of their victims using their sense of smell.

Some are related to Hob's victims and serve him hoping for news of their loved ones; some belong to a cult which worships Hob, hoping that one day he will return their wives or children to them in perfect new bodies. Others are spies who scratch out a living by supplying Hob with information or acting as go-betweens in contacts with certain citizens of Gindeen.

It is the behaviour of this last group which resulted in the name tassels, which are fringed knots on the hem of Hob's cloak. The name was given in mockery because they are a fallen and degraded group, but the idea of knots is appropriate because they are also part of the tangle of conspiracy and counter-conspiracy as the various groups within Midgard struggle to achieve their goals.

Trader

The Trader is Midgard's only source of lacs and new wurdes of Nym to enhance the patterning of lacs.

Trigladius

This is fought within Arena 13, the highest level of combat within the Wheel. Three lacs face a lone lac in a contest where victory results from the spilling of human blood. A human combatant stands behind the three in what is known as the 'mag' position; his opponent stands behind the lone lac in the 'min' position. They present themselves as targets for their opponent's lacs. Victory is marked by a ritual cut to the arm of the defeated combatant. Although the intention is not to kill, accidents do happen. In addition, grudge matches are fought which end in the decapitation of the loser.

Ulum

This is a sound-code used within the Trigladius Arena to communicate with and direct a lac, delivered by taps of the combatants' boots on the arena floor. Each combatant develops his own version of Ulum and keeps it a secret.

Wheel

The Wheel is situated in the city of Gindeen, within the Barrier. It is a huge circular building, and within twelve of its combat arenas gladiatorial contests take place between lacs. Arena 13, the highest ranked zone, is where the Trigladius occurs. The combat there involves both lacs and humans.

Wurde

The wurde is the basic unit within the ancient patterning language called Nym. Wurdes contain other wurdes, and to call one wurde is to call all that is embedded within it, both manifest and hidden.

JOSEPH DELANEY

 facebook.com/**josephdelaneyauthor**

josephdelaneyauthor

Read on for a sneak peek of the first episode
of Joseph Delaney's bestselling *Spook's* series,
The Spook's Apprentice

CHAPTER 1
A SEVENTH SON

When the Spook arrived, the light was already beginning to fail. It had been a long, hard day and I was ready for my supper.

'You're sure he's a seventh son?' he asked. He was looking down at me and shaking his head doubtfully.

Dad nodded.

'And you were a seventh son too?'

Dad nodded again and started stamping his feet impatiently, splattering my breeches with droplets of brown mud and manure. The rain was dripping from the peak of his cap. It had been raining for most of the month. There were new leaves on the trees but
the spring weather was a long time coming.

My dad was a farmer and his father had been a farmer too, and the first rule of farming is to keep the farm together. You can't just divide it up amongst your children; it would get smaller and smaller with each generation until there was nothing left. So a father leaves his farm to his eldest son. Then he finds jobs for the rest. If possible, he tries to find each a trade.

He needs lots of favours for that. The local blacksmith is one option, especially if the farm is big and he's given the blacksmith plenty of work. Then it's odds on that the blacksmith will offer an apprenticeship, but that's still only one son sorted out.

I was his seventh, and by the time it came to me all the favours had been used up. Dad was so desperate that he was trying to get the Spook to take me on as his apprentice. Or at least that's what I thought at the time. I should have guessed that Mam was behind it.

She was behind a lot of things. Long before I was born, it was her money that had bought our farm. How else could a seventh son have afforded it? And Mam wasn't County. She came from a land far across the sea. Most people couldn't tell, but sometimes, if you listened very carefully, there was a slight difference in the way she pronounced certain words.

Still, don't imagine that I was being sold into slavery or something. I was bored with farming anyway, and what they called 'the town' was hardly more than a village in the back of beyond. It was certainly no place that I wanted to spend the rest of my life. So in one way I quite liked the idea of being a spook; it was much more interesting than milking cows and spreading manure.

It made me nervous though, because it was a scary job. I was going to learn how to protect farms and villages from things that go bump in the night. Dealing with ghouls, boggarts and all manner of wicked beasties would be all in a day's work. That's what the Spook did and I was going to be his apprentice.

'How old is he?' asked the Spook.

'He'll be thirteen come August.'

'Bit small for his age. Can he read and write?'

'Aye,' Dad answered. 'He can do both and he also knows Greek. His mam taught him and he could speak it almost before he could walk.'

The Spook nodded and looked back across the muddy path beyond the gate towards the farmhouse, as if he were listening for something. Then he shrugged. 'It's a hard enough life for a man, never mind a boy,' he said. 'Think he's up to it?'

'He's strong and he'll be as big as me when he's full grown,' my dad said, straightening his back and drawing himself up to his full height. That done, the top of his head was just about level with the Spook's chin.

Suddenly the Spook smiled. It was the very last thing I'd expected. His face was big and looked as if it had been chiselled from stone. Until then I'd thought him a bit fierce. His long black cloak and hood made him look like a priest, but when he looked at you directly, his grim expression made him appear more like a hangman weighing you up for the rope.

The hair sticking out from under the front of his hood matched his beard, which was grey, but his eyebrows were black and very bushy. There was quite a bit of black hair sprouting out of his nostrils too, and his eyes were green, the same colour as my own.

Then I noticed something else about him. He was carrying a long staff. Of course, I'd seen that as soon as he came within sight, but what I hadn't realized until that moment was that he was carrying it in his left hand.

Did that mean that he was left-handed like me?

It was something that had caused me no end of trouble at the village school. They'd even called in the local priest to look at me and he'd kept shaking his head and telling me I'd have to fight it before it was too late. I didn't know what he meant. None of my brothers were left-handed and neither was my dad. My mam was cack-handed though, and it never seemed to bother her much, so when the teacher threatened to beat it out of me and tied the pen to my right hand, she took me away from the school and from that day on taught me at home.

'How much to take him on?' my dad asked, interrupting my thoughts. Now we were getting down to the real business.

'Two guineas for a month's trial. If he's up to it, I'll be back again in the autumn and you'll owe me another ten. If not, you can have him back and it'll be just another guinea for my trouble.'

Dad nodded again and the deal was done. We went into the barn and the guineas were paid but they didn't shake hands. Nobody wanted to touch a spook. My dad was a brave man just to stand within six feet of one.

'I've some business close by,' said the Spook, 'but I'll be back for the lad at first light. Make sure he's ready. I don't like to be kept waiting.'

When he'd gone, Dad tapped me on the shoulder. 'It's a new life for you now, son,' he told me. 'Go and get yourself cleaned up. You're finished with farming.'

When I walked into the kitchen, my brother Jack had his arm

around his wife Ellie and she was smiling up at him.

I like Ellie a lot. She's warm and friendly in a way that makes you feel that she really cares about you. Mam says that marrying Ellie was good for Jack because she helped to make him less agitated.

Jack is the eldest and biggest of us all and, as Dad sometimes jokes, the best looking of an ugly bunch. He is big and strong all right, but despite his blue eyes and healthy red cheeks, his black bushy eyebrows almost meet in the middle, so I've never agreed with that. One thing I've never argued with is that he managed to attract a kind and pretty wife. Ellie has hair the colour of best-quality straw three days after a good harvest, and skin that really glows in candlelight.

'I'm leaving tomorrow morning,' I blurted out. 'The Spook's coming for me at first light.'

Ellie's face lit up. 'You mean he's agreed to take you on?'

I nodded. 'He's given me a month's trial.'

'Oh, well done, Tom. I'm really pleased for you,' she said.

'I don't believe it!' scoffed Jack. 'You, apprentice to a spook! How can you do a job like that when you still can't sleep without a candle?'

I laughed at his joke but he had a point. I sometimes saw things in the dark and a candle was the best way to keep them away so that I could get some sleep.

Jack came towards me, and with a roar got me in a headlock and began dragging me round the kitchen table. It was his idea of a joke. I put up just enough resistance to humour him, and after a few seconds he let go of me and patted me on the back.

'Well done, Tom,' he said. 'You'll make a fortune doing

that job. There's just one problem, though . . .'

'What's that?' I asked.

'You'll need every penny you earn. Know why?'
I shrugged.

'Because the only friends you'll have are the ones you buy!'

I tried to smile, but there was a lot of truth in Jack's words. A spook worked and lived alone.

'Oh, Jack! Don't be cruel!' Ellie scolded.

'It was only a joke,' Jack replied, as if he couldn't understand why Ellie was making so much fuss.

But Ellie was looking at me rather than Jack and I saw her face suddenly drop. 'Oh, Tom!' she said. 'This means that you won't be here when the baby's born . . .'

She looked really disappointed and it made me feel sad that I wouldn't be at home to see my new niece. Mam had said that Ellie's baby was going to be a girl and she was never wrong about things like that.

'I'll come back and visit just as soon as I can,' I promised.

Ellie tried to smile, and Jack came up and rested his arm across my shoulders. 'You'll always have your family,' he said. 'We'll always be here if you need us.'

An hour later I sat down to supper, knowing that I'd be gone in the morning. Dad said grace as he did every evening and we all muttered 'Amen' except Mam. She just stared down at her food as usual, waiting politely until it was over. As the prayer ended, Mam gave me a little smile. It was a warm, special smile and I don't think anyone else noticed. It made me feel better.

The fire was still burning in the grate, filling the kitchen with warmth. At the centre of our large wooden table was a brass candlestick, which had been polished until you could see your face in it. The candle was made of beeswax and was expensive, but Mam wouldn't allow tallow in the kitchen because of the smell. Dad made most of the decisions on the farm, but in some things she always got her own way.

As we tucked into our big plates of steaming hotpot, it struck me how old Dad looked tonight – old and tired – and there was an expression that flickered across his face from time to time, a hint of sadness. But he brightened up a bit when he and Jack started discussing the price of pork and whether or not it was the right time to send for the pig butcher.

'Better to wait another month or so,' Dad said. 'The price is sure to go higher.'

Jack shook his head and they began to argue. It was a friendly argument, the kind families often have, and I could tell that Dad was enjoying it. I didn't join in though. All that was over for me. As Dad had told me, I was finished with farming.

Mam and Ellie were chuckling together softly. I tried to catch what they were saying, but by now Jack was in full flow, his voice getting louder and louder. When Mam glanced across at him I could tell she'd had enough of his noise.

Oblivious to Mam's glances and continuing to argue loudly, Jack reached across for the salt cellar and accidentally knocked it over, spilling a small cone of salt on the table top. Straight away he took a pinch and threw it back over his left shoulder. It is an old County superstition. By doing that you were supposed to ward off the bad luck you'd earned by spilling it.

'Jack, you don't need any salt on that anyway,' Mam scolded. 'It spoils a good hotpot and is an insult to the cook!'

'Sorry, Mam,' Jack apologized. 'You're right. It's perfect just as it is.'

She gave him a smile then nodded towards me. 'Anyway, nobody's taking any notice of Tom. That's no way to treat him on his last night at home.'

'I'm all right, Mam,' I told her. 'I'm happy just to sit here and listen.'

Mam nodded. 'Well, I've got a few things to say to you. After supper stay down in the kitchen and we'll have a little talk.'

So after Jack, Ellie and Dad had gone up to bed, I sat in a chair by the fire and waited patiently to hear what Mam had to say.

Mam wasn't a woman who made a lot of fuss; at first she didn't say much apart from explaining what she was wrapping up for me: a spare pair of trousers, three shirts and two pairs of good socks that had only been darned once each.

I stared into the embers of the fire, tapping my feet on the flags, while Mam drew up her rocking chair and positioned it so that she was facing directly towards me. Her black hair was streaked with a few strands of grey, but apart from that she looked much the same as she had when I was just a toddler, hardly up to her knees. Her eyes were still bright, and but for her pale skin, she looked a picture of health.

'This is the last time we'll get to talk together for quite a while,' she said. 'It's a big step leaving home and starting out on your own. So if there's anything you need to say, anything you need to ask, now's the time to do it.'

I couldn't think of a single question. In fact I couldn't even think. Hearing her say all that had started tears pricking behind my eyes.

The silence went on for quite a while. All that could be heard was my feet tap-tapping on the flags. Finally Mam gave a little sigh. 'What's wrong?' she asked. 'Has the cat got your tongue?'

I shrugged.

'Stop fidgeting, Tom, and concentrate on what I'm saying,' Mam warned. 'First of all, are you looking forward to tomorrow and starting your new job?'

'I'm not sure, Mam,' I told her, remembering Jack's joke about having to buy friends. 'Nobody wants to go anywhere near a spook. I'll have no friends. I'll be lonely all the time.'

'It won't be as bad as you think,' Mam said. 'You'll have your master to talk to. He'll be your teacher, and no doubt he'll eventually become your friend.
And you'll be busy all the time. Busy learning new things. You'll have no time to feel lonely. Don't you find the whole thing new and exciting?'

'It's exciting but the job scares me. I want to do it but I don't know if I can. One part of me wants to travel and see places but it'll be hard not to live here any more. I'll miss you all. I'll miss being at home.'

'You can't stay here,' Mam said. 'Your dad's getting too old to work, and come next winter he's handing the farm over to Jack. Ellie will be having her baby soon, no doubt the first of many; eventually there won't be room for you here. No, you'd better get used to it before that happens. You can't come home.'

Her voice seemed cold and a little sharp, and to hear her speak to me like that drove a pain deep into my chest and throat so that I could hardly breathe.

I just wanted to go to bed then, but she had a lot to say. I'd rarely heard her use so many words all in one go.

'You have a job to do and you're going to do it,' she said sternly. 'And not only do it; you're going to do it well. I married your dad because he was a seventh son. And I bore him six sons so that I could have you. Seven times seven you are and you have the gift. Your new master's still strong but he's some way past his best and his time is finally coming to an end.

'For nearly sixty years he's walked the County lines doing his duty. Doing what has to be done. Soon it'll be your turn. And if you won't do it, then who will? Who'll look after the ordinary folk? Who'll keep them from harm? Who'll make the farms, villages and towns safe so that women and children can walk the streets and lanes free from fear?'

I didn't know what to say and I couldn't look her in the eye. I just fought to hold back the tears.

'I love everyone in this house,' she said, her voice softening, 'but in the whole wide County, you're the only person who's really like me. As yet, you're just a boy who's still a lot of growing to do, but you're the seventh son of a seventh son. You've the gift and the strength to do what has to be done. I know you're going to make me proud of you.

SPOOK'S

THE WARDSTONE
CHRONICLES

*Dare
you read
them all?*

The dark rises anew . . .

THE FIRST EPISODE OF
THE STARBLADE CHRONICLES

An army of beasts is gathering in the north.

They will invade our lands . . .

enslave our people . . .

and spread their terror to the far corners of the earth.

**A terrifying new chapter in the
Spook's legend is about to begin**